Last year there was Perry's
nationwide bestseller,
The Butcher's Boy

"A brilliant suspense thriller, reminiscent of Graham
Greene!"

—*Washington Post*

"Shrewdly planned and executed thriller!"

—*New York Times*

This year he tops even his own success
with
Metzger's Dog

"Brilliantly plotted . . . should please fans of Graham Greene,
fans of Cheech and Chong, and most anyone in between!"

—*Newsday*

"Total pleasure and satisfaction!"

—*The New Yorker*

Charter Books by Thomas Perry

THE BUTCHER'S BOY
METZGER'S DOG

THOMAS PERRY
METZGER'S DOG

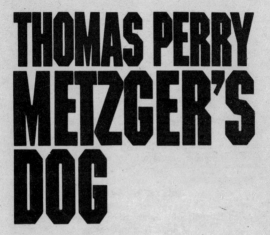

CHARTER BOOKS, NEW YORK

This Charter Book contains the complete
text of the original hardcover edition.
It has been completely reset in a typeface
designed for easy reading, and was printed
from new film.

METZGER'S DOG

A Charter Book / published by arrangement with
Charles Scribner's Sons

PRINTING HISTORY
Scribner's edition / 1983
Charter edition / August 1984

ISBN: 0-441-52867-8

Charter Books are published by The Berkley Publishing Group,
200 Madison Avenue, New York, New York 10016.
PRINTED IN THE UNITED STATES OF AMERICA

For the Perrys, the Goltzes,
and the Lees.
With thanks to Dr. Jo.

⩓ 1 ⩓

CHINESE GORDON WAS fully awake. He'd heard the clinking noise again, and now there was no question the cat was listening too. The cat, Doctor Henry Metzger, had assumed the loaf-of-bread position on Gordon's blanket, his ears straight up like a pair of spoons to catch the sound and lock onto it. Doctor Henry Metzger sat up and licked his paw, then froze as he detected some variation in the sound that Chinese Gordon's ears couldn't hear.

"What is it?" whispered Chinese Gordon. "Somebody trying to break in, isn't it?"

Doctor Henry Metzger turned from the sound, walked up Chinese Gordon's chest, and stepped on his forehead on the way to the spare pillow. He'd identified it as a human sound, which placed it outside Doctor Henry Metzger's sphere of interest.

Damn, thought Chinese Gordon. Burglars. He slipped out of bed, moved quietly to the doorway, and listened. He could hear from downstairs the faint squeaking of the garage door to the shop moving on its rollers. His eyes strained, but he could see nothing below except the familiar dim shapes of the shop ma-

1

chines. Then, as the garage door opened farther, he saw a man silhouetted for a moment. The man entered, followed by another, and another.

Chinese Gordon stayed low, watching from the upper landing without moving. There were three of them. The gun was locked in the bottom of the tool chest in the back room downstairs, which meant it was worse than nothing because if he gave them enough time they'd find it.

He could tell they were just inside the garage door now, probably standing there waiting for their eyes to adjust to the darkness before trying to move into the shop. It was a lousy situation, thought Chinese Gordon. They might be just kids or winos or junkies trying to score a lot of expensive tools and machinery, but that didn't mean they wouldn't kill him if he switched on the light or made a noise.

Beside him he felt Doctor Henry Metzger rubbing against him, purring. When Doctor Henry Metzger stopped purring and stared down into the shop, Chinese Gordon knew the men had begun to move. He watched the cat's face, the intent unblinking eyes focused on the darkness below. Then Doctor Henry Metzger crouched low and peered over the edge of the landing, his ears back so his head would have no silhouette. One of them must be directly below, looking up at the power tools hanging on the pegboard on the wall. Chinese Gordon listened, and he could feel the shape of the man below him, leaning forward over the bench, his face staring up at the tools to assess their value, weight, and bulk. Now he would be reaching up for the electric drill.

Chinese Gordon felt a twinge of guilt about what had to be done. He knew it wasn't fair, and there would be resentment, there might even be consequences he couldn't·imagine. He gently placed his hand on Doctor

Henry Metzger, feeling the thick, soft fur. Then, without warning, he scooped the cat up and dropped him. Doctor Henry Metzger screamed as he fell, the terror, surprise, and anger howled into the darkness in a high-pitched screech.

Chinese Gordon could tell immediately that he'd judged the trajectory correctly. Doctor Henry Metzger could only have dropped five or six feet before the tone of the howling changed and the human scream joined it. The cat had definitely landed on the man's head, scrambling desperately with claws out for a foothold, from the sound of it tearing great gashes, because the man's shouts weren't just terror, they were pain.

There were other sounds now too. The shouts of both of the man's companions competed with the howling and screaming. "What?" one yelled. "What? What?" Then he ran into the lathe, which rocked slightly although it was bolted to the pavement, and must have injured himself somehow, because then his voice came from the floor in a breathless, inarticulate moan. The other screamed, "Hold still! Freeze, you bastard!" as though he were either contemplating shooting someone or merely advocating keeping calm.

On the landing Chinese Gordon lay flat on his belly and listened. The man on the ground said, "We've got to get out of here."

"What the hell happened?" said the one with the commanding voice. "It sounded like a baby."

"God, I'm bleeding!" said the other.

Chinese Gordon heard them move away, then peered over the edge to watch them, one by one, escape under the partially opened garage door. A few seconds later he heard car doors slam and an engine start.

∧ 2 ∧

THE SIDEWALKS ON the campus of the University of Los Angeles were crowded and chaotic. John Knox Morrison disliked that part of it, the sense of all these people wandering about according to no visible pattern, sometimes two or three abreast so he had to sidestep to let them pass. The bicycles added an element of danger to the matrix as they knifed through any momentary openings in the crowd at unpredictable angles and at speeds that reduced control to the art of picking a gap and aiming at it. Whenever John Knox Morrison visited a university campus he tried to arrange a way to avoid this feeling: have someone pick him up at the airport and take him to the right building. But Los Angeles was difficult because he had too many people to see on different campuses. Back in Washington it was easy to forget what it meant to come west. It was hard to envision a city eighty miles long and eighty miles wide.

At least here at ULA he knew where he was going. If it hadn't been so near to lunchtime he'd have stopped in the romanesque revival building on his left for a doughnut. He knew the place better than most of these young people, he supposed. He'd been coming here

4

since most of them were babies. A young girl with a worried expression on her face stared directly into his eyes as she passed. That one was an example: a child whose self-absorbed, unconfident gaze rested on the tall, gray-haired man in a gray suit making a measured way through the crowds. For an instant he wondered if she envied him his age. She probably thought he was a dean or vice-president, someone whose gray hair and presence here meant that he had long ago passed the mid-term examinations, written the papers that seemed so awesome to her now.

It almost made John Knox Morrison smile to himself as he turned the corner and walked down the broader, easier expanse of University Avenue. The irony appealed to him—the child would have been puzzled and disappointed if she could have known who he really was. But he was more important on this campus than any dean or vice-president. If that little girl took a course in physics or chemistry or biology, the equipment she used would be the equipment that came here because he'd willed it. If she took a course in any of the social sciences, it would probably be held in the building he'd approved in 1968. The list was too long to remember at the moment, and it included a number of items he found distasteful to contemplate, investments that might not yield any discernible return before the end of the century. When he arrived on a university campus, he brought with him the force of the greatest determining factor in human history. John Knox Morrison was one of four senior executive officers of the federal government's National Research Foundation, by far the largest and richest of the agencies that dispensed government research grants. When he spoke with professors, deans, department chairmen, there was little doubt that John Knox Morrison spoke with an authority that obliterated all titles and institutional structures, reduced them to ephemeral and meaningless local customs. He spoke with the power of money.

WHEN Morrison reached the Social Sciences Building he took the elevator to the third floor and walked directly to Ian Donahue's office. On the door was printed only "300-307 Professor Donahue." Inside, there were an anteroom and a short hallway opening onto a complex of small rooms. Morrison passed one room where a young, bearded man was staring angrily at the display screen of a computer terminal, and another where two girls were drinking coffee and cataloguing what looked like machine-scored answer sheets for some kind of examination.

Donahue was waiting for Morrison in his private study at the end of the hall. Donahue's round, unlined face flashed a grin as he closed the door. "Great to see you, John," he said. "How've you been?"

"Fine," said Morrison. "Just fine." Donahue's manner always confused him at first. He supposed that he probably was Donahue's friend, in a way. When they'd met, Donahue had been an Assistant Professor in the fifth year of his appointment, with no significant publications and not much hope of doing anything remarkable enough to justify his receiving tenure in two years. In those days Ian Donahue's office was a dark little closet of a room that he shared with a truculent and abrasive young colleague who, judging from the disordered assortment of clothes and toothbrushes, must have been in the habit of spending nights there with women. It must have been a hopeless time for Donahue. The only thing he had going for him was a short article that had appeared in an obscure academic journal called *Sociometry*, which he had attached to a grant application to the National Research Foundation. It hadn't attracted any attention among the probably twenty or thirty sociology professors who'd read it, but it had been enough to cause something of a stir in Morrison's office. Morrison even remembered the title—"The Jalisco Famine of 1946: Toward a Quantification."

What had intrigued Morrison and his colleagues wasn't to be found in the major portion of the article. That was only an interpretation of demographic statistics. What interested Morrison was a speculation that it was possible to identify and isolate certain intangible ideas peculiar to a culture, assign them numerical values, and work out which ones cause people to behave irrationally. The Jalisco famine was by then a standard problem in the field: In the middle of the summer of 1946, when the crops were growing well in the fields, the weather was perfect, and no trouble was in sight, the rumor of a famine swept through Jalisco, causing twenty thousand small farmers to abandon their farms and flee the area. Because they did that, the crops failed, thousands starved, and the famine rumor came true.

Ian Donahue, an unknown and unpromising Assistant Professor, had hit upon an idea that had stimulated Morrison's imagination. If cultural fears could be assigned numerical values in retrospect in this single instance, they could be assigned numerical values in the present. If Donahue could explain past behavior, his formulae could also predict future behavior. Morrison perceived, if some others didn't, that if the quantities were known they could also be adjusted. If they could be adjusted, mass action could not only be predicted, it could also be precipitated. Morrison knew a number of people who would be very interested in Donahue's research.

That had been the real beginning of Donahue's career, a string of successes that had stretched over twenty some years. The complex of offices assigned to Ian Donahue in the Social Sciences Building was larger and more lavish than the offices of the whole Sociology Department.

MORRISON sat in the chair that looked out over the campus, the trees and lawns like a tiny park inserted in the midst of the sprawling, grayish city. "It's already November, Ian," he said. "In Washington it's November, anyway. Here it always seems to be August."

"I know," said Donahue. "I'll have the final draft of the report to you by December first. I promise. It'll be on your desk before Thanksgiving if there are no surprises."

"The report is not why I came here," said Morrison, his hand raised. "I had to come through to talk to somebody at USC, and I thought it would be a good time to see you. It'll also give me a chance to fill in another on-site visit."

Donahue nodded. He'd read in the newspaper a few days before that one of the Congressional committees was examining travel expenses of government officials. Even a man like Morrison must have to make every trip look as full of business as possible.

Morrison said, "The big thing, though, is that the Latin America grant is going to terminate on January one. I wondered what you had in mind after that."

Donahue shrugged. "The usual. As I said, the final report will be in a month early. Apply for a renewal.

We're in a very productive phase right now; I don't think you'll be in doubt when you see the paperwork.''

"I know you're right, Ian, but I don't think you understood what I said. It isn't just your grant that terminates in January. It's the whole project, the Latin America Outreach. Over a week ago the House subcommittee on Science and Technology let the request for continuation die."

"But that always happens!" said Donahue. "The administration always calls in a few favors and the money comes through. You told me that years ago."

Morrison stared out the window and shook his head. "Not this time," he said. "I've checked. This time the administration isn't going to pursue it. They've decided to change the emphasis to Africa for the moment."

"Damn! So that's it. Now I know who you saw at USC. It's that pompous fool Graham Baker, isn't it?"

Morrison said nothing, only stared out over the trees toward the distant freeway.

"I see," said Donahue. "It's because he's younger than I am, isn't it?"

"No, Ian, of course not. You know that age nonsense only happens in chemistry and physics. It really is the Africa thing. The Latin America project is just getting too much scrutiny this year. And the smart money is saying the Africa thing is going to need the attention."

"All right, but I'm warning you. I have no idea what Baker can do for you, but he's no scientist."

"It's not my decision," said Morrison. "I'm telling you, it's not. I don't make policy. Believe me, it sometimes makes me unhappy. Next year a tenth of my budget is already earmarked for linguistics research—specifically to develop quick ways of teaching Americans to speak languages like Somali, Bemba, Tswana, Luo, and Dinka."

"That's absurd," said Donahue. "I'm being cut loose to fund a project to teach a dozen unrelated languages of doubtful use? John, there are more Spanish-speaking people in Los Angeles than there ever have been speakers of Luo in the world."

"I know that, Ian. There are others who know it too. And I have connections with a few of them, people in private foundations that don't have to rely on the whims of subcommittees for their existence. I have a few suggestions for you." Morrison produced a card. "I think this one is your best bet," he said. "The Seyell Foundation. You've heard of them?"

"Of course," said Donahue.

"If I were you I'd give this man a call," said Morrison, handing Donahue the card. "Benjamin Porterfield. I've known him for years. He's the new president of the Seyell Foundation, and something of a specialist on Latin America himself. I'm sure he'd like to hear from you."

Donahue took the card. All it had was the name and a telephone number, printed in raised black letters. "Thanks. You're a real friend. Will you come out with me for dinner at Scandia? There's someone I'd like you to meet—a graduate student who's working with me on the final report. Her name is Grace Warner."

"Let me call you later on that, Ian," said Morrison. He rose to leave. "I'm going to stop back at the hotel for an hour or two and see if I can get out of another appointment. It's something I can probably take care of on the telephone."

As Morrison rode the elevator to the ground level he thought about Ian Donahue. In a week or two Donahue would collect himself and call Porterfield at the Seyell Foundation and be pleasantly surprised. The Seyell Foundation was now preparing to distribute the largest

set of grants in its history for studies like Donahue's.
Ian would probably even like Ben Porterfield, a quiet,
businesslike man in his late fifties who would appear to
Donahue to be an answer to his prayers. The image
struck Morrison as appropriate. That was what they
called the investors in the theater, wasn't it? Angels. In
the old days when Porterfield had been the Company's
chief Special Operations officer in Guatemala, that had
been the name his band of guerrillas had given him—El
Ángel de Muerte. But Ian Donahue would never get to
hear that. If Donahue tried to find out about Porterfield
he'd be able to learn that he was a respectable business
executive, a former president of a small airline, a former
vice-president of a major food corporation who'd been
on the board of directors of the Seyell Foundation for
years. It would never occur to him that the Foundation
had been converted, year by year, into one of the CIA's
client companies. Donahue might even feel some relief
at the ease of dealing with private research funds after
so many years of federal audits and on-site visits.
Porterfield's personality would probably be a relief too.
He was hard headed and aloof. Donahue might even be
able to get out of the business of finding female graduate students who didn't mind spending an evening in
the Beverly Wilshire with a middle-aged visitor from
Washington. That part was a pity, Morrison thought,
but it had to be. The orders were that the Latin America
project was ready to go underground. From now on no
funds that could be traced to the taxpayers would end
up in Donahue's research accounts. It was the end of a
long and mutually satisfactory association. Los Angeles
would never be quite the same for John Knox Morrison.
He wondered if the person who'd written the orders in
Langley had an inkling of the fact that he was destroy-
ing the best portion of Morrison's sexual history since

Harvard in the spring of '47. Those orders had passed Donahue, perhaps the most talented procurer in America, from Morrison, a man with spirit and taste and appreciation, to whom? Porterfield was a man who had eaten armadillo. That said it all. He wouldn't even consider accepting one of Donahue's graduate research assistants, because he wouldn't want to take the trouble to explain the knife scar on his back. The legend was that Porterfield was very happily married to the woman he'd been with since the early fifties, but John Knox Morrison didn't accept that. Porterfield clearly had no human feelings. He had the mind and tastes of a Soviet political commissar, the sort they sent into desert countries to train terrorists on a five-year tour of duty. Donahue's young students would be wasted on him. It was a pity.

⚛ 3 ⚛

"DOCTOR HENRY METZGER!" shouted Chinese Gordon. "You're a psychotic moron!" Trembling with fury, he shook his overalls over the balcony.

He spotted Doctor Henry Metzger sitting on the workbench along the wall of the shop where a patch of morning sunlight warmed the sheet metal surface. Chinese Gordon hurled the wet, reeking overalls at the cat. With the strength of his rage Chinese Gordon managed to propel the wad of denim halfway to the workbench. Doctor Henry Metzger raised his head to stare at Chinese Gordon for a moment, then turned his attention to licking his genitals.

Chinese Gordon looked around him for something else to throw, but with the thought came the awareness that he'd strained his shoulder with the first throw. He leaned over the railing and yelled, "You're purring, you son of a bitch!" Doctor Henry Metzger slowly stretched his body, then walked along the bench to the end, sprang to the windowsill, and stepped through the empty panel.

Chinese Gordon turned and stomped into the kitchen to make himself some coffee. It was a hell of a bad start,

13

he thought. The burglary had been bad enough, but this was ridiculous. He couldn't believe Doctor Henry Metzger could be so mean spirited. Sure, there was such a thing as a difference of opinion on tactics, or even a disagreement. This was nothing less than revenge. As he waited for the water to boil, Chinese Gordon contemplated the meaning of Doctor Henry Metzger's gesture. To a cat, a man's overalls must seem like a cat's fur, a neck-to-ankle cat suit. What depths of contempt must be expressed by pissing on a man's fur?

He decided not to brood about it. Today was too important to permit him to spend time distracted with personal problems. For months he'd been preparing for this, measuring and figuring, then grinding and drilling and shaping the steel, then oiling and polishing the parts, assembling and reassembling them, then cycling the whole machine by hand, sliding the flat cam forward and back to make the cylinder turn. Then he'd taken the whole thing apart and searched for the burrs or scratches that meant something was out of balance or fitted wrong. He'd done practically nothing else when he'd been alone for the best part of a year. Chinese Gordon was a master tool-and-die maker, a man who could make a thing like this in a matter of days, but he was making only one and it had to be right.

Chinese Gordon took his coffee downstairs to the shop, opened his van, and took a look at what he'd made. It was done right and he knew it. It had been an act of will to keep himself from making it perfect. He was accustomed to precise measurements, to machining parts to such close tolerances that they seemed to have grown together. This job was different—the parts had to be fitted loosely so that when it was operated the rapid buildup of grime and residue didn't cause it to freeze up, and of course there was the heat expansion too.

He had no doubt about this piece of work. Once again Chinese Gordon had succeeded where others hadn't even been crazy enough to try. As his eyes moved along it, part by part, he felt proud: the butt of the cam with its powerful return springs, the smooth cylinder, then down the long, black tube to the end. There was no question about it, he had reproduced it in every detail —a working M-39-A1 automatic aircraft cannon.

He reached in and checked the feeder again, jiggling one of the star wheels to line it up with the one beside it, then examining the belt stripper. Just for luck he flipped the extractor with his thumb before he closed the van door.

Even the pride of the craftsman and the pride of ownership together weren't enough to drive out the feel of the cold cement floor on his bare feet. Chinese Gordon climbed upstairs to search for something to wear. As he reached the top he saw Doctor Henry Metzger slip back in through the window. When Chinese Gordon stopped, Doctor Henry Metzger stopped.

"That's right," said Chinese Gordon. "You're better at this guerrilla shit than I am, because you're an animal. But that's also your flaw, Doctor Henry Metzger. You don't even know it's Saturday, you shithead. I don't wear overalls on Saturday. If it had been me, I'd have pissed on your blue jeans and shirts." He laughed as he walked into his bedroom to dress.

He reappeared, buttoning his shirt, just as Doctor Henry Metzger finished defecating on the overalls lying on the shop floor and began his pantomime of burying the droppings by scratching the pant legs over the pile.

• • •

CHINESE Gordon sang "Old Dan Tucker" as he drove the van along the Pearblossom Highway. Then they swung onto Route 18 at Victorville. Just as they drove past the Roy Rogers Museum, where the gigantic statue of Trigger pawed the dry air of the Mojave Desert, Kepler poured Immelmann's can of beer into Chinese Gordon's boot, so it made a sucking noise whenever he lifted it off the gas pedal. Chinese Gordon launched instead into another favorite: "She lives on a cattle ranch," he sang, "and she shits like an avalanche." Kepler and Immelmann tolerated countless verses, but as they left Joshua Tree and moved toward Twentynine Palms, Immelmann began to glare at him, so Chinese Gordon switched to "Bongo, Bongo, Bongo, I Don't Want to Leave the Congo." This made Kepler glare at him. Chinese Gordon was puzzled until he remembered that Kepler had spent part of 1965 as a mercenary in the eastern territories around Lake Tanganyika. He drove on in silence, turning south again at Twentynine Palms into the Pinto Basin.

He didn't slow the van until he neared Fried Liver Wash, where the Hexie Mountains jutted to the west and the country to the east stretched off into forbidding, empty flats that shimmered in the heat.

"This is?" said Immelmann.

Chinese Gordon didn't answer. He swung the van off the highway and held onto the steering wheel as they bounced along the desert floor into the dry bed of the wash. They kept going until they reached the place Chinese Gordon had found weeks earlier. Two hundred yards up the wash there was the rusting abandoned hulk of a 1954 Ford F-100 pickup truck. When Chinese Gordon had found it he hadn't been able to decide whether some fool had parked it there just before a flash flood or just driven it there, taken the tires off, and left it.

"This is the perfect spot," said Chinese Gordon. "There's nobody within fifty miles of us."

"No argument there," said Kepler, placing a cold beer can under each armpit. "A germ couldn't live out here. Let's get it over with so we can bury you before dark."

Chinese Gordon wasn't willing to be rushed. He turned the van around and lined it up on the pickup truck. "See?" he said, "I can aim the thing using this mirror on the dashboard with the crosshairs. All I have to do is steer the van so the target is lined up."

"Clever," said Kepler, suppressing a yawn. "Big fucking deal. You can line it up, but you can't fire it or you'll blow your own ass off the planet."

"Not true," said Chinese Gordon patiently. "I've got it all figured out." He flipped a switch under the dash, and a panel in the rear of the van slid open to bare the muzzle of the M-39.

"Hold it," said Immelmann. He and Kepler scrambled out of the van and stood a few yards off. "Go ahead," said Immelmann.

"Really," said Chinese Gordon, "I can do it." He flipped a second switch, and the converted air conditioner fan added its hum to the purr of the van's engine. "See," he said, "this vents the gases and smoke. Now the generator." He flipped a third switch, and there was a whining sound. "The firing voltage is 310 AC, so I couldn't use batteries."

The others nodded and looked at each other. Immelmann took a long swallow of the beer and burped thoughtfully. Then he said, "We should have come in two cars. We must be two hundred miles from Van Nuys."

Chinese Gordon ignored him. He put on his earphones and picked up the hand switch that was dangling at the end of a telephone cord. He moved the van forward a few inches, steering so that the crosshairs of the mirror were on the center of the cab of the derelict pickup truck, then put the van in neutral and gently pressed the hand-switch button.

There was a roar that lasted almost a whole second. It sounded to Chinese Gordon like *Ooowoow*. For an instant he thought the van had blown up, but it was only the recoil of the automatic cannon kicking the van forward about ten feet before his foot hit the brake.

Before his head snapped back he saw that he hadn't missed the target. The pickup truck had sat palpably and clearly in the crosshairs, then it had disappeared in fire and flying dirt. It looked as though the earth under it had exploded.

Chinese Gordon set the hand brake and looked back at his companions. Immelmann was sitting on the ground looking dazed, his hands still over his ears. Kepler was already running toward the place where the pickup truck had been. It was now just a charred and smoking hole with large pieces of twisted metal strewn about.

Chinese Gordon sauntered up to Immelmann. "I guess it works," Chinese Gordon said. Immelmann's mouth moved, but Chinese Gordon couldn't hear anything. He wondered if he'd gone deaf, but then he remembered he still had the earphones on.

He snatched the earphones off and yelled, "What?" glad to hear his own voice.

"An elephant fart," said Immelmann.

"What?" shouted Chinese Gordon.

"It sounded like an elephant fart," said Immelmann. His eyes widened and he shook his head again. "Exactly. Not rat-tat-tat. More like Woooooow."

Kepler was sprinting back toward them, shouting and

hooting. "You're a genius, Chinese. A genius! What was that?"

"Fifty rounds of high-explosive incendiary," said Chinese Gordon. "Ball ammo would have done it, but we don't have any."

Immelmann stood up, threw his beer can, and said, "A nasty weapon, Chinese. You're not the sporting gentleman you once were—you're a fucking mad scientist. What do you say we stop in Palm Springs for a drink before we pick up your Nobel Prize?"

"Okay," said Chinese Gordon. "It'll give us a chance to look at some banks."

ᴧ 4 ᴧ

THE OFFICE OF the president of the Seyell Foundation
was a room fifty feet long and forty across, with a
vaulted ceiling eighteen feet above. The room was
dominated by an antique desk of reddish maple with a
hand-rubbed surface so vast that Porterfield had at first
glance mistaken it for a billiard table that had unaccountably been flooded with blood.

The office had been perfectly reconstructed to look as
it had when Theophilus "call me Ted" Seyell had sat at
the desk to fire three hundred employees on New Year's
Day, 1932. The furniture, the old Persian rugs, even the
leatherbound books that lined the walls had been moved
from the old Seyell Building in New York before it had
been demolished in 1946 and set down intact here in
Washington. It was as though the shrine to the personality of Theophilus Seyell must remain inviolate or the immense fortune he'd amassed would no longer cling to
the bank accounts that bore his potent name. Seyell had
begun the Just Perfect Toy Company in 1904, making
wooden cutout toys with a jigsaw at night after working
as a bank teller all day, then hired an immigrant laborer
after a year to help him. Soon there were salesmen,

20

more laborers to work a day shift, and the J.P.T. Company began to grow. Through the early part of the century it flourished and diversified until the average person didn't remember what J.P.T. stood for, although employees continued to refer to it as "Just Plain Ted" long after it ceased to be possible that many of them could ever have seen Theophilus Seyell. J.P.T. retooled to make rifle parts for World War I and distilling equipment at the end of Prohibition. It was investigated after World War II for war profiteering, but by then Theophilus Seyell had died and the entity that had been J.P.T. was already undergoing its final transformation to the Seyell Foundation. Its board of directors had become trustees and executors, its assets were converted to numbers in account books of the philanthropic and scientific foundation that Seyell had described in his will. There were no stockholders to buy out, no relatives to consult: J.P.T. had always been Just Plain Ted.

BENJAMIN Porterfield sat at the desk examining the weekly financial statement. He felt vaguely uncomfortable. He knew he'd get used to sitting in old Theophilus Seyell's throne room. The names and titles the Company had invented over the years had brought him to worse places, but at the moment the size of the empty space around him seemed to create a vacuum that must inevitably by natural laws be on the verge of being filled. Every few seconds he found himself looking up toward the distant oak door to see who had come. The aspect of this assignment that worried him most was that it was too easy. It had been represented to him as an emergency. He was the most appropriate agent in place who could credibly move into the presidency of a major research foundation in a month's time without some sort of publicity. He was an expert in moving Company money. When the word had come through that many of the Latin America projects must be made to disappear from government budgets, he'd been the obvious one to handle the transition. The Company had been preparing the Seyell Foundation for years, placing votes on the board of trustees, tinkering with its portfolio, waiting for the day when the Foundation would quietly become a Company asset.

When the day had come they had picked Benjamin Porterfield, and that annoyed him. The choice made too much sense, fit the pattern too well. Most of Porterfield's contemporaries were chiefs of station somewhere or even running regional desks at Langley. That part didn't bother him. He'd always been a field man, beginning in Special Operations in the fifties and then moving into Domestic Ops in the seventies. His last three assignments had been like this one—a quick meeting with one of the bespectacled innocents who stepped off a commuter flight with nothing but an empty briefcase, gave orders in the Director's name, and caught the next flight home. Porterfield would be appointed president of a small airline in Miami, vice-president of the Canadian subsidiary of a large food corporation, and now president of a foundation. Always it was an emergency, always he was to head the transition team. They were pulling him closer and closer to Langley, using his gray hairs to build him a deeper and deeper cover, putting him in charge of operations so large and crucial that he couldn't possibly move without Langley's logistical and technical support. Having Langley's support was like being encased in cement. In the old days the Company had been different. In 1953 he'd been given a suitcase full of currency, an airline ticket, and a list of telephone numbers to memorize. A year later his little army of mercenaries was in the Guatemala jungles. That had been another time, a different world.

The telephone didn't ring, just lit up. He picked up the receiver.

"Mr. Porterfield, it's Mr. Bartlett of Crabtree and Bacon to speak to you about the audit," said Mrs. Goode.

"Tell him I'll call him back," said Porterfield. It was another annoyance, but only a temporary one. Until the communication between the Foundation and Langley could be moved to a safe wire of its own, he'd have to follow the procedure. In fifteen minutes he'd call back from a telephone booth in the neighborhood.

"He says it's very important and he's got to leave his office to catch a flight this afternoon," said Mrs. Goode.

"Right," said Porterfield, and pressed the button on his telephone. "Porterfield."

"It's okay now," said the voice. "The wire is installed."

"Good. Is that all?"

"No. We're calling about one of the projects Morrison has passed to you." The "we" was perfect, thought Porterfield.

"Which one?"

"It's a Professor Ian Donahue at ULA. The Director himself read the grant report and ordered the whole operation placed under the highest classification. Since three this morning we've had someone writing a replacement report. The Director called for Morrison to be here by ten-thirty," the voice said smugly.

"What about me?"

"You've got until eleven."

⟁ 5 ⟁

KEPLER READ ALOUD, " 'UFO Reported in Desert. Two residents of the community of Cottonwood Pass, California, have reported finding what they believe to be the site where a flying saucer made a crash landing. David Greeley, sixty-two, and his wife Emma, sixty, came upon a shallow crater with bits of burned metal wreckage in Fried Liver Wash, a remote area east of the San Bernardino Mountains, last Tuesday while on a rock-hunting expedition. In an interview Mr. Greeley predicted that an analysis of the wreckage would reveal that it was made of a metal not known on Earth. He further stated that a second spacecraft must have landed nearby to rescue survivors and salvage the critical components of the wrecked saucer, including its precious power source. "If only we'd been there on Saturday," said Mr. Greeley, "we might have solved America's energy problems forever. But it wasn't meant to be." Officers of the California Highway Patrol dispatched from Palm Springs to the site reported that it was the wreckage of an old pickup truck which had apparently been set afire by vandals.' "

"Vandals?" said Immelmann. "I guess so." He stared out the car window.

"Where are we going, Chinese?" said Kepler. "You're getting to be a pain in the ass, always driving us around to—" he read from the newspaper, " 'a remote area east of the San Bernardino Mountains' or some damn place like it was a scavenger hunt."

"Nothing remote today," said Chinese Gordon. "Just over to East L.A. to see a guy."

"Who?" said Immelmann quietly. "What kind of guy?"

"Well," said Chinese Gordon, staring ahead as he turned off the freeway, "not a very nice guy, I guess, but a guy who can help us. His name is Jorge Grijalvas."

"Whore-hay?" shouted Kepler. "Did you say whore-hay?"

"Approximately," said Chinese Gordon.

Immelmann said slowly, "Chinese, this disturbs me. We already have the three of us, and no doubt you'll tell Margaret. Each person we add is costing me an hour of sleep every night. This better be the last one, because this makes five."

Chinese Gordon chuckled. "This is my greatest stroke of genius. Jorge Grijalvas isn't in on our project at all. He's going to be our ally. Jorge Grijalvas, for your information, is one of the biggest bastards in East L.A. He is a sort of underboss of the Mexican Mafia."

"Shit," said Kepler. "I hate that. There's the Mexican Mafia, the Israeli Mafia, the Irish Mafia, the black Mafia. Why the hell can't people call it something else? Leave the word 'Mafia' to the Italians. I can hardly stand to read the paper anymore. And what the hell do we need this guy for?"

"We don't," said Chinese Gordon. "At the moment we have no use for him at all. The man is a walking case of urban blight—no redeeming social value."

Immelmann studied Chinese Gordon. "Go on." They drove down a block of crumbling, empty buildings.

"I'm providing, as they say, for a Better Tomorrow. This guy can do a number of things for us, based on his rather slimy enterprises. One, he can launder huge amounts of money if we need it, because he is a dealer in brown heroin, the scourge of the poorest of the poor. Two, he can make us disappear whenever we want, if the price is right."

"That's just what I was thinking," said Kepler. "Will you look at this neighborhood? I wouldn't walk a Doberman here—afraid somebody'd throw it to the ground and eat it." A dark blue 1961 Chevrolet with an impossibly shiny metal-flake finish and chrome-spoke hubcaps pulled up beside them. It was built so low to the pavement that it threw sparks as it accelerated at the corner.

Kepler eyed a group of a dozen young men wearing bandannas on their foreheads who were lounging in front of a hardware store, then pulled his pant leg up to reveal the knurled handgrip of the .357 Magnum stuck in his boot. Immelmann smiled.

Chinese Gordon continued. "You see, there's also the fact of history. You know there are already more people of Mexican descent in Los Angeles than there are Anglos? In five years most of southern California will be Spanish. By getting in touch now with Jorge Grijalvas we're making the smartest move you can imagine, getting into a growth stock on the ground floor. The world is one big commodities exchange and we're taking a plunge on Chicano futures."

•   •   •

HIS hand held out in front of him, the Director stood up and bounced across the room to meet Porterfield. But the Director's eyes were on the thick, flowered carpet at his feet. There had been speculation in the Company that Director William Blount used the flowers on his carpet as actors use marks on a stage to block out their movements. If that were true, thought Porterfield, this was a notable occasion. The Director advanced a dozen giant camellias to hold out his moist, pudgy hand before scuttling back behind his desk.

There was no greeting, only "Good. You're here," as though Blount were speaking to his feet.

"What's the problem?" asked Porterfield.

The Director's face took on a kind of dignity and repose when he was safely seated. "Probably nothing," said Blount. "It's a simple security problem if it's handled tactfully and intelligently. We've been going over some of the standing items in Morrison's inventory and discovered a certain lack of—discretion? imagination? I suppose that's accurate." The Director nodded to signify his agreement with himself.

Porterfield said, "The Donahue grants."

"Yes," said Blount. "Those projects should never have been carried on the books of the National Research Foundation to begin with. Have you read them yet?"

"No, sir," said Porterfield.

"This man Donahue has a complicated mentality. He seems to have started out as a young man studying mass psychological reactions as historical phenomena. As his work became more theoretical it also became more speculative."

"What sort of mass psychological reactions?" asked Porterfield.

"Social alienation of particular subgroups, in some of his milder research. In other instances it's economic panics, political upheavals, mass hysteria—fear of earthquakes, floods, volcanoes, and so on. He attracted attention when he started working out systems for quantifying the forces at work in these phenomena. Once he had a way of working out equations for a particular area, he seems to have turned to the empiricist's test, comparing his assessments with later events."

Porterfield nodded. "He started predicting."

"Precisely," said the Director, his face still inclined toward the blotter on his desk, his eyes lifting in their sockets to fix on Porterfield. "He also learned to refine his equations when the quotients didn't come to fruition in facts. Porterfield," said the Director, "this man actually has a grid, a kind of flow chart that he calls 'The Terror Index.' He's on record as receiving NRF grant money to perfect it by developing a blueprint for the destruction of Mexico."

Porterfield smiled. "It's easy enough to fix. The first step is to get him off the National Research Foundation's books, and Morrison's already done that. Welby told me on the telephone you had someone rewriting the reports, so that's covered too. We can be sure there's no future connection between him and the government. If you'd like, we can stop him from doing his research at all."

The Director drummed his fingers on the desk without taking his eyes off Porterfield. "For heaven's sake, Porterfield. So heavy handed. I don't want to destroy the man."

"Then what do you want?"

"I want to protect the Company."

"Is that all?"

"I want to protect the Company," repeated the Director.

Porterfield stood up. "And Donahue knows how to make the bogeyman come out in the daytime. He's part of the Company. Has anything been done?"

"I'm sending a man now. He should be in Los Angeles tomorrow to begin the security survey."

⚤ 6 ⚤

CHINESE GORDON PULLED the car over to the curb in front of an old white stucco apartment house with a high, narrow, wooden door. Wrought-iron grillwork covered the glass of the windows on the first floor. The flower boxes on the sills had potted azaleas sitting in them.

Kepler said, "If this is it, I'll stay with the car. That building belongs in Hollywood. They probably stole it."

"Don't be silly," said Chinese Gordon. "The car is safer here than in the parking lot at the Federal Building."

"It's your car," said Immelmann.

At the steps they could see that the lintel over the door was once inscribed "The Mont St. Michel," but the letters had been plastered over with clean white cement. Chinese Gordon rang the bell and there was a buzz to unlock the door. Kepler and Immelmann hung back to let Chinese Gordon enter first.

Inside was a tiny foyer decorated with pots and baskets, a pair of horns from a longhorn bull, and a few yellowing photographs of old *caballeros* with drooping moustaches. There was an open door with a brass plate engraved "Grijalvas Enterprises."

The receptionist at the desk said, "May I help you?"

Chinese Gordon said, "Mr. Gordon to see Mr. Grijalvas. These gentlemen are my colleagues, Mr. Kepler and Mr. Immelmann."

"Please be seated and I'll let him know you're here. He's in a conference at the moment." She walked around the corner and they could hear the sound of her spike heels for a distance of thirty or forty feet before a door opened.

Kepler stood up and paced around the room, looking at plaques, framed newspaper clippings, photographs. "Look at this," he hissed, and the others joined him before a frame that held a laminated article from a magazine. The headline read, "*Los Quatros Gros Años* of Jorge Grijalvas: Janitor to Millionaire in Four Years." Beside it were a certificate from the Chamber of Commerce "awarded to Jorge Grijalvas for his efforts in renovating low-income housing in the Los Angeles Barrio" and a black plastic sign that said "Member, Better Business Bureau."

Immelmann said, "Chinese, we're out of our depth."

"Right," said Kepler. "Not only owns real estate, but a man with 'Four Fat—' "

"Quiet," said Chinese Gordon. The receptionist's heels could be heard approaching up the long hallway. The three men sat down on the long leather couch. She reappeared, still smiling, and directed them to the door at the end of the hall.

Inside, a short, stocky man with a smooth, almost luminous tan complexion smiled and held out his hand. "I'm pleased to meet you, Mr. Gordon," he said, and ushered them to chairs along the wall opposite his desk. "Can I offer you a drink?"

Chinese Gordon said, "Mr. Grijalvas, this is Mr. Im-melmann, Mr. Kepler." Out of the corner of his eye Chinese Gordon saw Kepler nod, and then he heard him say, "Just beer."

Grijalvas pressed a button on his desk and snapped *"Cerveza"* into the intercom, then sat back and smiled, his hands folded on his stomach. "So, what can I do for you gentlemen?" he asked.

"We're looking for a chance to make a small invest-ment," said Chinese Gordon. "We felt that you, with your business connections, would perhaps be interested in helping us in exchange for a percentage."

"Perhaps," said Grijalvas, staring above their heads.

The door opened and a young man entered carrying a tray of beer bottles and tall glass steins. "Oh, the beer. Excellent, Juan. Thank you very much." Juan was thin at the waist but had the bulging arm muscles and thick neck of a weight lifter. As he turned his expressionless face toward them they could see a small blue tear tat-tooed below one eye, on his high cheekbone.

Grijalvas continued, "What sort of investment did you have in mind? Money for commerical property is extremely scarce at the moment—"

"Oh, no," said Chinese Gordon. "It wasn't real estate we were thinking of. We're expecting an embar-rassingly large inflow of capital in the near future and we'd like to try something more speculative. Although we have confidence in the long-term value of real estate, the turnover is so slow."

"Well, then," said Grijalvas, sipping his beer, "perhaps a partnership with someone who is willing to take on the risks of entrepreneurship."

"That's right," said Kepler. "We're in, we're out, everybody does his part, and we all have a beer." He poured the glass of beer down his throat without swallowing and grinned.

"What we were thinking of," said Chinese Gordon, "was something like financing a venture in pharmaceuticals—imported pharmaceuticals."

Grijalvas slammed down his stein like a gavel. "Good day," he said.

"Huh?" said Kepler.

"Get out."

"Wait," said Chinese Gordon.

"No, gentlemen," said Grijalvas. "It's ridiculous. The entrapment you people stoop to is so crude it's insulting. You come in here like you were born yesterday and try to get me to say something you can take to a grand jury. You don't even have the sense to take the gun out of your boot. Do you realize who you're dealing with? See that?" He pointed to an ornate western saddle with hammered silver studs that hung on a stand in the corner of the room. "I'll be sitting on that to ride in the Rose Parade before you make lieutenant."

Kepler whispered to Immelmann, "He'll need three more for his Four Fat—"

Grijalvas was still speaking. "You want to bust somebody for drugs, go out to ULA. Here," he shouted. "Take it with you." He tossed a folded newspaper on Chinese Gordon's lap.

Juan held the door open, so they stood up and went out. Kepler held onto his beer, which he finished as he walked down the hallway. When he set the stein on the receptionist's desk she smiled at them in confusion.

At the car Chinese Gordon said to Immelmann, "You drive," and sat in the back seat.

They drove in silence for a few minutes until Kepler said, "That was a hard way to get a free beer, Chinese."

"Shut up and listen," said Chinese Gordon. " 'Drug Research at ULA Campus,' " he read. " 'Spokesmen in the office of the president of the University of Los Angeles announced today that the controversial research on the effects of various controlled substances would continue in spite of resistance from alumni groups and even some members of the board of trustees. "The issue here is academic freedom," said Dale Crollett, Assistant Vice-President for University Relations. "Professor Gottlieb and his colleagues have secured the grants, the necessary approvals and licenses, and it is the position of the University that there will be no internal interference with scientific research." The controversy was touched off on Wednesday when the Drug Enforcement Administration turned over to the researchers one pound of the purest cocaine, which will be used in experiments to treat migraine headaches. Officals estimated the street value of the cocaine at over one million dollars when it was confiscated in a raid in East Los Angeles last July.' "

"Interesting," said Immelmann, "but not meaningful."

"Don't you see?" yelled Chinese Gordon. "He was taking us up on it! We have a deal!"

Kepler turned to Immelmann. "This man's optimism is getting on my nerves." To Chinese Gordon he said, "Do you think he sent Tiny Tears in there just to bring us a couple of beers?"

"No," said Chinese Gordon. "Actually, the tattoo just means he's served time. Probably that's where he got hooked on doing pull-ups. If he thought we were cops, would he even let us see an ex-convict in his office?"

"Probably," said Immelmann.

"This is a terrific opportunity," said Chinese Gordon. "If they confiscated the cocaine in East L.A., it probably belonged to Grijalvas. He's given us a challenge. He wants to buy back what was taken from him, that's all. If we get it, we have a deal—the start of a long and profitable relationship."

"What do you think?" said Immelmann to Kepler.

Kepler opened another beer can. "I think," he said, "that once upon a time there was a helicopter pilot in Viet Nam who got a bit off course and got shot down. As he climbed from the wreckage he said, 'What a break! Now we know where the bastards were hiding.'"

⩗ 7 ⩗

As CHINESE GORDON worked in his shop he tried to keep Doctor Henry Metzger in his sight. It had been a week since he'd installed the steel shutters on the windows and the automatic lock on the sliding door, both without consulting Doctor Henry Metzger. Now what was beginning to bother Chinese Gordon was that Doctor Henry Metzger didn't seem to be aware that anything had changed. The entire building had been closed so tightly that Chinese Gordon would have believed nothing larger than an ant could possibly break into it. Still, a dozen times a day Doctor Henry Metzger would disappear from the shop and reappear a short time later, ostentatiously cleaning his fur of the dust and seeds and leaf particles he'd picked up walking through the tall weeds in the empty lot next door.

At first Chinese Gordon had tried to ignore it, but Doctor Henry Metzger showed him no mercy. If Chinese Gordon didn't acknowledge immediately that he'd returned, Doctor Henry Metzger would spit out the debris from his fur and sneeze and shake himself so hard that his ears made a noise flapping against his head. Once, to emphasize the ease with which he eluded

Chinese Gordon's security measures, he brought back with him a pair of panty hose, a feat of such difficulty that it amounted in Chinese Gordon's mind to a major taunt.

There was a loud rap on the sliding door, and Chinese Gordon shouted, "Yeah!" as he went to slide the bolt aside. Immelmann slipped in, already talking, and closed the door behind him.

"Chinese, I've been thinking about this thing a lot lately, and I think we ought to put it off for now."

"We can't. Tonight is perfect. I've checked the place out and we can do it. There's no moon, the night will be cloudy, and everything is set. If we wait too long those professors will have cut all of Grijalvas's cocaine into lines and pumped them up the noses of five hundred degenerate bums who claim to have migraine headaches."

"I'm starting to get a migraine myself," muttered Immelmann. "Chinese, I just don't feel lucky."

Chinese Gordon started carefully hanging his hand tools on their pegs along the wall. "What happened?"

"Nothing," said Immelmann. "I didn't get much sleep last night and I don't feel sharp. You shouldn't do something big if you don't feel sharp."

"Why didn't you sleep?"

"There was a party in the apartment across the court. It was unbelievably noisy. The music was so loud I could feel it, and people kept going outside and then when they came back they'd have to shout louder than the music to get somebody to open the door. Then I called the police."

"So?"

"So I dialed the number and a very strange voice came on. It was slow and deep and kind of gravelly, like this: 'Who . . . is . . . this?' I said, 'I'd like to make a

complaint.' The voice, honest to God, Chinese, it
sounded weird, like a big fat ghost. 'Who . . . is . . .
this?' again. Three times. I said, 'I'd like to file a complaint.' Then the voice said in that same way, 'Go . . .
fuck . . . yourself.' Then he hung up.

"Then I called the phone company and they said
they'd connect me. As soon as I heard it ringing I knew
it was the same voice: 'Go . . . fuck . . . yourself,' before
I could say anything. I didn't sleep at all."

Chinese Gordon suddenly realized he'd lost sight of
Doctor Henry Metzger, who had gone out through his
secret exit again. "Don't be a fool," Chinese Gordon
said. "It's just nerves. This thing will only take an hour
or so, and then you can sleep tonight and the next few
days after that. You could even spend the night calling
the same number and giving him a hard time."

Immelmann pondered the idea. Then he shrugged and
said, "I'm going to go try him right now," and stomped
up the stairs to Chinese Gordon's living quarters.

Kepler didn't knock, just kicked the door and yelled
"Yo!" When Chinese Gordon let him in, Doctor Henry
Metzger scampered in among the feet, and Chinese Gor-
don glared at him in anger.

Kepler said, "Hello, Doctor Henry," and the cat
rubbed its body against him and leaped up on the
workbench. Chinese Gordon clenched his jaw and
turned away so Kepler wouldn't sense his annoyance.
Kepler said, "You know, Chinese, I wouldn't have put
all those steel shutters and bolts and things on if I were
you. It makes burglars think you've got something in
here they'd want. What did it cost you, anyway?"

"Not much," Chinese Gordon lied. "I did it myself,
of course."

"Well, if you need any more of the quarter-inch steel,
let me know. I can get it cheap. Free, practically."

"Thanks," said Chinese Gordon, "but—"

Immelmann was coming down the stairs.

"Well?" said Chinese Gordon.

Immelmann said, "This time it was a different voice. The voice said, 'Los Angeles Police Department.' I have it figured out, though. There must be something wrong with my phone. When I dial the police number it registers wrong and gets The Voice."

"Sounds possible," said Chinese Gordon. "They can send a guy to fix it tomorrow."

"Fix it?" said Immelmann. "Hell, no. I'm going to leave it that way. I can call him up any time I feel like it—in the middle of the night, of course."

Chinese Gordon wondered how long it would take Immelmann to realize that he'd have to be awake to call the number, or that the second call had been placed by an operator. He hoped it would take at least twenty-four hours.

CHINESE Gordon drove the van past the campus gate, and the uniformed parking service man gave a nod. It was four-thirty in the afternoon, and Chinese Gordon had known the man wouldn't look carefully enough at the ULA parking sticker to notice that it was three strips peeled off another vehicle and pasted on. At this hour the traffic was all in the exit lane, and the parking men were beginning to relax.

Chinese Gordon drove up the narrow street past a row of ten-story dormitories and into the parking structure. He pulled into a space marked "Service Vehicles Only" and left the motor running while Kepler and Immelmann applied magnetic signs to the sides and rear door of the van. When Chinese Gordon had insisted on a yellow revolving emergency light on top of the van,

Kepler had said, "But Chinese, it's ridiculous. The signs say 'Klondike Air Conditioning Service.' " Chinese Gordon had replied, "Have you ever seen a repair truck without one of those?" Immelmann had agreed, so now he stepped on the front bumper and applied the finishing touch, a big yellow light in the center of the roof above the windshield.

"Not yet," said Chinese Gordon. "The ceiling's too low. We'll never get out of the ramp."

"Oh," said Immelmann, and climbed back in the van.

Chinese Gordon drove out of the parking ramp and stopped to let Immelmann slide the light into its brackets. Kepler glanced at his watch, a big Rolex with a face like a gauge from an airplane cockpit. "Four thirty-nine."

"Good," said Chinese Gordon. "We'll be parked outside the building at five when they all go home, so the night security will think we've been around all day."

"You're a clever man, Chinese," said Kepler.

"Devious," said Immelmann, squinting his eyes and pondering. "Odd that you should be such a jackass in other ways."

"It's one of the mysteries," Kepler agreed.

"Get down now," said Chinese Gordon. "We're coming to the Social Sciences Building." Immelmann and Kepler moved to the back of the van and crouched on opposite sides of the back door. Kepler sat back with his feet across the box covering the barrel of the M-39, glanced at his watch again, and said, "Four forty-six."

Immelmann lay down flat as though to go to sleep. He sighed and said, "You know, nobody gives a shit if it's four twenty-eight or four ninety-seven. Being with you two has been something of a religious experience for me."

"Oh?" said Kepler.

"It proves that God, in His bounty and generosity, always creates more horses' asses than there are horses to attach them to."

"Amen," said Kepler, popping open a beer can.

Chinese Gordon got out of the van and placed the red-and-white-striped sawhorse in front of the grille. He was pleased with it, even though the paint wasn't completely dry—it looked so official and businesslike, but it served no purpose. He buckled his tool belt and then placed a second sawhorse behind the van. He walked into the Social Sciences Building and began stalking the hallways. He'd been here two days before, but that had been just a preliminary trip to get a general idea of how to penetrate the building. Now he was here to study the rooms. The time to find out where somebody kept something valuable was the end of the day, when they locked it up. He knew nobody would pay attention to him because he had already assumed his disguise, a gray work shirt with a label that said "Dave" sewn over the pocket.

He knew exactly what he was searching for, so he wasted no time looking into classrooms and departmental offices. It would be a place with some activity, like a laboratory or a clinic, with more than one room, and right about now they'd be putting the cocaine into a safe. Chinese Gordon started on the top floor and began to work downward. It wouldn't be on the ground floor, because somebody would think of that as a security risk. On the fourth floor he found what he was looking for. The sign on the door said "Institute for Psychobiological Research. Director: Gottlieb." Stenciled in big red letters on the door was "Admittance by Appointment." Chinese Gordon admired that way of putting it: No sense offending those invited to come in for a free toot of cocaine, and no sense spending the day fighting off a crowd of marble-eyed beggars with noses like snorkels. Chinese Gordon kept moving. He knew that these people would be closing up for the day now, and they'd be in the hallways within minutes.

On the third floor things were about the same. There were a few classrooms, a lot of little offices, and not much else. Near the far end of the hall, he passed an office that seemed to have an unusual amount of activity. There were too many people coming out. The place didn't look big enough to hold them. Three of them were probably secretaries, women in their late twenties or thirties who wore high heels and makeup and expensive, conservative clothes. Then there were others, people too old to be undergraduate students, wearing work shoes and sneakers and boots, their outfits all reminiscent of lumberjacks or cowboys. He decided to wait near the stairwell. For something to do, he unraveled a few feet of insulated wire from the spool on his tool belt and began cutting and splicing it into insane patterns that would intimidate anyone who saw them.

At five-fifteen two men came out together. The first didn't look as though he belonged in a university. He was in his middle thirties, wearing a beautifully tailored gray suit and carrying a briefcase of lustrous Italian leather, so thin that it seemed designed to carry two-page letters or maybe contracts. The second man was older, his coat a worn and ageless tweed, and his briefcase was of the voluminous sort that might have held books, or the term papers of a fair-sized class. He was saying, "It's very disruptive."

The first man answered, "The work will be done this weekend. By Monday the whole security problem will be solved." As the two disappeared into the elevator, Chinese Gordon smiled.

• • •

WHEN Chinese Gordon returned to the van it was dark outside and the few cars that passed were moving as quickly toward the campus exit as the narrow, winding street permitted. He opened the door of the van and Immelmann and Kepler climbed out. Both were now wearing gray work shirts like his. Over the left breast pocket each had a patch sewn on that said "Dave." Immelmann had stolen them from a dryer in a Laundromat.

"Okay," said Chinese Gordon. "Make it look heavy."

The two lifted out a large cardboard box that said "HOTPOINT POWER PLUS" on it and followed Chinese Gordon into the building. The hallways were now empty, and the steps of the men echoed on the tiles. Chinese Gordon noted with satisfaction that the elevator was waiting on the first floor. Nobody had gone up, but somebody had come down.

The fouth floor was only dimly lit, another indication to Chinese Gordon that things were going well. He held the box while Kepler and Immelmann flipped a coin to see who would open the door. Kepler picked the two locks and then stood back.

"There must be an alarm. Let's check it out first," he whispered.

"I don't see any lights," said Chinese Gordon.

"How about strips?" said Immelmann.

"No, but there must be something," Kepler muttered. "My high school principal had an alarm in his office twenty years ago, for Christ's sake, and the locks were a hell of a lot easier to pick than this."

"That was when you were there," Chinese Gordon whispered. "Besides, maybe he kept more cocaine than these guys." He pushed past them into the room and set the box on the floor. The others followed.

In the dim glow of the single window, the room looked like the waiting area of a doctor with an impoverished practice. There were couches and mismatched chairs arranged to face a receptionist's desk. A few worn magazines and crumpled newspapers were inexpertly stacked on a coffee table.

"My turn," said Immelmann, who knelt to pick the lock on the door to the inner room, then slowly pushed the door open. "No alarm here either, but this could be the place."

"Why?" said Kepler.

"There's a little safe in the corner."

"Of course that's it," said Chinese Gordon. "Do you see any other rooms? Watch it with the safe. That's sure to be wired."

Kepler and Immelmann walked up to the safe. Kepler chuckled. "Beautiful. Just beautiful."

"What?" snapped Chinese Gordon.

"Go down and start the engine, Chinese. There aren't even liquor stores with these things anymore. It's a joke. It's wired, all right. Come here."

He pulled a length of wire from the spool on Gordon's belt and snipped the wire off, then looped it and taped it to the strip of wire on the wall. Then he yanked off the wire to the safe and said, "Now it's not."

"I have something to do," said Chinese Gordon. "Wait for me here."

"Don't take too long," said Immelmann. "We'll have the safe in the box in a minute. Just have to cut some bolts."

Chinese Gordon took the stairs to the third floor. It took him only a moment to find the office he had noticed earlier, and he had no trouble opening the lock. He had expected things to be easy, but this reminded him of a dream he'd once had in which the walls of buildings were made of a thick, soft concoction like cheese.

Inside, he found a line of doors on a long hallway. He studied the doors and the placement of the rooms and decided on the one at the far end of the hall. It would be either a broom closet or the boss's office. It must be on the corner of the building, so that meant a chance for two windows. The professor he'd seen before was definitely of two-window rank.

He opened the lock and smiled. It was the boss's office, all right. There was a big desk and an old manual typewriter. No secretary would use a machine like that. The walls were lined with books, the sort of books that cost too much unless you got them free. Chinese Gordon scanned the office. There was no safe, no display case for something rare and valuable. He moved his face close to the painting on the wall, but even in this light he could see it was only a commercially printed reproduction of an Utrillo street scene. He'd stayed in a motel once where the same print hung over the bed.

Maybe it was a waste of time. They could have been talking about bolting down the office machines. He sat on the desk and thought. The younger man wasn't the type for bolting down typewriters. In a five-hundred-dollar suit he wasn't selling burglar alarms, either. Whatever it was had to be valuable. Upstairs Kepler and Immelmann were loading a million dollars in cocaine the university had been keeping in what amounted to a jewelry box, but the man hadn't been up there. He'd been down here.

Chinese Gordon rushed into the hallway and began opening doors. He peered into each room for some sign that it might hold something worth stealing. There was nothing. In the fourth room he stopped. Inside was a computer terminal. Shit, he thought. What if they were just worried that somebody would come in and access their fucking data base? For an instant he considered smashing the screen of the terminal. It would have given him pleasure, but he controlled the impulse.

Everything about the way the rooms were arranged would induce the feeling that the farthest office was the safest. It had to be there.

Chinese Gordon went back to the boss's office and stood in the doorway. There were books on the desk. When he tried the desk drawers they weren't even locked, so he didn't search them closely. Then he noticed the row of filing cabinets. There were four. The lock button was pushed in on the third one only. The time was going by. If this wasn't it, then he'd have to forget it.

Chinese Gordon picked the lock and flung open the top drawer, which contained nothing. The second drawer was empty too. In the third drawer was a box the size of a ream of paper. He tried the last drawer, and it was empty.

There was no strong reason to take the box, but there wasn't a strong reason not to, either. God knew he'd done enough work for the damned thing. He left the office with the box under his arm and ran up the stairs to the fourth floor.

IMMELMANN and Kepler were already in the hallway holding the carton between them. When Chinese Gordon appeared, they moved into the elevator.

"Problems?" asked Kepler. "If there's a security guard with a broken neck, I'd like to know."

"No," said Chinese Gordon. "Just thought I'd pick this up on a hunch. I'll tell you about it later."

The elevator door opened and they stepped out. The

first-floor vestibule was still empty. Somewhere in a distant hallway they could hear the metallic clanking of a bucket and the squish of a mop wringer. They moved quickly out of the building. As the others made their way down the walk to the van, Chinese Gordon gently guided the door shut. It locked behind them automatically, and he smiled to himself. He liked it when things were as he'd expected them to be.

Chinese Gordon drove along the dark, deserted, winding road across the campus, stopping at every corner to obey the signs that protected the thousands of pedestrians who crowded the walks in the daytime. He started singing, "Look out the way, Old Dan Tucker," as he made the long curve that led to the exit gate.

He was building to his favorite part when he'd get to sing about old Dan Tucker comin' to town, when the headlights settled on the figure of a man in the road. It was a uniformed parking attendant, and he was setting up a sign that said "Exit Closed." As the van drew nearer and the headlights brightened on him, the man raised his hand and squinted. His face and hands looked unnaturally white.

"Shit!" said Kepler. "It's the same one." He pulled up his pant leg and grasped the grip of his pistol.

"One of these times you're going to blow your foot off," Immelmann observed.

Kepler turned to Chinese Gordon. "You said they'd change shifts."

Chinese Gordon said, "No problem. See?" The man stepped back and waved them on. "We're going to make it."

Suddenly the man's face changed. The squinting eyes widened, the pinched expression flattened, and the mouth hung open as the man disappeared from the glare of the lights and the van glided past.

Kepler was holding the .357 Magnum in his hand now. First he lunged across Immelmann to reach the side window, but Immelmann's long, lanky shape was trapped in the way. Immelmann bent his elbows like wings and tried to pull his bony knees to his chest, but he only succeeded in jerking a kneecap into Kepler's chin. Chinese Gordon could hear Kepler's teeth clap shut with a click. Kepler dropped to the floor and scrambled toward the back of the van.

Chinese Gordon studied the dark silhouette of the security man in the rearview mirror. The man was running now, a fat trot that seemed to bounce and jolt his body up and down without bringing it much nearer to the van.

Kepler shouted, "I've got the box off, Chinese!"

Immelmann said, "What for?"

"He's going for the kiosk, you idiot! The telephone!"

Chinese Gordon stopped at the traffic light and glanced ahead for an opening in the stream of cars. Kepler was waving his pistol and shouting, "You've got to take out the kiosk, Chinese! Now, before he gets to the phone!"

Chinese Gordon pressed the three buttons under the dashboard. The generator whirred, the fan hummed, and the back door slid open. In the mirror he could see the lighted parking kiosk, a tiny outpost in the darkness, centered in the crosshairs. He could see the parking guard's chubby shape trotting along, his hat now gone. Chinese Gordon grasped the remote-control switch in his right hand. Ten minutes could make all the difference.

He said, "Hold onto something," and flicked the switch with his thumb. The gun roared, the van jolted forward, and Chinese Gordon's view was obscured by flame and smoke and movement. When he looked through the rearview mirror again, he could see that the kiosk was gone. Strewn along for a distance of a hundred feet beyond were pieces of burning wood and chunks of pulverized cinder block. He could see the parking guard crawling on his hands and knees down the center of the street at amazing speed.

Chinese Gordon stepped on the gas pedal and pulled out into traffic, the van trailing smoke out the back door and side vents. Cars along the boulevard had pulled over and stopped, as though the terrible noise had stunned them. Chinese Gordon turned on the flashing lights and leaned on the horn as he hurtled down the street among them. He squealed around the corner on two wheels and headed for the freeway entrance.

Immelmann moved to the rear of the van to help Kepler close the door. "I wonder what they earn," he said.

"What?" shouted Chinese Gordon.

Immelmann smiled. "You know, those parking guys."

ᴧ 8 ᴧ

CHINESE GORDON'S BODY was hunched forward over the steering wheel, his right foot still on the gas pedal and his teeth clenched as the van knifed into the space between two cars and shot up the Harbor Freeway. He drove with ferocious tenacity, first shuttling from lane to lane to dodge slower cars that floated by like drifting swatches of color, then easing into the wake of a long-haul semi that moved up the left lane with a frightening gallop that meant an empty trailer and the driver's firm intention to keep the engine straining at least until he had to gear down on the grapevine at Bakersfield.

Kepler said, "Figure seven or eight minutes for that sorry bastard back there to realize he's not dead. Figure a minute to remember to call the police, and maybe five minutes from them to decide he's not crazy and start trying to do something constructive."

Immelmann thought for a moment. "Fifteen minutes, then. That's about what I figured. We've used up about five." He smiled. "So in about ten minutes either they'll have us or they won't get us."

Chinese Gordon said, "We can't make Van Nuys in ten minutes, even following this maniac."

"True," said Kepler. "They'll have the choppers over the freeway before then anyway." He turned to Immelmann. "Thank the good Lord that Old Chinese has a plan."

"I do?"

"Of course," said Kepler. "You always do."

"Well, I don't exactly have one at the moment, but I've been thinking about it."

"See?" said Kepler to Immelmann. "What'd I tell you? He doesn't have the faintest idea of how to get out of this, but he's thinking."

Chinese Gordon took the ramp from the Golden State Freeway behind the semi and then veered to the right lane, picking up speed. He passed two more exits before he saw the sign he remembered. "Good," he said. "How long since we left the campus?"

Immelmann said, "About six or seven minutes."

Chinese Gordon drifted onto the exit ramp and coasted onto another ramp at the end. He drove north on the Glendale Freeway to Foothill Boulevard and then cruised up Foothill Boulevard.

"I see your plan," said Kepler. "You're going to keep turning onto smaller and smaller roads until finally the road and everything on it just disappears."

"Close," said Chinese Gordon as he passed a hamburger stand. He brightened. "It's right up here." He drove along what seemed to be empty fields for a distance onto a gravel drive and followed it a hundred yards into the trees and stopped before a chain link fence.

"What's this," asked Immelmann, "a garbage dump?"

"No," said Chinese Gordon. "It's a junkyard. Get the lock on that gate." Immelmann jumped down and trotted to the gate. He examined the padlock for a moment, seemed to fondle it in his hand, and then tugged it open.

"Amazing, isn't he?" asked Chinese Gordon.

"Yeah, just like Houdini," said Kepler. "What are we doing here?"

"I know it's not a great plan, but it's all I could think of." Chinese Gordon glanced at his watch. "It's been about fifteen minutes and we've put a good fifteen miles between us and the college. That's something, but by now they'll have helicopters, maybe even roadblocks on the freeways. If we don't do something, we're finished."

"Agreed," said Kepler. "Three Fools Killed in Shootout with LAPD."

Immelmann was waving them forward, and Chinese Gordon obeyed, inching along with the headlights off. Immelmann closed the gate and snapped the padlock, then climbed into the van.

They drove up and down the aisles of car bodies, some crumpled and distorted, others merely pillaged, a hood or a bumper gone. There were automobiles of all kinds, some sitting stranded on blocks without tires, others looking as though they had been parked just for a moment. There were whole sections of the place devoted to cars of one brand, other areas that seemed to defy classification. Chinese Gordon drove on until he saw a zone where the rusting hulks of metal seemed to rise higher than usual, then turned down the aisle toward it.

There were campers, pickup trucks, even two tow trucks, and then the vans. There were vans of every make and description, every combination of colors. He found an opening and parked next to a van that lay on its side like a sleeping hippopotamus.

They got out and stood in the darkness. Immelmann

removed the magnetic signs from the van's sides and the yellow light from the roof and stowed them neatly inside, while Kepler peered into the cooler. The three sat down in a row on the ground beside the van. Kepler popped open a can of beer that sounded unnaturally loud, and passed it to Chinese Gordon, then popped two more. In the huge expanse of abandoned, rusting metal there was no motion, no sound. In the unnatural silence Chinese Gordon could hear the sizzling sound of his beer foaming out of the top of the can and dripping onto his lap, but he was too deep in concentration to be distracted. The next stage of things had to be perfect. It had to be something that—

"Listen," whispered Immelmann.

There was only the sound of the beer fizzing in the hollow cans, a quiet, comforting, metallic sound. As Chinese Gordon listened, the sound seemed to swell, to grow. Something else seemed to be adding to it, augmenting it, a deeper, more rhythmic sound. He whispered, "Into the van."

They scrambled in and huddled around the warm barrel of the automatic cannon. They all knew the sound too well, had heard it too often in too many places to mistake it for anything else. As they watched through the windows they saw the tiny red spot appear over the hill and float slowly toward the junkyard, sometimes sweeping smoothly for a time, then stopping, hanging in a swaying arc above the vicinity of the freeway and then moving on. As it approached, the noise grew louder, first to a high humming, then deeper and deeper until the growling noise of the engine could be distinguished from the beat of the whirling rotors. As they watched, the red spot paused, hovering, and a bright beam of white light shot downward to the ground, then swept a few hundred feet, and then flicked off. In the distance now they could see the red running lights of other police helicopters moving methodically back and forth over the roads. Now and then one would shine its searchlight on the ground, and a circular pool of light would transfix whatever was beneath in its glare, and then sweep on.

"Looks like Da Nang," said Chinese Gordon.

"Here it is," said Kepler. The helicopter hovered over the junkyard and turned on its searchlight. The disc of bright light shot around the fence, lingered for a second on the shack near the gate, and then moved on.

For a long time none of them moved. Two more helicopters passed overhead and then moved back over the road and followed its course to the northeast.

"GONE," said Kepler. "Now what?"

"Now we think," said Chinese Gordon. "That poor schmuck back there must have been a lot clearer than we thought if they're already making a sweep this far out. We have to assume he gave them some kind of description of the van, so they think they know what they're looking for."

Immelmann shrugged. "Three men in a white air-conditioner repair van, armed and dangerous, et cetera."

"I don't like leaving the van," Kepler said. "We might get lucky and the guy who owns this place won't notice it for a day, but more likely he will. People who deal in worthless shit always think it's great and hate to part with it, so they go around and visit it whenever they've got a minute."

"We could smash it up a little," Immelmann said.

"We could open the safe here."

"There's the armor plate that Chinese bolted inside, and the gun," Kepler said. "Everything about it says 'Call the Police.'"

"We may as well get started," said Chinese Gordon. "There are only four cans of that spray paint we used on the sawhorses. There's tape in the toolbox. We've got to use everything carefully. Don't waste it, don't leave anything lying around. I'll start taping the chrome and the windows. You two see if you can find anything around here that will change the way the van looks, even if it's only hubcaps or some damned hood ornament."

"You're going to paint the van red?" said Kepler. "In the dark? With cans? Chinese, think about it. Pretend you're a cop. You've been listening to the radio. Some hysterical parking guy says he saw a white van blow up his outhouse with an automatic cannon from an airplane. Then you hear the reason it happened was because the van is carrying the Gross National Product of Peru. Say you're not some rookie, but a real honest-to-God twelve-year veteran. It's three in the morning and nobody has seen the white van yet. What are you going to do if you see a red van coming your way?"

"At three in the morning, sure," said Immelmann.

Chinese Gordon shrugged. "You said yourself we can't leave it here. We can't take it out as it is. We can't do anything but change it and head for home in the rush-hour traffic tomorrow morning, when there will be more white vans on the road than there are police."

Kepler and Immelmann moved into the darkness, carrying screwdrivers and wrenches. It was difficult to see at first, but as they walked among the battered shapes of trucks and vans, they began to discern the accessories, some practical, others vain: A truck had a trailer hitch, a van had a rack to hold its spare tire on the back door. Another had a set of spoke hubcaps and wooden door handles.

"This is sort of fun," said Kepler as he unscrewed a set of mud flaps under a Volkswagen minibus. He heard Immelmann give a snort, and he supposed Immelmann was right. Then he heard Immelmann say something unintelligible. He rolled out from under the Volkswagen and looked up at Immelmann, who was standing in the empty path between the rows of car bodies, staring at something off in the darkness. He was muttering, "Oh shit. Oh shit. Oh shit," so quietly that Kepler could barely hear it. Kepler lay on the ground and peered into the silent shadows. Then he heard it, far away at first, and then louder and louder, a tick-tick-tick, faster and faster, and then he caught a glimpse of it.

It was the black shape of a huge dog, so big it seemed to brush its shoulder against the hood ornament on a '57 Chevy as it passed, but he knew that wasn't possible. It was just the distance and the darkness, but that made it even worse, because a dog that charged two men from a couple of hundred feet instead of stalking them was something worse than just big. Then he remembered why junkyards never have night watchmen, something that had slipped his mind when he'd been hiding from the helicopters and wondering why he always listened to Chinese Gordon's schemes. Kepler lay on his belly and pulled the .357 Magnum out of his boot. He steadied the pistol in both hands and leveled it on the sound, the "huff, huff, huff" of the charging beast's eager chest. He knew he'd see it, if only for a moment when it was about ten or twelve feet from Immelmann. It would jump hugh for the throat because it was surely that kind of dog, the kind the owner would starve and beat and abuse until it hated the smell of a man so much even he couldn't go near it when he came to open the gate in the morning, so he had to lure it into an enclosure with food. There would be time for only one shot, but Kepler didn't expect to need more. After it blew the dog apart, the slug from the .357 Magnum would crack the engine block on the car across the aisle.

He held the gun steady on the sound, waiting for another flash of vision, something to focus on. The dog sounded like a freight train—"huff! huff! huff!"— more than heavy breathing, and not a bark, more like the dog was talking to itself, maybe even laughing. He felt an instant of regret—the poor crazy animal, waiting all this time finally to sink his teeth into somebody, and—

"Don't shoot it," said Immelmann.

"What?"

Immelmann walked calmly across the aisle and stood beside an old bread delivery truck. He opened one of the back doors wide, climbed inside, and Kepler lost sight of him. Just then the animal appeared, dashing at terrible speed, taking eight or ten feet at a leap, its mouth open wide, its lips rolled back to bare a set of teeth from some nightmare. It overran the truck by some twenty feet in its insane ferocity, then seemed to turn in the air to scramble to the open door. It leaped inside, giving voice to a snarl that sounded like something being torn.

Kepler jumped to his feet and sprinted for the truck, but as he did, he saw Immelmann get out of the driver's seat and slam the door, then walk around the truck and close the back door. An instant later the dog hurled itself against the door so hard the truck shivered.

"Pitiful," said Immelmann. He looked in the window and said, "Sorry, you poor bastard." The dog's face pressed against the glass, its front teeth trying to bite the surface. The dog threw himself against the door again and again, making a booming noise and shaking the truck. Then he tried to bite the glass again, and his rage grew into a titanic frustration at not being able to open his jaws wide enough.

Immelmann looked at the dog's face and said sadly, "He wants to bite the world, doesn't he?"

Kepler stifled an impulse to shoot him through the glass. "Come on," he said, putting the pistol back into his boot. "If we get out of his sight maybe he won't hurt himself trying to get at us."

They returned to the van to find Chinese Gordon already painting. He had taped paper over the windows and lights and was carefully spraying with an even, steady motion of his forearm, back and forth. Immelmann set down his burden of chrome and picked up a can of paint. They worked in silence for what Kepler judged to be three hours. After a little while Kepler stopped hearing noises from the bread truck three aisles away. He kept himself working, even after he judged the van was as red as it ever would be and Chinese Gordon insisted on doing all the cutting and screwing that was making his van look like a fire truck designed by a mental defective, by thinking about the owner of that dog opening the door of the bread truck. The man would arrive at seven-thirty and call the dog to its cage. He'd lay steak in sight, then wait. He'd whistle, he'd make every noise he could think of. At eight or eight-thirty he'd be sure the dog was dead or at least too sick to move. Then he'd come inside, walking on tiptoe. By then he'd have stopped being afraid and be thinking about a new dog—a puppy, probably, that he'd have to start teaching to kill people, start abusing and starving. But he'd still have to start looking for the old dog because a two-hundred-pound carcass rotting in your yard would be a horror. At some point he'd find the bread truck and open the door. Kepler leaned into the van, pulled a beer can out of the cooler, and popped it open. He poured a stream of beer down his throat and smiled to himself.

As the sky in the east began to lose its purple and brighten into a metallic gray, Immelmann stood up and said, "Chinese, I could use a hand with that horse trailer over there."

"What for?"

"It's a hell of a disguise, for one thing."

Kepler nodded. "It is, Chinese. It'll just about completely change the way the van looks from the air. Here, let's pull it over and hook it up." The two picked up the trailer's hitch assembly and started pulling it out of the line.

"Wait," said Kepler. "Where are we going? The van's over there."

"I always wanted a dog," Immelmann said.

"Oh no, Immelmann. You can't. The fucking thing is a monster. It'll kill you. For that matter, Chinese Gordon'll kill you."

Immelmann leaned against the weight, moving the trailer by himself. "It just needs a friend."

Kepler stalked along beside him, bending down to talk into Immelmann's ear. "You live in a one-bedroom apartment. An animal like that needs a place to run. Like Africa."

Immelmann grunted as he pulled the trailer. "I've made up my mind. You can get Chinese Gordon into an uproar about it if you feel like standing around arguing until the guy who owns this place comes to work. You could also shut up and help me."

Kepler moved to the rear of the trailer. In the growing

light he could read the two bumper stickers. At one time they'd said, "Have you hugged your horse today?" but someone had changed them to, "Have you hugged your whores today?" and "Have you fucked your horse today?" He decided to remember to tear them off before they drove the trailer onto the road.

They backed the horse trailer to the rear of the bread truck and the dog woke up. This time it didn't bark, just threw its body against the back door, rocking the truck, then getting up in silence and leaping against the door again.

"I'll open the truck door, you slam the trailer door," said Kepler. "The timing has got to be right."

"Of course." Immelmann took his position beside the trailer, his hand poised on the open door.

Kepler listened to the sound of the huge dog throwing itself against the truck door, then walked to the front of the truck. The dog's toenails scratched the metal truck bed as it gathered speed for another leap, and Kepler flung the door open. When he saw the black shape lunge past, he knew he'd miscalculated. The dog's leap carried it to the roof of the trailer, where it scrambled for a foothold, then whirled and poised to leap down at Kepler. At that moment Immelmann said quietly, "Down, boy," and pushed the dog's haunches hard. The dog slipped on the roof and sat down.

In the dim light Kepler could see the sitting dog sliding past with what seemed to be a look of puzzlement on its face, and Immelmann pushing it so quickly it couldn't stand up. As it went off the edge of the trailer and saw that it was falling back into the bread truck, it writhed and twisted in midair. As it landed, the dog dashed into the horse trailer eagerly, and Immelmann closed the door.

They pulled the trailer up the aisle, but the dog inside

was silent. Immelmann beamed. "He's strong as a man and weighs as much. He's fast, he's got teeth like a Rototiller, and he's not afraid of anything that breathes."

"All true," said Kepler. "Hell of a pet for a man who's afraid his yard will be infested with cows."

THE sun was already above the level of the ridge to the east when Chinese Gordon drove past the gate and onto the gravel drive and waited for Kepler to replace the lock. As Chinese Gordon eased the van onto the highway, the sound seemed to grow louder for a moment, then fade into the hum of the engine and the rush of the wind and the more unfamiliar rattle of the trailer. He knew the sound hadn't gone away. He listened intently, trying to separate it from the other sounds and identify it. There was a high-pitched whine for a few seconds that seemed to go down the scale to a growl. It wasn't too surprising that a horse trailer in a junkyard needed a grease job, maybe even needed wheel bearings. It was the shaking that worried him. Every ten or fifteen seconds he felt something happen to the horse trailer. It shook as though its weight had shifted suddenly, and that could only be trouble. He was glad when he saw they were getting close to Van Nuys, because by then he'd decided there was something wrong with the way the trailer was mounted to its axle. What it felt like was that the trailer wasn't empty. It felt as though it had a horse in it and the horse was getting mad as hell.

ᴧ 9 ᴧ

WHEN THE TELEPHONE rang, Porterfield was awake and alert. His left foot pushed off on the floor and he lifted himself out of the bed carefully to keep from moving the blankets over Alice. There was a slight twinge in the left knee, a stiffness that wasn't yet a tremor or a pain, but a reminder. Alice stirred slightly in her dream, sighed, and tugged the blanket up to her neck.

He closed the bedroom door and lifted the receiver. "Yes?"

"Please call in." It was a man's voice, the toneless, clear, quiet voice.

Porterfield turned on the hallway light and squinted against the glare to dial the familiar number. "Benjamin Porterfield. Any messages?" He waited while the computer, somewhere in the communications center, compared the recording it had just made with the master print of his voice in the memory bank. Then the man said, "Can you be in at six?"

Porterfield's eyes were beginning to adjust to the light. He glanced at his watch without surprise. It was four-thirty. "Yes." He hung up and slipped into the bedroom, leaving the door ajar to cast a sliver of light on the closet.

He could see Alice's shape on the bed, a small, compact lump with the covers clutched around her, her face empty and innocent of thought—a face watching the pretty pictures of a dream. Alice was becoming a little old lady, he thought, a sweet little old lady. She was nearly as old as he was, although time didn't appear to be using her up as quickly. She seemed to feel his eyes on her and let part of herself come to consciousness to acknowledge him.

"Ben?"

"What?"

"That wasn't one of the kids?"

"No, baby. Nothing to worry about. I just have to go in early."

"Trouble?"

"No. Go back to sleep. I'll call you later."

Alice sat up in bed and rubbed her eyes. "I'll make you some breakfast." She looked like a child in the dim light. He leaned over and kissed her cheek.

"Thanks anyway. I've got to have a breakfast meeting with somebody." He sat on the bed and put his arms around her, then gently pushed her back on the pillow. "Now go back to sleep."

He showered and dressed in the bathroom, trying to be as quiet as possible. It made him feel good to think of Alice in the bed, warm and soft, by now sleeping again, her face calm and somehow still beautiful almost thirty years after he'd met her.

When she heard the front door closing, Alice got out of bed and padded quietly to the living room in her bare feet. She stood in silence and watched the car pull out of the driveway and creep up the dark, empty street. Alice stood absolutely still, staring out the window for a long time after the car had disappeared, her face calm and thoughtful. Then she lit a cigarette and went to the kitchen without turning on the lights, and started the coffee. Soon the birds would start singing, she thought, and then the cold, bluish tinge of dawn would warm to yellow, the sun itself appearing first right over the chimney of the house across the street.

PORTERFIELD entered the Committee Room and classified the problem at a glance. There were no junior people scurrying in and out with earnest expressions, which meant the problem hadn't yet reached the moment when nothing could be done about it—the great flurry of pointless activity hadn't begun.

He noticed Hadley, who ran the Domestic Operations arm of Clandestine Services. He was predictable enough, and Pines, the Deputy Director, was no surprise. Their presence only certified that the trouble was worth getting out of bed at four-thirty to talk about. Kearns had had some shadowy relationship with the Latin America desk for so long nobody even thought about what his actual job was anymore. When Porterfield saw Goldschmidt he became curious. Goldschmidt was chief of Technical Services. If Goldschmidt was here it meant the problem was serious enough to draw his attention away from all the spy satellites and the research facilities built into Company proprietaries and affiliates, the arsenals, and nobody but Goldschmidt knew what else. Then Porterfield noticed John Knox Morrison sitting at the far end of the table and snorted. Morrison had managed, at this hour, to select a red necktie with a pattern that at first seemed to be white dots, but on second examination were small, perfect copies of the Harvard seal, with even the motto *veritas* legible from eight feet away. If Morrison was here, it was a disaster. Morrison wasn't someone who'd be called in to discuss strategies or solve problems. His only value was that he was someone who could be placed in positions that required the right family, a certain kind of influence. The fact that he appeared to be a fool was part of his protection as an operative; the fact that he was a genuine fool meant the disguise was impenetrable. Morrison's tanned, beefy face was looking uncomfortably pink, and his pale blue eyes darted furtively up occasionally to stare in secret alarm, first at Goldschmidt, then at Deputy Director Pines.

Pines spoke to Porterfield. "Hello, Ben. We've got troubles. We don't know what kind yet, but they're real enough to start figuring the options."

Porterfield nodded, and glanced at Morrison, who was intently tracing the grain of the wooden conference table with a pudgy forefinger.

"You're familiar with the Donahue psywar grants?"

"The Director mentioned them the other day," said Porterfield. "I've read most of the reports."

"Last night—early evening, actually—some kind of terrorist group attacked the campus of the University of Los Angeles. We don't know much about it yet. It was apparently something on the order of a commando raid. They blew up a parking service kiosk. That points to foreign groups, because if they picked that they probably thought it was a police guard post."

"Is that it?" asked Porterfield.

"They broke into the Social Sciences Building. That's Ian Donahue's building. It was early enough to make the eleven-o'clock news in Los Angeles."

"Great."

"Fortunately, they didn't want this kind of publicity

any more than we do. They covered it by breaking into a research lab and running off with—get this—a million dollars' worth of cocaine:''

"What was that doing there?"

"It's nothing to do with our projects, just some damned medical research thing that was easier to run from there than from the ULA hospital complex. I double-checked. We've got nothing to do with it.''

"What did they get from Donahue?"

"That's part of the problem," said Pines. He glared at Morrison. "We don't know yet. We know something is gone, that they were in the office. That's all we do know. They went in and got into two rooms in a building that has two hundred.''

Porterfield turned to Morrison. "What could they have gotten?"

Morrison leaned from side to side, staring off at the wall behind Porterfield's head, deep in thought, as though the question had never occurred to him before. "Oh, that's hard to say. I would imagine there are copies of his yearly reports to the National Research Foundation, maybe a few grant proposals.'' Morrison was becoming more and more uncomfortable under the gaze of the five men around the table. "And then there was his correspondence with NRF. With me, really— no connection with Langley, nothing to worry about, really.''

Goldschmidt looked at Porterfield, his lips pursed and his eyes bulging as though there were an immense pressure behind them.

Porterfield said quietly, "You really don't know what Donahue had, do you?"

Morrison chuckled, nervously. "No, of course not, not exactly, but—''

"Oh shit," said Kearns.

Pines said, "Thank you, Morrison." He glanced at his watch. "Wow! Almost six o'clock. We'd better get you out of here before we blow your cover. There's a car waiting."

Morrison seemed about to protest. He looked around the table and for some insane reason settled his gaze on Hadley, as though Hadley would assert Morrison's right to stay. Porterfield had watched Hadley's jaw flexing and loosening rhythmically for the past few moments. It was the same unconscious gesture a cat made before it leaped on a bird, while it imagined the feeling of grinding the bird's fragile bones. Morrison nodded to a spot somewhere near the middle of the table, grinned stupidly, and said, "Good point, thanks," as he left the room.

"So," said Porterfield. "Worst case?"

Pines turned to Goldschmidt, who said, "Impossible to say, really. What amazes me most about this is just that. That man"—he paused and looked around the room—"that . . . man . . . has been supporting the . . . research . . . of this Donahue person for upward of twenty years. He seems to have had some authorization for it." Goldschmidt's gaze settled on Pines, and it was a look of hatred. "We have to assume that what these people have is the sum of what Professor Donahue knows, what he has proposed, what he imagines, and what that insufferable moron has let him know. What we're sure of is an embarrassment. What we don't know may be a catastrophe."

Porterfield waited, and Kearns spoke. "We're pretty sure that what he had in that office included a lot of psywar tactical information that has been used in Latin America. It also probably included a lot of stuff nobody has ever used—some of it so crazy we wouldn't have considered it, some of it right out of the contingency plans."

"It may not be that bad," said Pines. "Ben, you've read the abstracts this guy Donahue wrote. It's really pretty amateurish stuff. He tries to find out what form the bogeyman takes in a country and devises means to make the bogeyman come to life. It's a mixture of stating the obvious and a pseudoscientific quantifying of things that can't be measured."

"Preposterous," Hadley agreed. "The real problem is that there seems to be a pretty sophisticated team of terrorists capable of operating in L.A. We don't know what they are, where they came from."

"Sounds right," said Porterfield, but he was watching Goldschmidt and Kearns as he said it. They were both staring hard at Pines. Kearns was blowing short breaths of air out through his nose like a bull. Goldschmidt's face had assumed an empty expression, as though he had never seen Pines before and wondered what he was doing there. Porterfield understood. "Who used the Donahue reports?"

"Used them?" Pines repeated. "Why, nobody."

"Ridiculous," said Hadley.

Porterfield ignored them and turned to Goldschmidt. "Who?"

Goldschmidt sighed. "It seems that's true, Ben. They weren't used operationally. But from what I've been able to gather, my distinguished predecessor ran some tests."

"Where?"

"One in Argentina in the early sixties, one in Zaire about ten years ago, once" —he paused and stared at Hadley—"it appears he tried it in Tennessee. There were at least three experiments in Mexico. There may be more, but that's all I've found.''

"How did it work?"

"Perfectly, of course. It scared the hell out of people who already had plenty to worry about, and in most instances the teams seem to have been able to focus the panic to make large segments of the population fulfill the predicted behavior. For the psywar teams it was just target practice. The problem is that the whole idea was to give Donahue a chance to compute reliability coefficients, play with real statistics to see how many variables could be plugged into his equations and accounted for.''

"So he had to do his predictions in advance," said Porterfield. "I suppose they let him figure his own results."

"You see it," said Goldschmidt. "He wrote the program the field teams followed, then got the statistics on each of the variables he was interested in. Then he'd come up with empirically tested validity figures and report those back."

Hadley was impatient. "We don't know at this moment whether anything about that was even in the office, and it's damned unlikely that the people who broke in knew about it or would recognize it if they found it. For Christ's sake, they blew up an empty parking shelter. Chances are they don't even speak English."

"That's a good point, Bill," said Pines. "They may really have been after the cocaine. It costs a hell of a lot of money to get far in the armed lunatic business these days, and cocaine is better than money. If they were after documents in Donahue's office, they'd have photographed them, maybe copied them on the office machine." He looked satisfied with himself, his head moving rapidly to look first at Porterfield, then at

Kearns, a lock of hair displacing itself to remind them
that he was one of the new ones, the young geniuses who
seemed to appear from nowhere with impossible records
of achievement in some totally irrelevant endeavor—
advertising or investment banking or the stock market.

Kearns said quietly, "Very true. At the same time,
they picked two offices out of two hundred, the only
two that contained anything worth stealing, probably.
Then, if I remember the tape of the interview with the
parking man correctly, it was only after they'd driven
past the campus gate that they blew up the kiosk. They
had driven past, and he decided to make a run for the
telephone in his kiosk. What's it sound like, Ben?"

Porterfield considered, then shrugged. "Most likely a
hand-held rocket launcher. The Russians have a little
beauty they've been passing out like candy, and of
course there's no guarantee our own disposable one they
used in Viet Nam isn't coming back to haunt us. God
knows enough of them were left there in '73. What's it
called again?"

Goldschmidt answered wearily, "Mark-360. In any
case, there is no homemade aimable weapon that will
disintegrate a building from a distance of fifty or sixty
yards. The point is established. We'll know the exact
nature of the armament used in an hour or two. The Los
Angeles Police Department has asked for federal assistance on that portion of the case, and they've received
more than they know."

Kearns continued. "Okay, so they did all this, then
disappeared. That was . . ." he glanced at his watch,
". . . at least eight hours ago. I say we have to assume
that they have enough to make us damned uncomfortable, maybe worse, and that they are funded and guided
by some power capable of giving them military weap-

ons, a power that won't have any trouble figuring out what to do with the Donahue papers."

"The LAPD is a pretty good force," said Hadley. "There's a chance they'll catch up with these people in an hour or two longer. A foreigner can hide at night, but he really sticks out in the daylight."

Kearns shook his head in disgust. "If they were going to catch them, they'd have done it by now. It might even be better if they didn't. A squad car with two cops armed with revolvers against what—an antitank gun? Rocket launchers? No." He turned to Pines. "I'd like a meeting with the Director this morning. What I'm going to say is that I'm pulling back about half my people —everyone whose cover is even remotely susceptible in Mexico, Guatemala, El Salvador, Nicaragua."

"But that's an immense pain in the ass," Pines protested. "There's no reason to imagine they'll be in any danger. We don't know if these people have anything at all, let alone something that compromises anyone in particular."

Kearns spoke patiently. "That's exactly the problem. Obviously, we have to find out who they are, what they have. While we're doing that, I don't see an alternative to arranging some vacations, business trips, prolonged illnesses, and maybe speeding up some transfers."

Goldschmidt nodded. "A wise course. The worst-case reaction seems the only reasonable one. The approach is too mannered to ignore. They knew enough to find Donahue's office, which means they are capable of receiving and acting on fairly sophisticated intelligence information. They provided a cover by stealing cocaine, which keeps the police and the press occupied. And yet they blow up an empty parking booth with a military weapon. It's all rather too precise, isn't it?"

Pines spluttered, shaking his head. "You're saying they're picking their adversary, aren't you? That's crazy."

"They knew the police would be satisfied that it was a banal drug theft, something we can't very well get involved in unless we reveal what it is we believe has been stolen, which they know we won't do. They employed, apparently for effect, the most rudimentary terrorist tactics in the center of our second largest metropolitan area. In fact, they seem to have been sending us a message."

Hadley groaned, but Goldschmidt ignored him. "The fact that we're sitting here at this hour worrying about it is proof that the message has been received. And now they know that we must do what they intend: We can't have the Donahue reports turning up as evidence in a spectacular drug trial in Los Angeles. They know we will do what is necessary to keep that from happening."

Porterfield looked around the table and saw that everyone but Goldschmidt seemed to be deep in thought. Hadley's lips were moving silently, as though he were adding up long columns of figures in his head. Then his eyes seemed to focus again. "Okay. Assume it's a major league group. I guess then Kearns is right that we have to lower our profile in the regions we know are mentioned in these damned papers. That much we can do now."

Pines said, "All right. I'm sure the Director will agree to that, but the priority has got to be finding out exactly what these people have." He turned to Porterfield. "You're our link with Donahue, aren't you?"

Porterfield shook his head, frowning. "I've never had any contact with him. Morrison was supposed to steer him to me, but so far—"

"But you're listed right here," Pines said. He pointed

to a line on a sheet of paper in front of him, alarmed. "My God, Ben, this is no time to turn coy. Am I supposed to put that ass Morrison in charge of something like this?"

"He seems to have been for the past twenty years."

"You'll damned well take charge of this," said Pines. "You're the only one who can possibly do it, and I don't see what else you can do. The Director said it had to be you."

"So I'm in charge? Of what?"

"Of the whole operation. Whatever has to be done to cut our losses on this," said Pines, surprised. The others nodded.

Porterfield glanced at his watch and then stared at Pines, his eyes suddenly very cold and distant. "Then go call my office and tell them I'll be in at noon, and arrange to have me see the tapes of the L.A. news and get copies of the police reports."

Pines stood up and left the room, his ears turning bright red, his neck stiffening. He walked quickly, his shoes echoing on the tile floor in the empty hallway. He knew he hadn't heard anyone laugh. They wouldn't. They weren't the sort of people who might. He wasn't afraid of Porterfield. That was absurd, he was sure of it. What he was feeling was something else: anger, he decided, and distaste. He'd heard the stories, read the files. The man was little more than a common thug, a borderline psychotic. There was no reason to feel anything about him at all. He was an anachronism, a leftover from the days when things were cruder, the days when . . . Pines was beginning to feel calmer. He was the Deputy Director, after all. It was his duty to get this operation moving, and he was doing it. He wasn't taking orders from Porterfield, he was giving him orders, even if they were really the Director's orders. Pines felt better as he turned into the communications wing, with its computers, cryptographic decoders, and satellite monitors providing a barely audible whisper of electronic sound. This was the real world, his world. It seemed almost humorous that he should be setting up an operation for a man whose file said he'd been known to guerrila bands in Guatemala as the Angel of Death. Pines had been—what? Nine years old then.

ᐃ 10 ᐃ

DOCTOR HENRY METZGER walked easily along the narrow balcony railing, staring with uncritical interest at the commotion in the shop below. Doctor Henry Metzger's large, unblinking yellow eyes encompassed the scene, alert but revealing nothing more than an intention to watch. Much of it was familiar—Chinese Gordon and the others moving around and making noise, and the return of the big smooth surface of the van, a little different now. This time behind the van there was a new thing, big and smooth too. As Doctor Henry Metzger studied it, the pupils of his eyes narrowed suddenly to thin black crescents and his tail whipped back and forth.

Chinese Gordon sat down abruptly on the cement pavement, leaning against the base of the drill press. "I know I shouldn't be surprised."

Kepler edged nearer to the wall, slightly to Chinese Gordon's right side. Chinese Gordon, he remembered, was right-handed. "There wasn't much choice, Chinese. You would have done the same thing. He wouldn't leave without it."

Immelmann stood beside the van, smiling. "I know

75

after you think about it you'll see I was right. He's a great animal."

Chinese Gordon looked up at him and spoke very slowly. "Magnificent. I'm surprised he hasn't broken out of that trailer yet, a fine animal like that. It must be an off day for him, with all the travel and excitement. Have you thought about what you're going to do when he does?"

Immelmann stared at the ground, looking annoyed. "You're a hard man, Chinese. I just spent the night being chased around town by every cop in southern California because the king of the bean bandits gave you his secondhand newspaper instead of wrapping garbage in it, and now you decide it's time to be an asshole. All I ask for is the kind of favor you'd do for your fifteenth cousin twice removed."

Kepler spoke from somewhere to his right and slightly behind him, and Chinese Gordon wondered how he'd gotten way over there. "Fact is, Chinese, we've got the damned thing. I don't know what we can do but see if Immelmann's right. If we have to whack it out I'd rather do it here than in public."

Chinese Gordon nodded. "I've got four steaks up in the refrigerator."

"Thanks, Chinese," said Immelmann, and bounded up the stairs toward Chinese Gordon's living quarters.

"What do you think, Chinese?" said Kepler. "We could lace one of the steaks with rat poison just in case the first three don't cheer him up."

"Immelmann?"

"No, for Christ's sake. The Hound of the Baskervilles."

"I don't keep poison around. Doctor Henry Metzger handles that kind of thing. Sometimes he brings me the heads and feet as a present. He seems to think it's funny. It's enough to make you faint—little tiny pink hands . . .''

"That's okay," said Kepler, screwing the silencer onto the barrel of his pistol. "It's better to go quick anyway. I'd just hate to miss and have bullets bouncing around in here."

Chinese Gordon was about to answer, but Immelmann was coming down the stairs waving the steaks.

"Okay," Kepler said. "Here's what it looks like to me. We rig the door with a rope. We all go up the steps, give the rope a tug and let him out. Then we give him a steak or two and see if we can work out a deal with him."

"Sounds good to me," said Immelmann. "That's probably the way he's been fed before."

"What's to keep him from going up the stairs and taking your leg off?" said Chinese Gordon.

"I've been thinking," said Immelmann. "A dog can't climb a ladder."

"Oh no," Chinese Gordon said.

"Don't be so damned lazy." Immelmann examined the wooden steps. "We could take off this bottom section whole and put it back afterward. A couple of new four-by-fours and it'll be stronger than it is now."

Kepler and Immelmann, working with crowbars, pried out the spikes and moved the bottom section of the steps aside. Then Kepler wedged a short section of a two-by-four between the handles of the trailer door, tied Chinese Gordon's clothesline to it, and they all climbed the ladder to the balcony. Chinese Gordon sat in silence in his kitchen while the others worked, consulting loudly about the best way of tying the knots, when to pull, what to do next.

When the two stopped talking, Chinese Gordon knew it was time. He walked to the balcony and peered over the edge as Immelmann tugged the clothesline and the two-by-four clattered to the floor.

The trailer door swung open and the huge black dog leaped out, already running. His teeth were bared and his eyes wild as he dashed about the shop. He never barked. The only sound was the deep "huff-huff-huff" of his panting in anticipation of the horror he longed to perpetrate.

When Kepler saw him he seemed even worse than the night before. In the dark he'd hoped his imagination had added something to the size and maybe even more to the ferocity of the beast. He said, "You're sure dogs can't climb ladders? That is, no dog can climb a ladder?"

The dog looked up at the three men and bared his teeth still more, uttering a long, low growl.

Immelmann tossed a steak down to him. It made a wet, flapping sound as it hit the pavement beside the animal's feet, but the dog didn't look at it. Instead the dog made a leap for the end of the steps that Immelmann and Kepler had left intact. His forepaws almost touched the last step. He gave a low rumble of frustration and tried again. This time Kepler heard a toenail scrape on wood and felt the hair on the back of his neck begin to rise. "What do you think? Shall we fire a warning shot across his bow?"

"It'll only piss him off," said Immelmann. "We don't want to make him think we're scared of him or he won't respect us."

"You'd have to be a moron not to be scared of that thing," said Kepler. "For Christ's sake, it doesn't even look like a dog."

"It'll eat in a minute, and then we'll try to talk to it," Immelmann said.

Doctor Henry Metzger had watched the black dog

and the men long enough. He spent some time cleaning his fur, then decided to investigate the broad, smooth surface of the unfamiliar trailer. He jumped off the balcony and landed with a light thud on the roof of the van.

Chinese Gordon, Kepler, Immelmann, and the dog all jerked their heads toward the van in unison. "No," said Chinese Gordon. Doctor Henry Metzger looked at him without interest, then crouched and leaped to the roof of the trailer.

The dog walked slowly toward the trailer, his forelegs stiff, his eyes on the cat. "I guess this has gone on long enough," Kepler said, flicking the safety on his pistol.

It was Chinese Gordon who said, "Wait."

Doctor Henry Metzger crouched at the edge of the trailer roof and peered down at the dog, motionless. The dog slowly lifted his head and sat down, his tongue like a long slice of ham hanging out. In a movement like lightning, the cat was on the ground. The dog fell backward and ran around behind the van, but Doctor Henry Metzger shot under the van, and both disappeared from view. Kepler was poised with his arm steadied on the railing, the pistol aimed at a spot a foot beyond the van's grille, waiting, but neither animal reappeared.

There was no sound. At last, Doctor Henry Metzger walked slowly into view and sat down to lick his paws. Then he noticed the steak a few feet away and trotted over to examine it. In a few seconds he was trying with little success to nibble off bits of it.

The dog walked around the rear of the van and approached Doctor Henry Metzger. When the dog was still six feet away he lay down on the pavement and rolled over on his back. The three men stood in shocked immobility as Doctor Henry Metzger sauntered over to the great black beast and then walked back with it to the steak. The dog clapped its big jaws onto the slab of beef, tearing and grinding it happily.

When Doctor Henry Metzger decided it was time to tour the inside of the horse trailer, the big dog dropped the steak and followed. While Doctor Henry Metzger prowled about the trailer, the dog sat outside, waiting. When Doctor Henry Metzger was satisfied that he knew what there was to know about the trailer, he and the dog returned to finish the steak.

Immelmann climbed down the ladder cautiously, the second steak clamped under his arm. As his foot hit the floor the dog poised for a spring, his teeth bared. Doctor Henry Metzger walked up to Immelmann and rubbed his body against Immelmann's leg, purring, and the dog sat down. Then, unaccountably, as though from some dim memory, the great black dog rose on its haunches, its big jaws open, and begged.

∆ 11 ∆

MARGARET'S LONG BROWN hair lay in swirls and arabesques around her head on the pillow. It was a sight that made Chinese Gordon's eyes water in joy, admiration, awe. He even detected a slight impulse toward gratitude but decided that probably wasn't normal and concentrated on the marvelous, smooth white shape, the sheer beauty of her. It struck him as miraculous. He was chosen, for the moment, at least, to be in possession of the most beautiful thing on earth.

He leaned down and kissed her eyelids, softly. The lashes fluttered slightly and then the clear green eyes opened and stared at him. "Chinese, have you—uh—done something?"

"Nothing that compares with this. You could be a movie star, or at least a model or something."

"I know. I could have been a contender. Cut it out and tell me what you've been doing."

Chinese Gordon lay down beside her, teasing himself with the feel of her warmth, her skin. "Nothing much. You met Doctor Henry Metzger's dog. If it is a dog."

"He's sweet. Every cat should have a two-hundred-pound dog. But what else? Chinese, you have the work habits of a snake. You swallow an animal whole and then hibernate for months. At the moment I don't see any of your playmates, and all of a sudden you're getting that self-satisfied look again.''

Chinese Gordon stared at the ceiling. ''Mr. Gordon's smugness remains a mystery. Mr. Gordon could not be reached for comment.''

''Just tell me this much: Are you in danger? I mean, this time have you and your merry men signed up to go to some country that smells like cow dung and teach little brown people how to murder each other, or did you just swindle somebody?''

''Neither. I plan to stay here, marry you, keep you pregnant all the time, get fat, the whole thing.''

Margaret sat up, and Chinese Gordon knew he couldn't keep from staring at her breasts, so he didn't try. She reached to the dresser for her cigarettes, lit one, and turned away. Chinese Gordon kissed the back of her neck, but she went on. ''Okay, smartass. I've got it figured out. I read the papers before I came here. I knew something was coming, but I had hoped it might be something legal, or at least minor. I do that, you know —read the papers before I see you. Did you know there were over sixteen hundred bank robberies in southern California last year? I think I read all sixteen hundred, just to see if—''

''Bank robberies? What the hell are you—''

''That's what I figured you'd do when you finally got bored enough.''

''That's insulting, Margaret. The only people who rob banks are addicts and psychotics.''

''Don't worry. I've figured it out. Just tell me, should I be expecting the police to burst in here any minute, or what? If so, I'd like to get dressed.''

''No.''

"What are you going to do with the cocaine?"

Chinese Gordon picked up his silver Rolex watch and squinted at it. "Pretty soon I'll get a call with an offer for it. The offer will be lousy, but that's no problem. You might say I've got Los Angeles by the nose."

Margaret puffed on the cigarette and slowly blew smoke toward the ceiling. "I once read an article that said antisocial behavior peaked at age seventeen. I wonder what you were like at seventeen."

"Let's see . . . I guess I was in the army. That was the year after the Tonkin Gulf thing, and the big deal was 'interdiction.' That's what they called it. They'd fly a few little groups of us in helicopters to spots on the Ho Chi Minh Trail they called 'chokepoints' and then pick us up before it got dark. Since nothing ever moved on the trail before sunset, it wasn't too bad. I wasn't yet the world's greatest lover—I don't think I actually got the championship officially until I was a little older and more sensitive."

The telephone rang, and Chinese Gordon slowly got out of bed, still talking. "Youth and enthusiasm count for something, of course, but if I remember correctly, it was only when I was twenty-five or so that the United Nations Sexmaster General sent a bipartisan commission to—." He picked up the receiver. "Hello."

"Congratulations, Mr. Gordon." The voice was Jorge Grijalvas's.

Chinese Gordon said, "Well, thank you, but I'm not really interested in buying anything over the telephone. You people always say I've won something and then I have to buy a bunch of aluminum siding or go to hear a sales pitch in a hotel dining room. Good-bye." He hung up and kept talking but stood beside the telephone. "—to study what the British delegate, Lady Bunsworthy, called my 'prowess.' " He ducked the pillow, which thudded against the wall, picked up the telephone, and walked out into the kitchen, closing the door behind him.

The telephone rang again and he said, "Yes?"

"This is Jorge Grijalvas, Mr. Gordon."

"Oh, hi," said Chinese Gordon. "What can I do for you?"

"Let's not waste time. You have it, and I'm making an offer. Two hundred thousand cash."

"Sorry. You've got the wrong number."

Grijalvas hesitated. "Isn't this seven-six-nine—"

Chinese Gordon interrupted. "No, the other number."

Grijalvas chuckled. "I can take it, but this is simpler."

"You're welcome to try," said Chinese Gordon. "Fair's fair, after all. That's how I got it. You've got twenty-four hours to make me a decent offer. After that it'll be gone."

"Don't make me laugh. Who else can pay even that?"

"According to the last poll I took, there were only three people in Beverly Hills who wouldn't. Two of them have asthma, and the other has an artificial nose —a terrible war accident, you know. Bitten off by a prostitute in Marseilles."

"What do you want for it?"

"The police assessed it at a million. That'd be enough."

"Surely you know that the papers exaggerate these things. And what do I get out of it at that price?"

"Something to mix with your powdered sugar and baking soda for the suckers."

"I'll think about it."

"Always nice to hear from you." Chinese Gordon hung up and went back into the bedroom. "Where was

I? Oh, yes. The United Nations. The whole issue was put best by Colonel Anna Liebchen of the East German Luftpizzle when she said—moaned, actually—''

"Where did you get this, Chinese?" Margaret was lying on her stomach on the bed, staring at something in front of her.

"No, what she said was—"

"Shut up. This is crazy."

Chinese Gordon walked to the bed. He could see now that she had the box open, and sheets of paper were scattered on the pillow. "You shouldn't snoop, you know."

"What is it?"

"I don't know, to tell you the truth. I haven't had time to do any reading in the past couple days. First there was Immelmann and his evolutionary freak of a dog, then I had our financial future to think about."

"Where did it come from?"

"I liberated it while I was taking a plunge in the pharmaceutical industry the other night at the university. It's probably not worth anything, but while I was there two guys were making some kind of deal on a security system, so I thought I'd check it out. That was the only thing that had a lock on it, so here it is. Most likely it's a statistical study of the incidence of venereal disease in sixteenth-century nuns."

"The hell it is. You got this at the university? In some professor's office? Jesus!"

"Well, one of them had to be a professor. He was too pompous to be anything else. The other one looked like a salesman. What's the big deal? Does it look like it's worth something?"

Margaret rolled over to face him, still clutching several pages. "Tell me, Chinese, does 'psywar' mean what it sounds like?"

⩕ 12 ⩕

PORTERFIELD HAD TO sidestep twice to avoid the electricians on ladders installing the security gear in Donahue's laboratory. Bits of wire and boxes with molded foam padding littered the hallway. When he reached the end of the corridor he saw the one who must be Donahue sitting behind a desk and talking, the telephone cradled on his shoulder. The man held up a finger to Porterfield but didn't smile.

Porterfield waited in the hallway. He was glad it was Saturday. It would be only Donahue and the technicians, and he was sure he'd seen one of them with Goldschmidt at Langley only a month ago. He watched as the man spliced something into a line that led nowhere near the security equipment, then stuffed it back behind the drilled-out plaster and began to seal the hole.

"Mr. Porterfield?"

He turned and saw Donahue in the doorway. They shook hands and went inside.

"I'm terribly sorry about this," said Donahue. "There's been a burglary in the office, and as luck would have it, the damned electricians are just now installing the alarm. I think they're finished with the noisy part, though, so we may be able to talk."

"Burglary?" said Porterfield. "Too bad. I hope they didn't get anything that can't be replaced."

"Oh no. Actually, they missed everything you'd have thought would attract them—office equipment, the petty cash. They stole several unpublished manuscripts of mine. Thank God I had them on storage disks for the word processor. I can retrieve them at six hundred words a minute whenever I choose. The problem is— and I know I can trust you to keep this confidential —much of the material had a certain national security interest, so I'm a little concerned about seeing that it's recovered."

"I see," said Porterfield. "I hadn't realized you were much involved with the Defense Department."

Donahue shrugged and smiled but said nothing. Porterfield had checked the history of the payments to Donahue, and all of them had been made through the National Research Foundation. Porterfield said, "I see. Perhaps I'm wasting your time. Mr. Morrison had mentioned to me that you were doing some research that was of interest to the Seyell Foundation and that the funding for it was becoming difficult. If—"

Donahue held up his hand. "Don't misunderstand me. At the moment I'm preparing some proposals with the Seyell Foundation in mind."

Porterfield stood up and smiled. "Very good. Just send them along when they're ready and I promise they'll get plenty of attention. They'll be high on our agenda for next year, which would mean that the actual funding could come through the year after that. It's been a pleasure." He turned to go.

"Two years?"

Porterfield stopped. "Well, not two years, Professor Donahue. More like a year and a half."

"But even the government is faster than that."

"The deadline for this year's screening committee is already past, and while I could return to Washington tomorrow with something to slip into the mass of material they have to deal with, after that it would be impossible. Meddling with deadlines would jeopardize our tax-exempt status."

"I can show you some things that would change your mind," said Donahue. "Things I was working on for the National Research Foundation." His desperation seemed to be swallowed for a moment by some other emotion that wasn't immediately identifiable. "It's going to knock them on their asses." Then he added, "If there's anyone there qualified to read it."

Of course the little bastard would be this way—bitter, waiting for the chance to revel in some personal triumph over people who certainly never thought about him, probably never even heard of him; but that too would be part of it. These people spent their lives telling themselves they had international reputations because they were quoted in a journal with two hundred subscribers. He'd forgotten about that part of it. "Of course, for a distinguished scientist like you we might be able to deal with a body of work, at least until a specific contract could be constructed."

Donahue beamed. "When does your plane leave?"

"Late this evening—ten forty-five."

"I can have the manuscripts out of the machine by six." He reached in his desk drawer and began fumbling with a row of word processor disks in gray envelopes.

Porterfield moved to the door. "Eight will be fine."

He passed along the corridor to the end of the suite of offices. The electricians seemed to have gone, although there still was a toolbox on the floor near the door. When he turned the corner, Goldschmidt's man was waiting for him. Porterfield said quietly, "It's all on word processor disks in his office. We'll need his access code."

"Do you need to talk to him some more?"

Porterfield glanced at Goldschmidt's man as he walked. He was definitely one of the ones Goldschmidt had trained to be what he called professional. He always found them in their early twenties, intelligent and athletic like this one, and somehow induced in them that strange, attentive look. This one had to be thirty or more, which made him something of a veteran. Porterfield thought about Donahue for a moment, then shrugged. "No. He's nothing."

CHINESE Gordon lifted the telephone receiver.

"Mr. Gordon."

"Hi there, Jorge. You certainly took a long time making up your mind."

"I had arrangements to make, people to talk to. You know how it is, I'm sure. I'd like to make you an offer."

"Okay."

"Seven-fifty."

"Fine."

"What?"

"I said yes, I'll take it. I've got other things to do, and I don't want to be a pig about it. I'll call you at ten. But Jorge?"

"Yes?"

"Don't be too ambitious. It hasn't been anywhere you could find it for some time, so all you would do before ten is get somebody killed. Just be ready with the cash. You can bring as many people as you can fit in one car, all heavily armed if that seems good to you, but remember it's going to be a public place."

"Of course. It would be."

Chinese Gordon hung up and dialed Kepler's number. "Time to go."

Chinese Gordon walked across the shop to the door. Doctor Henry Metzger was curled in a furry ball on the metal welding table, but stretched himself and lashed his tail from side to side. "See you later, baboon ass," said Chinese Gordon. Beneath the table Doctor Henry Metzger's dog stirred. The large, alert, pitiless eyes opened, and the upper lip curled to bare the jagged array of teeth. "You too, you mental case." The dog's horrible maw widened into a yawn, and then the broad, untroubled face settled into sleep.

Chinese Gordon made his way down the alley to the back door of the grocery store. There was no sign that anyone was watching. He supposed a man like Grijalvas could probably connect an unlisted telephone number with an address easily enough, but this was about the time he had walked to the grocery store every day since the arrival of Doctor Henry Metzger's dog. He walked through the shop to the counter, bought a pack of cigarettes, and went out the front door to the street.

At the curb he got into Margaret's car and drove off. Since it was a beautiful, sunny Sunday morning, he decided that he favored "Bringing in the Sheaves." As he coaxed the bright yellow Volkswagen to sixty and eased into the center lane, his voice reached maximum volume, but he had already sung the only verse he knew. Undaunted, he amused himself by inventing obscene lyrics until he reached the Hawthorne Boulevard exit ramp.

Chinese Gordon drove on in silence until he reached the beach, then parked and waited for a half hour, watching to be sure no one had followed. Then he drove onto the vast parking lot set in the sandy hillside above the ocean and got out of the car, leaving the keys under the seat.

By the time he reached the entrance gate there were three buses in the loop spewing their hordes of passengers onto the walkways. In the distance he could see families beginning the long trek across the parking lot, the tall pairs of parents moving with straight, unswerving purpose toward the entrance, while smaller shapes scampered and cavorted about them in a reckless, random expenditure of energy. Chinese Gordon sighed. Judging from the size, they'd all be named Joshua or Laura and their mothers would be Kathys or Karens.

Inside the park he made the first telephone call. "Be at the phone booth at the Griffith Park Observatory at eleven."

"Shit, *amigo*. Are you going to do that to me? It's embarrassing."

"I can't help it. I need the insurance."

"I understand."

By eleven he'd seen the others. Immelmann was at the head of a line of people and was buying a long string of tickets to the Skyride, a shaft that rose over two hundred feet in the air and served as the track for a glass elevator. He looked excited and happy as he folded the string of tickets, hung his binoculars over his neck, picked up his knapsack, and wandered off. Chinese Gordon tried to convince himself that Immelmann's expression was different from that of the ten-year-old boy who came to the window next, but he was distracted when he heard Margaret's voice beside him. "I suppose you wrecked my car."

"No. Everything's fine. See you at noon."

The telephone rang only once at the Griffith Park Observatory. Chinese Gordon said, "The telephone booth outside the Museum of Science and Industy in Exposition Park in half an hour," and hung up.

A few seconds later the telephone in Chinese Gordon's booth rang and Kepler's voice said, "He still hasn't called anyone else. He's got three with him, no second car. Got to go."

Chinese Gordon bought a hot dog and stared out at the ocean. A squadron of brown pelicans skimmed the calm, shining surface a few hundred yards offshore, pumping their wings several times in unison and then gliding in single file and finally soaring upward to bank and plummet into the water. He shared the hot dog bun with an inquisitive sea gull and then went off to make the final telephone call. "Ocean Land," he said.

"I'm getting tired, *amigo*. This is the third park."

"You'll love it," said Chinese Gordon. "You'll be in time for the twelve-o'clock dolphin show."

At twelve o'clock Chinese Gordon was eating popcorn and sitting in the last row of the gallery surrounding the dolphin pool. Below him two young men who looked like lifeguards were taking turns talking in abnormally cheery voices into a public-address system that made their p's and b's explode in the ear: ". . . we want to remind you ladies and gentlemen that everything the animals do here at Ocean Land is absolutely natural. It's not a trained animal act, it's an exhibition of several of their natural behaviors. And now let me introduce two of the members of our cast, two Pacific bottlenose dolphins, Perky . . . and . . . Jerky!" Chinese Gordon watched as two dolphins approached the trainer by balancing on their tails in the water, churning their flukes furiously to remain erect. Strapped to their heads were two oversized plastic hats, one a top hat and the other a fireman's helmet.

Chinese Gordon turned away to scan the crowd.

Lined up at the railing were Jorge Grijalvas and three other men, all wearing suits. "Jerky!" shouted the trainer in exaggerated frustration. "Why can't you be more like Perky?" Chinese Gordon watched as one of the dolphins did a one-and-a-half flip through a hoop and the other spit water at the trainer.

Then Immelmann sat down beside him. "It looks clean. All four together in plain sight, one car. They haven't been near a phone, according to Kepler."

Chinese Gordon glanced up at the rail and saw Kepler standing behind Grijalvas and his men. Chinese Gordon followed Immelmann up the concrete steps, past Grijalvas and across the plaza beside a pool where the fat, leathery shape of a walrus rolled off a ledge into the water.

They entered a building marked "Aquarium," and walked along a dark corridor lined with windows opening into luminous blue. Now and then a large fish would glide past, a big unblinking eye would scan across them without surprise, and then there would be a flurry of smaller fish, fluttering like bright birds to scatter ahead into other windows before the cruising monster. The corridor curved and rose, a spiral ramp circling the tank. At some of the windows parents held small children up to peer into the lighted water, the children's faces glowing blue in the dim hallway.

At the top of the ramp there were three doors along the wall. Chinese Gordon and Kepler entered the door marked "Men" and waited.

When Grijalvas and his companions came in, Kepler stood at the door. "I'll watch for interruptions."

Chinese Gordon was settled on a toilet. "Hi, Jorge. Sorry about all this."

"Let's get it over," said Grijalvas. "Let's see the cocaine."

Chinese Gordon lifted his shirt and showed an array of plastic bags taped to his body. "Your turn."

One of Grijalvas's men reached into his coat, but Kepler was on him, the barrel of his pistol jammed against the man's throat. Kepler pulled open the coat to reveal a shoulder holster. Chinese Gordon said, "Now dig deeper. There better be money somewhere near that gun."

"There is," said Grijalvas.

Chinese Gordon waited while Kepler extracted an envelope, examined it, found another and another. "All right," he said. "Unload."

Each of the four men pulled six envelopes from various pockets and tossed them on the floor. Chinese Gordon examined each carefully and put it into the knapsack at his feet. Finally he stripped off the bags of cocaine and stood up to stretch while Grijalvas and his men loaded their pockets.

Kepler snatched up the knapsack and tossed it onto the floor outside. He watched as the door of the Ladies' room opened and Margaret walked out, picked up the knapsack, and disappeared down the dark corridor.

"Now what?" asked Grijalvas.

"Now we have a nice afternoon," said Chinese Gordon. "You saw the dolphins, Perky and Jerky. Now we're going to see one more show and then go our separate ways." He glanced at his watch. "Come on."

They filed through the doorway to the upper deck, where there was another gallery surrounding another large pool. Another pair of young men were standing at the edge of the pool, and one was saying, "We'd like to remind you that this is not a trained-animal act, but a display of certain natural behaviors of these magnificent creatures of the sea, the killer whales." A gigantic black and white snout emerged from the water, and the

glistening black body rolled after it. A fin that appeared
to be the size of a car hood slapped the surface and
drenched the front row of the audience, who gasped and
giggled, but Chinese Gordon wasn't watching. He was
staring past Jo-Jo, the Madcap Joker of the Sea, and
into the distant parking lot. In the far corner, a tiny
bright yellow Volkswagen was moving past the exit gate
onto the coast highway.

⋀ 13 ⋀

"CAPTAIN RACINE, PLEASE," said Porterfield. He could hear the young policeman set the receiver down on something hard and walk away calling "Captain, phone," into a large space filled with other noises.

"Racine."

"Hello, John. It's Ben Porterfield. What time can you meet me?"

"Dinner is on you at Musso and Frank's. Seven-thirty."

THE polished wood walls didn't seem to end in a ceiling at all, just in a dimness somewhere above the level of the lights. Porterfield sat alone in his booth, thinking about how much Musso and Frank's reminded him of rail-roads. The waiters in their bright red jackets moving up the aisle at almost a run, their trays piled high with covered dishes, gave the impression that the whole long, narrow room was on its way to some destination, but there was an unmistakable feeling that when the passengers got there it would be another time, probably around 1925. It wasn't as though the restaurant stimu-

lated the imagination or evoked the past. There was
nothing archaic or antique about it. There was just the
simple, unarguable fact of continuity. Each day for the
past sixty years the stoves got lit and the tables set and
the waiters put on their red jackets and somebody un-
locked the door. When the red leather on the seats wore
out, the upholsterers came and replaced it, exactly as it
had been, as it always would be, taking care to be ready
for the next day, the next customer, paying no attention
to what year it might be outside the front door on Hollywood Boulevard.

Out there it had been a steadily evolving stream of
people walking past the windows, first orange growers
and next film people from the directors and actors to the
grips and gaffers and then almost instantly the multi-
tude who grew up around the studios, the film proces-
sors and advertisers and rental agents and drivers and
the people who sold them all clothes and food and
houses and cars and insurance, and next the ones who
were there to sell sex or drugs and finally, for the past
few years, ones who weren't even on the boulevard to
do that, people who were here because there were bright
lights that made it look warm, or maybe a parking ramp
nearby where you could sleep most of the night if you
still had enough of your brain left to memorize the
schedule of the patrol cars.

Inside the door it was still 1925, and the lineal heirs, if
not the original clients, were still ordering the big salad
and the side of oysters, and one of the fat men at the
booth across the aisle from Porterfield's was saying,
"My lawyer can piss rings around his lawyer," and
another answered, "Yeah, but his accountant can make
an elephant disappear up its own ass."

Racine followed a red-coated waiter up the aisle and
slipped into the booth before the next waiter overtook

him. "Well, Benjamin," he said, leaning on the table with both elbows, "I read one time that William Faulkner went behind the bar here to show them how to make a mint julep. Want to see if they wrote it down?"

"No, thanks," said Porterfield. "He was probably the last person to order one. Scotch."

Racine shrugged. "Martini." The waiter disappeared. "How did you get stuck with this one?"

Porterfield watched a waiter pass by with a tray of what looked like five identical steaks and felt a dull longing. He still wasn't used to the three-hour time difference. "Oh, proximity. I had already been scheduled to take on the project before it fell apart, so I guess that made me the only adult male with no way to say he was too busy."

"Take on the project? Have you read any of that guy's stuff?"

Porterfield nodded. "I suppose they'd have eased him out. They'd already gotten him off the public payroll, and eventually they'd have taken him off the foundation's list too. If not this director, the next one."

"It's too bad they didn't get around to it sooner."

"What have you got so far?"

Racine's voice dropped until it was barely audible above the steady hum of activity. "Not a hell of a lot. There's no question that whoever got the cocaine also has whatever was in that clown's office. We have no leads on who it was, just that it was three dark-skinned male Caucasians in a van who were pretending to be air-conditioner repairmen. The coke isn't enough to depress prices notably in a market this size, even if it's all sold the same day, so we won't know anything about it unless they take it to East Jesus, Kentucky."

"What about the explosion? What was it?"

"Hell, that's the best part. You'll love it. It wasn't an

explosion at all, at least not one explosion. This isn't going to be in the papers, so we can savor it all by ourselves for now. It was caused by HEI rounds from a twenty-millimeter automatic cannon.''

"You're joking.''

"No, I'm not.'' Racine's face was suddenly old and tired. "I wish to God I were, but the ballistics people found the remains of a dud pumped through one of the bricks in the rubble. It also explains why it looked so strange to the parking man. He said the kiosk sort of tore itself apart and blew backward.''

"So they're driving around with the gun from a fighter plane mounted in a truck.'' Porterfield shook his head. "Any way of telling who the original owner was?''

"They had to weigh and fluoroscope the dud to figure out what it was, and there were no brass casings lying around. They'd have to rig something in the truck to catch them, or they'd be beaten to death with hot brass and pieces of stripped belt.''

"Anything at all on the ammunition?''

"They're working on it, but nothing so far. Everybody with an air force has been using it since about 1950, a hell of a lot of wars ago. If we had a live round, Goldschmidt's people might at least guess what country manufactured it. Even that might not help, since I'm told that we make most of it and sell it or give it away, and the rest is a pretty close copy. No telling how much the Russians make or who has it.''

Porterfield's face was expressionless as they gave the waiter their orders and returned to their drinks. He wondered about the strange familiarity of it. It had been Costa Rica, the late fifties, when he'd been assigned to Special Operations. That time it had been Porterfield teaching a small group of dark young men, so earnest and serious that at least two of them would have passed for insane. He'd decided a truck was too conspicuous in a country where the cost of a five-year-old truck would have bought a village, so he'd settled for a series of fixed mountings in strategic places, then spent more time training the young men in breaking down the antitank gun into pieces small enough to carry on bicycles than in firing it. The man with the barrel had been a special problem in selection. He had to be so brave that his only human emotion was hatred. There was no way that Esteban Cabazon or any other man could have hidden the four feet of metal tubing on a bicycle. He'd lived a charmed life, at least for long enough. The police and Guardia Nacionale had been armed with old Enfield rifles. The terror on their faces as the vintage 1944 Jeeps seemed to jump backward and crumple—"Has the word gotten out to the police who are looking for these people?"

Racine sighed. "Probably. The ones on the scene were sworn to secrecy. National security and all that stuff, but you know how that works. Your buddy is out there in a squad car looking for a van he thinks has three Mexican drug dealers and maybe a stick of dynamite in it—"

"Sure. Tell me—"

"No, Ben. Wait. I've got to get out of here in a minute, and I've got to know what you want me to do about the absentheaded professor."

"What do you mean?"

He leaned forward so far his tie lay on the table in a coil. "When do you want us to find the body?"

CHINESE Gordon watched Margaret arch her back and then rock her hips slightly to get comfortable on the bed. She was definitely losing her suntan, the peculiar demarcation that seemed to intensify certain parts of her with a white light as though they glowed with an energy of their own, or as though some principle of evolution had caused them to be marked as areas of special interest, in the absurdly literal way that nature did things.

She plucked her glasses from the nightstand and opened the *Los Angeles Times*. He watched her peering down at the paper, leaning on her elbows, her long hair hanging down to veil the side of her face. "I think we should get married," he said quietly.

"That's sweet," she said to the newspaper. "I do too."

"No, I mean now. If you put things off when it's time to do them, then you get better and better at thinking of reasons to put them off, and—"

"Wait, Chinese. There's something here."

"A colossal once-in-a-lifetime sale at I. Magnin's," he said.

"Read this." She tossed a section of the paper on the bed and rolled onto her side to face him.

"You mean, 'Spoiled Little Smartass Ignores Marriage Proposal'?"

"I'm serious, you idiot. About the professor."

He picked up the paper. " 'Body of Missing Professor Found. In the second violent incident on the ULA campus within a week, the body of Professor Ian Donahue was found last evening in an overgrown drainage ditch within a few blocks of his office. The Los Angeles County coroner's office has issued a statement that the cause of death was suffocation due to a crushed trachea brought on by a blow to the throat. Police spokesmen declined to comment on whether Donahue's death was linked to the recent dramatic theft of cocaine valued at over a million dollars from the ULA Social Sciences Building but admitted that his office was near the one where the cocaine was kept. Captain John Racine of the LAPD told reporters that Donahue had not been listed as a witness to the theft, nor had his name been connected in any way with the ongoing investigation.' "

"Well?"

"It's the same one. Interesting."

"Is that all you can say?"

"It is interesting. A chop to the throat, and all that. It's not that hard to do, but the average person doesn't think to do it that way. Unless you're trained for it and have a little practice, it seems kind of chancy and inefficient. Of course, these days every little weasel with a big mouth who's ever been decked in a bar spends the next seven years going for a black belt, so—"

"Stop lying, Chinese. It's not a coincidence and you know it."

"Coincidence?" Chinese Gordon walked out to the kitchen and shook some coffee into the pot, then started boiling water. "No, it's probably not a coincidence. That doesn't mean I'm going to let it ruin my day."

She stayed with him, staring up at him in amazement. "Who do you think killed him?"

"I'd say there are three major possibilities. One is that somebody read the papers and got the idea there was something valuable to steal in every office on campus, and the other is that Donahue was planning to do something about the cocaine himself, and his partners thought he'd cut them out." He hummed a few bars of "I Went to the Animal Fair" and poured the boiling water into the coffee filter.

"You said three."

"Oh, the third we can ignore, just like the first two. It's not our problem. I'd say our problem now is how to invest a hell of a lot of cash without attracting too much attention."

"The third one is the only real one, Chinese. I read part of that report, so I know what it is. He was killed by somebody in the government. You, as usual, will lie to me and do what? Drop out of sight for a year?"

Chinese Gordon shrugged. "I'd miss you."

"Oh, Chinese. You're such a fool. They've just killed that man. If you get arrested they'll pin it on you, so there's no going back. There's probably no going forward either, because if what's in the rest of those papers is bad enough to murder him for, they'll never stop looking for you. So here you are, walking around like the village idiot making coffee. You think because I'm a woman I don't know anything and can't even learn it, but you're the one who never learns."

Chinese Gordon chuckled. "Do you have a better idea?"

"Of course I do."

" 'IN the field studies done under the ULTRA program, 1955-1970, in Oaxaca State (Mexico), Tennessee (U.S.), and elsewhere (see appendices I through IX), it was established that a battery of sociometric methodologies yielded surprisingly high indices of correlation.' "

"Where's the footnote page?" said Margaret, crawling across the bed to leaf through the box of papers. "Here it is."

"The coefficient of dullness is right up there." Chinese Gordon scratched his belly. "I'm not surprised somebody punched the little bastard in the throat."

Margaret knelt on the bed and read,

In the early tests it was found that traditional participant-observer methodologies yielded low interrater reliability figures. Beginning in the Tennessee studies of 1958, a system of statistical demograph-

ics was applied in which the number of displaced
persons was recorded at each stage of the stimulation period. A team of interviewers was placed in
the field stations where those who left the area went
to apply for temporary shelter, food, and other
necessities. Subjects were told that the questions
were intended to establish their eligibility for federal assistance. The reasons the subjects gave for
their actions were used to validate the hypothesis that a specific stimulus had been the independent variable, causing them to panic. It was found
that a sampling of as low as one percent yielded
correlation coefficients well within the acceptable
range (.65-.9) if the sample was at least one hundred subjects.

"We're getting nowhere," said Chinese Gordon. "He
waited for a flood and went down and asked people if it
bothered them."

"No. He calls it a 'stimulation period' in a 'target
area.' Maybe he explains it in an appendix. Where'd
you put the appendices?"

"They're in the box." He crawled to the foot of the
bed and stared into the box. Doctor Henry Metzger was
curled up on the thick stack of papers, already asleep,
his nose touching the toes of his hind feet, his tail fluttering slightly as he stalked some luscious prey whose
only habitat was Doctor Henry Metzger's dreams.
"Come on, you worthless pelt," said Chinese Gordon.
"Pile your flea-bitten ass on something else." He
reached into the box to lift the cat. Doctor Henry Metzger gave an annoyed little cry, and Chinese Gordon
froze.

It was his right leg, just above the ankle. He didn't
have to look. The instant he felt it, an image formed in

his brain. The hot, wet pressure clamped around his leg was enough. The teeth barely touched the skin, and the tongue was lolling out of the side of the gaping mouth, dangling against his heel. The great black beast made no sound. Slowly Chinese Gordon turned his head to look over his shoulder at the dog. A big black eye stared back at him. "He's got me," said Chinese Gordon quietly. "The goddamned cat has taught him how to climb stairs, and now the big son of a bitch is going to tear my leg off."

"Really?" said Margaret. "That's wonderful. What a clever kitty you are, Doctor Henry." She snatched Doctor Henry Metzger out of Chinese Gordon's hands and held him in her arms, petting him gently. Chinese Gordon could hear him purring smugly.

"I wish you hadn't done that," said Chinese. "When this monster kills me I want to take Doctor Henry Metzger with me."

"Oh, don't be such a baby. He's only play-biting. He thinks it's a game." She turned to the dog, and her voice became whispery and melodious. "Game's over, boy." She smiled at Chinese Gordon. "It's called on account of childishness."

Chinese Gordon felt the dog's jaws open and release his leg. Then the dog's huge tongue licked his leg from ankle to knee. He decided it felt like a paintbrush.

Doctor Henry Metzger jumped to the floor and trotted out of the room, his tail in the air. The dog slowly followed, like a huge black shadow passing through the lighted doorway. As it moved down the stairs it sounded to Chinese Gordon like the footsteps of a man walking on his toes.

Chinese Gordon held up his hand. "I don't want to talk about it."

Margaret reached into the box and thumbed through

the papers, extracting some from the bottom. "That's fine with me, Mr. Baby, sir. Here's an appendix."

Oaxaca. In these studies the stimuli were selected with reference to the standard ethnologies of the region (Smith, Gebhard, Rowlands). In the rural Tennessee studies the strong family bonding due to isolation and economic factors associated with sub-sistence farming, coupled with the history of the region, made the selection of a stimulus a simple matter: Theft of small children, combined with the rumor that this was being done by black city people for sexual purposes, was found to be sufficient. In the Mexican studies racial tensions were found not to be acceptable, nor was distrust of urban strangers found useful. The structure of peasant village society made visits from strangers pleasant occasions not to be feared (see Gebhard, 1947). There were, however, a number of exploitable vul-nerabilities.

Smith (1962) had noted an ingrained terror of cannibalism, which he attributed to a combination of factors, including the practice beginning in the sixteenth century of Roman Catholic missionaries making explicit reference to the eating of human flesh by the Aztecs. The idea had achieved immense importance in the folklore of the region, partially because the references were also used to explain the concept of transubstantiation and the sacrament of communion. The society was obsessed with the image of cannibalism, both as the image of what people did under the influence of evil (demonic possession) and what people did in order to achieve salvation. It is a particularly interesting case be-cause the village people of the region were ethni-

cally Mayan. Ritual cannibalism had not been a
characteristic of Mayan culture during the clas-
sical period, as it had been among the Aztec and
the Tlaxcala.

Margaret stared at Chinese Gordon. She tossed the
paper on the bed and took up another sheet. Now her
arms were entwined, her left hand gripping her right
shoulder as though hugging herself for protection from
what she was reading. " 'Working with the Psychological Warfare team supplied by the Central Intelligence
Agency, this researcher selected twelve villages with
populations between one hundred and two hundred. It
was agreed that the fear of cannibalism must be isolated
from other fears, so the form selected was the eating of
recently buried corpses.' " She threw down the sheet
and shuddered. "It's unbelievable."

Chinese Gordon shrugged. "So try another section if
that one's not to your taste."

She selected another and began to read.

The revision of the scale of measurement to en-
compass the competing factor of unforeseen genuine danger prompted the hypothesis that the
ULTRA could be used in more complex urban
societies. The 1954 coup in Guatemala was the first
for which the Central Intelligence Agency had kept
detailed sociological and methodological records.
In 1959, after the sophistication of the ULTRA
scales had reached a sufficient level, the Director's
office graciously made available to the project certain necessary records.

⋀ 14 ⋀

". . . THE DIRECTOR'S OFFICE graciously made available to the project certain necessary records." Porterfield set the paper on the desk. As he stood up to walk to the window he realized he'd been sitting in the uncomfortable desk chair for longer than usual. He could feel his left hip joint as he took the first step—not yet a pain, just an awareness of it, of the ball and socket moving. About once a year it was more than that, a dull throb that actually weakened the leg, as though he'd been kicked, he thought—age giving him a kick in the ass. He didn't have to remind himself that years were coming faster now, and if he measured them by the rate that things wore out, it was even faster.

Porterfield stared out at the gigantic parking lot and beyond it, at Los Angeles International Airport, stretching for miles into the morning haze. This place had changed since the early sixties. In those days the chief of station in Los Angeles had been Paul Cameron, a World War II OSS man who'd spent the fifties in the Philippines, going old-style from one remote village to another through the jungle on foot, tending his counter-insurgency program like a trapper making the rounds of his traps. In 1961, when Porterfield had met him,

Cameron must have been at least fifty years old but lean and hard, as though he'd been at war so long it was too late for him ever to turn slack. Porterfield in those days had been set up as president of a Miami air freight company that was largely spurious, its only asset a checkbook that paid for airplanes and parts and the salaries of pilots, more and more of them passing through Los Angeles on their way to Southeast Asia as the sixties wore on. Soon after that, Cameron had retired. It had been years before Porterfield learned that Cameron had signed the report to the President suggesting that the whole enterprise be given up before it grew too big.

Now even the place was different, still near the airport but indistinguishable from the offices of the corporations that had grown to comparable proportions in even less time and for the same reasons. The new building, all eight stories of tinted glass and structural steel, seemed to be full of the computerized hardware that monitored and directed the satellites. None of the faces he saw in the hallways had been here in the old days. Most of the people there were too young even to have heard of Paul Cameron. The chief of station here now was a man named Gossens, who had started out as some kind of electrical engineer in a company whose only customers had been NASA and the Air Force.

Porterfield forced himself to think about the assessments that had come from Langley. Los Angeles was a terrible place to have this happen. The place stretched eighty miles north and south from San Fernando to Mission Viejo, and another eighty east and west from San Bernardino to Thousand Oaks. What was called the City of Los Angeles was only a small part of the whole, a part where over four million people lived at night. At the beginning and end of each day nearly that many cars flooded the freeways. The figures Langley provided only increased the absurdity of it.

For this area, as big and crowded as some states, there was a city police force of five thousand, a complement of sheriff's deputies, and the California Highway Patrol. New York City had a police force of twenty-five thousand. The chance of the police finding a small band of terrorists in a place like this was so slim even Langley's dogged theoreticians had left it out of their calculations. Within the past year, there had been other incidents here—Armenians against Turks, two factions of exiled Iranians, three sets of Koreans, including a resident detachment from the KCIA tolerated by the Company in a reciprocity agreement, Irish gunrunners, Israelis against Palestinians, against Libyans, against Syrians. There were competing sets of exiles from Argentina, Chile, El Salvador, Costa Rica, Nicaragua, Peru, Bolivia, and Cuba, each of which was difficult to isolate or watch because they faded among the estimated one million resident aliens from Mexico. There were smaller factions too, among them French-Canadian separatists, Indonesians of the far left and far right, Filipinos, Vietnamese. The Soviet consulate had been attacked five times, by Kurds, Afghans, Poles, Turks, and a group that hadn't identified itself. Now three male Caucasians, reportedly of dark complexion, had made a raid on an undefended university building and disappeared. It wasn't a question now of catching them but of anticipating what they were going to do and finding a way to cut the Company's losses.

Porterfield returned to the desk and scanned the report from Langley again. The Company's people on the major newspapers and television networks had been briefed in case it turned out to be another Pentagon Papers revelation scheme. He wished the Director hadn't panicked and erased Professor Donahue from the equation. A denial from him, or failing that, a campaign to discredit him, might have helped if anything slipped through the mesh and made it into print. It was too late for that now. There was a team busily creating a medical history for the professor that documented repeated confinements in mental hospitals dating back to his days as an undergraduate at Michigan. There was another team using the same technique to create a bogus history of left-wing political activism, and Technical Services was putting together composite photographs of him entering both the Cuban and Soviet embassies in Mexico City in case it should be necessary to build a story of that sort. Any of the possibilities would have been more convincing if Donahue hadn't been killed, but there were people working on that part of the story too.

The main problem now was to devise a way of handling the people who had the Donahue papers. He stared out at the distant airport again. On the average day seventy-seven thousand people passed through Los Angeles International. There was no reason to watch. You had to know who they were before you could predict what they'd do.

PORTERFIELD glanced at the summons again. It was a printed card. "You are cordially invited. To. At. On." This time it was cocktails with the Cornell University Alumni, Los Angeles branch, at the Sheraton Universal, suite 702. Next time it could be a cardiologists' convention if the people coming all looked as though they might be doctors.

He knocked on the door of the suite and when it opened he said quietly, "You."

The tall black man nodded and closed the door behind them, then stepped to the television set and turned up the sound.

He looked the same, Porterfield thought. He must be nearly forty by now. "Who else is here?" Porterfield stared at the table beside the sliding glass door where two glasses of Scotch sat untouched.

"Nobody else is coming. I haven't seen you in four or five years, but you haven't improved. Still remind me of a nasty, fat old bull. Want to sit down?"

"Thanks, J.K." Porterfield took one of the drinks and sat at the table. "What are you doing in Los Angeles? New ambassador to Watts?"

J.K. shrugged and glanced at the television set. "I'm not in Los Angeles, Ben. If I were in Los Angeles I might be here to talk to you, and I've got nothing to do with you."

"You're here to do me a favor," said Porterfield. "You don't owe me a favor." He sipped his Scotch and waited.

"They're making some mistakes."

"They've been known to."

"First stage was when this university thing happened. They sent out a call to every chief of station in Domestic Operations to take a guess about who did it."

"I know. I stopped it when I came on. Too late, I suppose, but—"

J.K. chuckled. "Who whacked the professor? You do it yourself?"

"I'm getting too old for that, J.K. Is that the second stage?"

"Hell no. I don't think it was even a mistake. The mistake is more people know about this little problem than ought to know. Me, for instance."

"I'm not worried about you. What do other people know?"

"The general version that's going around is that this professor who worked on some psywar stuff and wrote it all down lost his papers. He was removed. But the papers are still in the hands of somebody who will find a way to use them. Is that much true?"

"Probably."

"What are the chances you'll be able to do something about it?"

"You know what these things are, J.K. The papers could be in Moscow Center by now. Or it could be an independent group that decides to go public by walking into one of the Company's client newspapers and handing everything over. It could go either way."

J.K. shook his head. "You ever think of retiring?"

"Every time I try to chew my food on the left side of my mouth. Maybe I'll get a partial plate instead."

"There are a lot of people who are worried about what might happen if whoever has the papers knows what to do with them. I've seen two requests for reassignment already, both of them from people who are afraid they'll be in semifriendly capitals the day everybody hears what they really do for a living."

Porterfield snorted. "Not surprising. I told the Director to try to get people like that out. Most of them are already retired."

J.K. stood up and walked to the window. "They're setting you up, Ben. Their responses to both requests were routed through my office, so I saw them. They turned both of them down. You know who signed the order?"

"Who?"

"You."

Porterfield said, "I see. Thanks for telling me, J.K."

"What do you want me to do?"

"Same as always. Use your brain. Anyone who thinks

he's in trouble, is. Get him out and sign my name to the paper. Word it as though I'm reversing my own order.''

"What are you going to do?"

"Ad-lib. Maybe I'll talk to the Director."

"If you can get to him."

"What do you mean?"

"I wasn't in the country the year they decided to do an audit. When was it?"

"Seventy-five."

"From what I saw in Langley yesterday, I'd say we've got a repeat. They're afraid, Ben. They're afraid somebody's going to take the Director off the count. He's got bodyguards with him in his office. They're afraid they've blown it so bad that somebody inside the Company is going to decide it's time for new management."

ʌ 15 ʌ

"WHERE ARE WE?" asked Margaret. "The Park in Rear bar." Chinese Gordon leaned his left elbow on the window and signaled for a left turn.

"The what?"

"See?" He pointed to the five-foot fire-red neon sign that flashed "PARK IN REAR." Above it, an unlighted but ornately filigreed script said the something Cafe and Bistro, but Margaret wasn't sure if she could have read it in daylight.

"Charming."

Chinese Gordon pulled the car into the shadowy alley and stopped it beside a 1968 Chevrolet painted mainly in gray primer dappled with red rustproofing. As Margaret got out she noticed that the parking lot was vast, stretching in a hundred-yard rectangle along the solid line of plain walls and loading docks, and that at least fifty or sixty cars were sitting at haphazard angles wherever their owners had felt like stopping them. "Looks like a demolition derby."

"No, just Friday night at the Park in Rear. We'll be out of here before they all try to get out that alley, so we'll miss most of the fun."

115

"I could pass up all of the fun."

"If we want to talk to Immelmann tonight, this has got to be it. He only goes to Ma Maison on Thursdays."

He pulled the door open, and the stale, smoky air of the place rushed out, bringing with it a tenor voice shouting in a southern accent over a driving bass guitar. Margaret shuddered involuntarily and looked around her. It seemed to be one cavernous room dominated by a marble bar that must have been a hundred feet long. She counted seven barmaids scurrying up and down behind it, and four men who stood along the back wall, big men with the hard, scanning eyes of policemen.

All over the room were tables where people sat drinking and yelling against the invincible solidity of the bass guitars. The music had already pummeled her senses so that she didn't hear it as music anymore. It was like being inside a great chugging engine composed of pounding pistons and some kind of undifferentiated roar. She followed Chinese Gordon through a crowd of tall men holding beer bottles, her face at chest level beside all of these bodies, and far too close, so her view was of plaid shirts and cowboy shirts, pockets with cigarette packs stuffed into them, wet underarms and then a greenish-blue tattoo of something with wings and a sword and some reddish flames. In front of her was only Chinese Gordon's back, and she felt an urge to cling to him but stifled it and only tried to make herself smaller to thread her way through behind him.

As she passed one man he was shouting along with the music, so she finally had the words blasted into her face along with an odorous, beery mist that seemed to go with the general smell of male sweat: "If that's all you want, little lady, you already got it." Perfect, she thought. Immelmann would be right at home. He always called his girlfriends "Little Lady" or "Sunshine'' because he couldn't remember their names.

At the tables there seemed to be a lot of people wearing hats—young women in cowboy hats, a man in a blue Dodger baseball cap, a few that bore trademarks like Caterpillar or Peterbilt. There was even an olive-drab one with sergeant's stripes stenciled on it in black.

She followed Chinese Gordon to a darker corner, where Immelmann and Kepler sat drinking beer out of bottles and then snapping their heads back to down shots of whiskey. Immelmann stood up when they approached, and he pulled out a chair for Margaret. Kepler nodded and held up a hand to call for the waitress, who seemed to be hovering nearby to watch the hand. She scurried to his side on impossibly high platform shoes that made Margaret wince, leaned over to listen, then strutted away in a parody of efficiency.

Chinese Gordon spoke, and she was surprised when she realized she could hear him. The noise seemed to have subsided imperceptibly. "We came to talk to you about another idea we've got.''

Immelmann smiled and waved a big hand in Kepler's direction. "That's a coincidence, Chinese. I wanted to talk to you about the same thing. I was just telling Kepler.''

"Don't listen to him, Chinese,'' Kepler said. "The man is a retard. It's an insult to have to take him seriously, and I do it only out of charity.''

"What's your idea?'' Margaret asked Immelmann.

"Thank you for asking, honey.'' There it was, she thought. He was probably too drunk to remember the name. "What we've got here is a chance for an investment. You remember I come from farm country.''

Kepler said, "I'd never have guessed.''

Immelmann ignored him. "Well, we've got a chance to triple our money—quadruple it in a year or two if we're willing to invest it now. There's a chance to buy a whole lot of land in Saskatchewan for very little right now.''

"No doubt," said Chinese Gordon. "It's fifty below zero there most of the winter."

"That's the beauty of it," Immelmann said. "That's why we can pick up prime acreage for the asking. Miles and miles of it."

"What's the idea? Oil? Minerals?" Chinese Gordon asked.

"Minerals? Shit!" he snorted, his long face breaking into a grin. Then he glanced at Margaret. "Excuse me, honey."

Kepler said, "God bless you." To Margaret he said, "Must be something he ate."

Immelmann leaned forward, talking barely above the buzz of noise around them. "It's not oil, it's not minerals, it's"—he glanced about and pronounced distinctly—"beefalo."

"Beefalo?" Chinese Gordon asked.

"That's right. Beefalo are a hybrid animal that has been developed by crossing beef cattle and buffalo. The meat tastes just like beef, but the animals themselves thrive in the roughest climate. I've been looking into this, and Saskatchewan is perfect. Way up north where cattle can't live and land is cheap."

Chinese Gordon stared at Margaret. She looked down at her hands in her lap.

Kepler leaned forward and said, "Immelmann, you are a grown man. When somebody tells you something tastes just like something else, you ought to know better than to believe him. You've been through survival school in the Marines, haven't you?"

"Sure."

"They told you snake tasted just like chicken, didn't

they? Well, you know goddamn well it doesn't. It tastes like snake. Armadillo doesn't taste like—''

"That's true," said Immelmann. "It's not like that. Everything disgusting is supposed to taste like chicken. If they said beefalo tasted like chicken, I'd know they were lying. It doesn't. It tastes like beef."

"That's what they say about horse, too," Kepler said. "You ever eat horse?"

Margaret looked up to see the heavily padded bust of the waitress appear between her and Kepler. The conversation was beginning to make her queasy, but maybe the drink would help.

Immelmann was insistent. "Look, at this moment the world is starving for beef."

The waitress eyed him uneasily. "Would you like to order something to eat?"

Kepler shook his head and handed her a bill.

Chinese Gordon sang, "I see by your outfit that you are a beefalo boy." Immelmann stared at him, one eyebrow lifted, so he moved on into "I'm an old beefalo-hand," which he changed quickly to "Beefalo gals won't you come out tonight and dance in Saskatoon."

"You're not a normal person, Chinese," Immelmann announced. "I'm offering you a chance to quietly convert your assets, which are a little precarious, if you know what I mean, into substantial holdings in land and stock."

"You know," said Kepler, "if you just took it to Las Vegas and played blackjack you'd have a little less than a fifty-fifty chance of making more."

"Is that what you're going to do?" asked Margaret.

"I'm not doing anything except drinking up some of the interest until I hear what you two have to say," Kepler said. "Chinese told me how to get it. Maybe I'll let him tell me what to do with it."

"I don't think we're going to need much money for this," said Chinese Gordon. "I just don't want to see you sink into inactivity, moral degeneration, and premature senility."

"Not more night classes?"

"I'm thinking about it. By the way, Immelmann, if you moved to a ranch in Canada you'd be able to take that big mutant—"

"Chinese!" said Margaret.

"Right. Yeah. It's an idea Margaret had, and we wanted to see what you thought." He leaned forward and spoke quietly. "All that paper I got Sunday night turned out to be some stuff the professor was doing for the CIA. Most of it's kind of long winded, but there's enough of it that's readable to make pretty good headlines."

"Blackmail them?" said Immelmann. "And you're afraid of a dog?"

"It has certain advantages. Secrecy is their middle name."

"No," Immelmann interrupted. "Intelligence is their middle name."

Kepler held up his hand. "I get it. I see what you're saying. They'd be more worried than anybody about keeping things secret. And because they're secret, they can pay off."

"That's what we were thinking," Chinese Gordon said. "If you try to hold up the mayor of Los Angeles, he can't pay even if he wants to because he—"

"They'll just kill us all," Kepler said. "Until now I was wondering who took that professor out."

"That just proves our point," said Margaret. "What we've got is important enough to be worth something to them."

"Get rid of it, then," Immelmann said. "Pretend you never saw it, Sunshine. Free yourself of this maniac and come with me to the land of the midnight sun.''

"Isn't that Sweden?" Margaret asked.

"Who cares?"

"Shut up," Kepler said. "It is an interesting idea. Is the paper good enough to work with?"

"Within limits," Chinese Gordon said. "I figure if we don't ask much more than it would cost to hunt us down, we might have a deal."

"What price range, roughly?" Kepler asked.

Margaret said, "I read in the paper it costs about five million dollars each time the President spends a weekend in Los Angeles, with the security and servants and things."

"I'd say in the ten-to-twenty range," said Chinese Gordon, holding his drink up to the light as though he were scrutinizing it for impurities. "No sense in pricing yourself out of the market."

"Let's go over to the shop and do some reading," said Kepler, tossing a sheaf of bills on the table.

They all stood up and began moving through the crowd. Margaret turned to Immelmann and whispered, "I thought you weren't interested."

He leaned down and answered, "First they'll get you, but it won't matter because your birth certificate has already disappeared so you don't exist. But then there may be people like me who think they might remember there was such a person. Only they couldn't be right, because pretty soon their birth certificate disappears and they don't exist either."

Margaret edged past a man who seemed to be wearing the skin of a woolly animal as a vest. "I suppose you think what you're saying makes sense?"

"No, I just think I'd better come along in case you need somebody tall."

"Tall?"

"Pretty soon you're going to be in deep trouble."

⋀ 16 ⋀

Utilization of Latent Terror Research and Analysis. 825074. The current phase of ULTRA is perhaps the most ambitious attempt to test the application of modern techniques of directed psychophobic behaviors. By implementing a plan developed by the Central Intelligence Special Operations Division, it will be, for the first time, possible to test with classic empirical methodology the validity of the psychometric predictions developed in the early phases of the ULTRA project.

Background: In 1978 the government of Mexico released previously secret geological reports concerning the Chicontepe Field, a strip of land seventy-five miles long and seventeen miles wide along the Gulf of Mexico between Tampico and Poza Rica. This area, it was revealed, contains potential petroleum reserves double the size of those on the Arabian peninsula. Because of the obvious economic and strategic importance of this Chicontepe Field, the Central Intelligence Agency was asked to develop tactical proposals for securing it.

• • •

Porterfield tossed the sheet on the table and rubbed his eyes. "This Professor Donahue had clearance to be given a contingency plan for the takeover of Mexico?"

The Deputy Director raised his eyebrows and shrugged, a gesture he might have practiced before a mirror. He was able to do it without disturbing the expertly fitted shoulders of the blue banker's suit. "As nearly as I can tell, he helped develop at least two alternative plans for that objective. He seems to have been in on the ground floor, and the clearances grew up around him and his research."

"Did Morrison know about these Mexico plans? Was he cleared?"

"I doubt it. At least not beyond the theoretical stage."

Porterfield froze, his hands still over his eyes. Slowly he opened his fingers and peered between them at the Deputy Director, his eyes cold and alert.

The Deputy Director sat in silence. He glanced around the room as though he'd never noticed it before, and was impressed. Then his eyes settled on Porterfield and widened in a pantomime of meeting an old friend far from home. "Of course there are plans, Ben. There are always plans, you know that. There are plans for everything."

Porterfield nodded, his hands folded now in front of his mouth.

"When I left my job with the brokerage to come here, do you know what the Mexico plans looked like? One of them was actually based on Woodrow Wilson's landing of marines at Veracruz. I guess they figured, 'Hell, it worked once.' " He chuckled.

Porterfield leaned forward. "So you and the Director decided—"

The Deputy Director held his hands out in a gesture

of modesty. "Not me, Ben. I was just one of many people who suggested that the Company had better get moving or some fine morning the only option we'd have would be to let the Russians take over the biggest oil field in the Western Hemisphere or blow seventy-five miles of Mexican coastline into the Gulf." He tapped the table with his forefinger. "You've got to remember what the situation has always been down there. In 1961, when everybody else broke off relations with Cuba, Mexico didn't."

"Okay," said Porterfield. "Now the plan, or enough of it, is in the hands of foreign terrorists, and has been for a couple of days now. It's blown. Now what?"

"That's what the Director wants you to tell him. It's a fumble, Ben. I'm not denying that. We're on our own fifteen-yard line, and this Professor Donahue fumbled the ball. It's up to you to pick up the ball and do whatever you can with it."

"What arrangements have been made for getting people out who might be compromised?"

"A couple of the division chiefs seem to have panicked and begun rolling up their own networks, but we've countermanded the orders. We've even met a few of these nervous Nellies at airports and turned them around."

"Why?"

The Deputy Director smiled. "Why?" he shook his head, still smiling. "Hell, you're an old hand, Ben. You spent a lot of years moving in and out of those Latin American countries, and you never ran out on an assignment. If we pulled out everybody who was afraid of Professor Donahue's reports, we'd lose half our people in five or six countries. And where do you stop? Most of our operatives down there aren't even Americans. Do you pull them out too? If we even hint that these papers exist, a lot of them will convict themselves by trying to run away.''

''Pull them out.''

''What?''

Porterfield said, ''Pull them out. If the report turns up, you can send them all back, or most of them. But it's been long enough now that we know we probably won't get the papers in any of the easy ways.''

''We can't do that, Ben. It's the one thing we can't do. It would take years to get back to the point we've already reached.''

Porterfield's hand moved across the table and cradled the Deputy Director's necktie, his thumb rubbing the smooth-textured silk as though he were considering buying it. He said quietly, ''You and the Director are morons. In a way you're a lot like the late Professor Donahue.''

''You're way out of line, Porterfield,'' said the Deputy Director. He sat limp in his chair, motionless and sweating.

Porterfield's hard eyes held him. ''You've been thinking about contingency plans and strategic objectives. Now I'd like you to think about what happens if these papers are sitting right now in the office of, say, the chief of internal security in Buenos Aires or Mexico City or Santiago. I've seen what happens when they roll up a network. Only this time it'll be different. You'd better be rooting for them. The death squads and the secret police are usually pretty good because they get so much practice, but they always miss a few.''

The Deputy Director jumped to his feet, but Porterfield's grip on the necktie tightened, and the Deputy Director jerked to a stop halfway up, giving an involuntary grunt, his eyes watering. Porterfield loosed his grip, and the Deputy Director straightened.

"Since you like the tie so much, I'll have my tailor send you one just like it next week."

"No, thanks. By then it might be bad luck."

"READ the section on the Mexico project," said Margaret. "We haven't gotten through it yet, but that looks like it could be the best."

Kepler leafed through the report, holding it far from his face and eyeing it warily. "Here. Tactics. That's at least something I can read."

It is essential to link the government in the minds of the populace with the privileged upper classes and to create a deep and inflexible hostility to both. At the same time, it is important to ensure that the government will be stimulated to react to each crisis by turning its power against the suspect lower classes. For Phase One of the program, the most useful vehicle is the Ministry of Health. For the past ten years the Ministry of Health has been engaged in a concerted effort to promote family hygiene in every way possible: vaccination, the draining of swampy areas, etc. . . .

"This is boring," Kepler said. He skipped a few pages and started to read again.

Particularly effective are those products which are vigorously promoted by the Ministry of Health and sold in modern chain stores wholly owned by members of the ruling upper classes. Typical examples are contaminated baby food and toxic tampons.

"What?" said Margaret.

"You heard right."

"I wish I hadn't."

"It's pretty sickening stuff, all right," said Kepler. "But it just isn't what we need."

"What on earth do we need?"

Immelmann spoke. "This is just enough to get us killed. It gets published and what happens? They deny it and it sinks out of sight. What we need isn't something that gives them a week of bad press. We've got to find something that'll keep them awake at night in a cold sweat."

"Isn't an invasion of a friendly country enough for that?" Margaret asked.

"No," said Kepler. "I'm sure they have plans like this for every country on earth, and Antarctica. This isn't worth anything unless they're actually doing it, and they're not."

Chinese Gordon said, "There's some of what you're looking for on page 435."

Kepler turned some sheets and read. " 'The assistant to the Minister's appointment secretary would be responsible for ensuring that the Minister's answer was the appropriate one of the four she had memorized.' " He skipped onward. " 'The chief of police of the village of Caliente would . . .' You're right, Chinese. This is the stuff—agents in place who can be identified."

CHINESE Gordon heard a scratching sound in the kitchen and turned his head to see Doctor Henry Metzger burying his food bowl with the throw rug, an elaborate and ostentatious performance that ended in his pretending to bury the rug too with an immense mound of imaginary material, interrupting his work occasionally to stare at Chinese Gordon.

"I'm busy, Doctor Henry. I'll feed you later."

Doctor Henry Metzger sauntered into the bedroom, rubbing his side against Margaret's leg and then making a wide circuit along the wall. He passed behind the men and then sprang to the bed, padded across the sheets of paper and onto Margaret's lap, where he walked in a tiny circle until his own tail brushed his face and he flopped down heavily.

It was then that they heard the sound downstairs. It was a hissing noise, a steady scrape as though someone were dragging something along the concrete floor. Then it seemed to be moving up the stairs, first only the hiss, but then a tapping began, something hitting on each step as it approached.

"It can't be," said Chinese Gordon.

At the sound of his voice the noise quickened, the staccato tap becoming a clatter.

"Too fast for a cop with a wooden leg," said Kepler.

The dog's big black muzzle appeared in the doorway. When he saw the gathering in the bedroom, his eyes seemed to flare with pleasure and his jaw hung open to let his tongue dangle out between the terrible white teeth. His breaths came in gruff, excited gasps, "Heh. Heh. Heh." He seemed unconscious of his tail slapping the door as it wagged.

Kepler turned to Immelmann. "He must have heard you had some beefaloes." His hand moved slowly to his right boot.

Doctor Henry Metzger lifted his head from Margaret's lap a half inch and opened his eyes, then closed them again, purring.

"He was tied up outside with a double half hitch on a

rope that would hold an aircraft carrier to a dock," said Chinese Gordon.

The dog moved into the room, his long toenails scratching on the floor, a thick rope tied to his collar and stretching around the corner toward the stairway.

"You tied that thing up outside?" said Kepler. "What if he got hungry and ate a mailman or a kindergarten class or something? The least you could do is tie a decent knot."

"Don't be mad at him," Margaret said. "He was just lonely for Doctor Henry Metzger and heard voices."

"Looks like he chewed through the rope, Chinese," Immelmann said.

"Yeah, and maybe you brought a monkey with you to untie it for him. Are you people deaf? He just dragged a four-inch ring bolt and probably half my garage wall up those stairs."

"Just proves my point," said Kepler. "No sane man leaves an animal like that outside, tied up or not."

"No sane man has an animal like that," Chinese Gordon snapped, "if there *is* another animal like that. And if he had one, you bet he'd let him go outside. Have you ever seen how much that dog eats? Well, he does everything else proportionately."

"Awesome," Immelmann agreed.

The dog walked up to Margaret and pushed his face close to Doctor Henry Metzger, who was now engaged in licking one of his paws. He placed the other on the dog's nose.

"Don't worry, Chinese," said Kepler. "Chances are if he eats a kid he'll probably eat his bicycle too, so there won't be any evidence. Now unless you want to bring in a few poisonous snakes first, or a crocodile, I suggest we get back to business."

With some difficulty Chinese Gordon moved his eyes to Kepler, but every few seconds Chinese Gordon glanced at the dog. "Okay. The papers and television people keep saying that we're terrorists. That poor scared parking guy at the university gave them a description of us that leaves it open whether we're black or white. I guess he's afraid of dark people and afraid of us, so—"

"I read that you might be a new Samoan independence group," Margaret said.

"I get the idea," said Immelmann. "Who should we be? We can send them a ransom note in Korean. I've got a girl who writes Korean and it looks great. It looks like O, I, and L all printed sideways and backwards, upside down, and on top of each other—"

"Save it," said Chinese Gordon. "We don't want to do that. If we do, your friend will know."

"No," Immelmann said. "You see, we give her a long thing to translate and just pick out the words we want, one here, one there."

"And then the answer comes back in Korean," Kepler said. "Brilliant. Chinese is right. They think we're terrorists, which means they think we're nuts, which is good. They don't know where we're from, which is also good. If they think we're from someplace in particular, they'll start thinking about what they have to lose in that place, and maybe they're not willing to take the chance by giving us money."

"The less they have to work with, the better," Chinese Gordon said.

The dog turned away from Margaret and walked toward Chinese Gordon. On the stairs there was a bump-bump-bump as the rope pulled its unseen burden three steps higher. "Damn," said Chinese Gordon quietly. "Damn." The dog placed its forepaws across

Chinese Gordon's legs and pushed off the ground. "Oh, God," Chinese Gordon said, and the dog gave a strange low growl as it pushed its nose close to Chinese Gordon's throat.

"Isn't that sweet?" said Margaret. "He wants to sit on your lap, just like Doctor Henry Metzger." Sadly she added, "He's just too big."

"Margaret," said Chinese Gordon in a calm, quiet tone, "this noble animal is preparing to tear my head off." The dog's jaws were clamped shut, but he could see the two front fangs barely obscured by the black lips.

The dog gave another long, low growl. This time it seemed to start somewhere deep in his massive chest and move upward to his throat.

Kepler said to Immelmann, "What do you think?"

Immelmann nodded, his brow furrowed judiciously. "She's right, Chinese. He's trying to purr."

⌃ 17 ⌃

PORTERFIELD WAITED FOR the fourth ring of the telephone. He could imagine Alice on the first ring putting down something she'd been reading and walking from the living room to the phone on the kitchen wall.

"Hello?" There was the slight reserve in her voice that made it a different voice, one he never heard except in the instant before she knew who it was.

"Hello, honey."

"Ben. I was just wondering if I should get in the bathtub or wait a few more minutes. I fooled you for once."

"I'll get you next time. Is everything okay?"

"Of course. Miss me?"

"I always miss you. I should be able to get back in a few days." There had been an edge in her voice—what was it? There had been thirty years of telephone calls, sometimes made from cities thousands of miles from the place they both pretended he was. She was holding something, almost as though it were an object he couldn't see. "What have you been doing?"

She sighed, and he could feel she was deciding to pass the object to him. "I went to dinner tonight at Pauline and Charles Compton's house."

"We haven't seen them in—it must be three or four years. What brought that on?" Charles Compton had been retired since the purge of 1977. Now he worked for an insurance agency. In the old days Charles and Pauline had been among the few people they could see socially. Only with other couples in the Company was there no awkwardness in the fact that nobody ever talked about business. There was no need to maintain the usual terrible watchfulness about dates and cities that came up in conversation. All four were comfortable confining conversation to the present—the children, this year's books, this week's movies.

Alice's voice was thoughtful. "I don't really know. Pauline called last night and said they'd tried the Foundation office during the day. I guess I was the consolation prize."

"Did you have a good time?"

"They were cordial. Pauline's a good cook."

"Sounds pretty dull. What's the problem?"

"He's changed. No, I know we've all changed, and I know I'm not the one to talk, with my hair looking like the topping on a fancy dessert. But you know, Ben, he was drunk."

"Well, he's probably feeling business pressure. The insurance companies must be in the same shape as everything else. What did he say?"

"Nothing. Not a thing that's worth mentioning. Most of the evening he just drank and asked questions about you. As I was leaving, he said the oddest thing. No, it wasn't odd in itself, it was just the way he said it. It was, 'Tell Ben not to abandon old friends.' "

"Oh, well. I'll give him a call when I'm home. He'll be okay. Maybe I'll have a few drinks with him, if that's what he's doing these days."

"If you have to. But just remember, don't abandon old wives."

"Never. I guess I'll turn in now and let you get that bath. I'll talk to you tomorrow."

"Good night, Ben."

"Sleep tight, baby."

Porterfield sat on the edge of the bed, staring out over the balcony at the vastness of the valley stretching far to the north, the millions of lights seeming to form a glow above the earth brighter here near the center, dimmer and less substantial in the distance. So it had gotten as far as Charles Compton already. The word was moving through the old boy network of retired agents and peripheral people, and some of them were worried. Some of them had things to worry about. He considered for a moment having someone pull out Charles Compton's file, but he dismissed the idea. It didn't really matter which chapter of Donahue's opus was the one that kept Compton awake at night. Compton was of no use to him.

CHINESE Gordon strolled across the vast lawn, feeling the thick, elastic layer of wet grass under his feet and smelling the warm, still evening air, fresh and moist. "Just like a golf course," he said. "The Official Federal Country Club of Wilshire Boulevard."

"Are you sure this is a good idea?" Kepler asked.

"It's brilliant, actually. You saw the gardeners leave when they turned off the sprinklers. The conditions are perfect—wet, healthy grass, a beautiful sunset, ideal wind conditions. You should learn to take pleasure in being a tiller of the soil." He took a deep breath and blew it out through his teeth. "And loosen up a little.

You're holding your trowel like you were going to stab somebody with it.''

Kepler contemplated the luminous deep purple sky beyond the massive white shape of the building. Chinese Gordon moved off a few yards to adjust the nozzle of his weed sprayer. After a few tentative squirts he had choked it to a thin, straight stream. Kepler heard him chuckle and then begin to hum a medley of Sousa marches as he clutched the spray tank under his left arm like a bagpipe. Kepler knelt down and carved out a circle of turf with his trowel, dug a few inches deeper, and buried the bottle. When he looked up he could see Chinese Gordon in the twilight walking back and forth with the sprayer, dousing the lawn with a steady stream of silvery fluid.

On the boulevard the continuous stream of cars was already a blur of headlights reflecting on polished metal, and the stores had lighted their windows. Here and there colored neon swirls had appeared on the shadowy sides of buildings.

As Chinese Gordon's march brought him closer, Kepler could see that a few inches above the lawn a slight haze like wisps of steam seemed to rise and then drift off into the night. Kepler stood up and backed away to make room.

Chinese Gordon stopped, turned off the valve on the weed sprayer, and said, ''As fine a piece of decorative gardening as this group of public servants will ever see.'' He smiled as he started the long walk across the lawn beside Kepler. When they reached the car he carefully wrapped the weed sprayer in a blanket and laid it in the trunk.

''What's the problem?'' Chinese Gordon asked. ''You haven't said anything in fifteen minutes.''

"No problem."

"Then what is it?"

"I was trying to think of the right word. You know how that is. You see something and you know there's a word for it but instead you keep thinking of other words that maybe sound like it but don't mean exactly what you want them to mean. And of course it doesn't matter because you know the right word exists, so you can't be satisfied until you remember it."

"Sure." Chinese Gordon made a right turn onto Wilshire Boulevard and then drove a block before the red light stopped them. "I have that happen a lot. It's like having one of those tiny bugs fly up your nose. You blow your nose and snort and maybe try to dig it out with your finger if you're alone. You can't stop until you succeed completely. What was the word?"

"Simpleton."

IT was nearly six o'clock. The sun was rising, and in a few minutes Donald Carney of the IRS would begin what he thought of as the quiet hours. Those last two hours of the late-night shift always seemed to be empty. Between twelve and six he always finished the work that required concentration. When the sun came up it was time for other people to start their turn. He usually made lists. There were lists of things he'd have to work on tomorrow night, things he had to pick up on the way home this morning, lists of messages to Blucher, the man who occupied this office during the day. This morning there would be plenty of messages. The Internal Revenue Service was moving into prime auditing season now, and even the quiet hours were filling up. He stood up and walked to the window. The cars were already flooding the boulevard, and the tiny shapes of people moved along the sidewalk, far below him, their shadows long in the bright, oblique rays of the sunrise.

The view from the twenty-third floor of the Federal Building was almost supernatural, like clairvoyance, or even omniscience. He could see the afternoon's weather approaching from the sea. If the air was clear he could sometimes even tell how heavy the traffic on the Santa Monica Freeway was going to be. Even the regular things looked different from up here. The painted numbers that people below never noticed on the roofs of buses and police cars were clearly visible. He leaned against the windowsill and sipped his coffee. In a little while the first of the day people would begin walking up that sidewalk from the parking lot.

Four long shadows suddenly appeared at the front of the building on the white pavement. He could barely see the tiny men who made them. As he watched, they began to run. The shadows, five or six times longer than a man, seemed to flicker and bounce and float. At first he thought they were running toward the street, but then the shadows fanned out across the green lawn. It was then that Carney saw it. In the center of the depthless green far below him, Carney could see the brownish yellow letters. The four shadows swept to the spot, then flickered along it and then crossed each other in frantic movements. Finally the shadows merged and stopped, all four of them flailing across the brownish-yellow patch, but the shadows didn't obscure it at all. It was perfectly visible from the twenty-third floor and just as legible as the numbers on the roofs of the buses on the street. It said, "DONAHUE." Donahue? He shook his head and gave a humorless snort. Whoever this guy Donahue was, within a day or two he'd be wishing he'd just written "FUCK YOU, IRS" the way the last two had—the way any normal person would.

Carney had worked out the first of his lists, drunk his coffee, and returned the file he'd been working on to its place in the drawer before he felt enough curiosity to look out the window again. Now there were more tiny men surrounding the spot on the lawn, this time men with shovels and wheelbarrows. They had already cut the turf into strips like carpet and rolled it into little strudels to be loaded into the wheelbarrows. By quitting time the new strips of turf would probably be laid in place and the spot would be indistinguishable from the rest of the lawn, at least from the twenty-third floor. The gardeners seemed to be very efficient at making things look as though they'd been growing for years. In a day or two the new turf would be rooted and healthy. At least it would be if it weren't too trampled to survive. From up here he could count seventeen shadows, only four of them working with shovels and wheelbarrows while the others watched.

PORTERFIELD stood at the office window, staring out at the airport. It would have pleased him to be over there now, looking at this building through the window of an airplane. The ten-o'clock flight arrived in Washington just about the time he usually came home for dinner.

"I'd say that the signs all point to a genuine break for the good guys," said Gossens.

"Meaning?" Porterfield said.

"Us." Gossens stretched it to two syllables, obviously annoyed.

"No. I mean what signs?"

"The fact that they did it in such an amateurish way, like vandals, for one thing. Writing on a lawn and leaving a note buried in a bottle—why, it's downright infantile. And they did it at the Federal Building down-

town. That's especially telling. If it were some group af-
filiated with a major power, or even independents with
some sophistication, they'd have to know that the Company has no office down there. The place is entirely
devoted to civilians—the IRS, Immigration, that kind
of thing.''

Porterfield sighed. He said wearily, ''What would
have happened if they'd come to this complex to leave
us a message?''

''They'd have been snatched up, of course. Nothing
comes within a thousand yards of this building without
coming under surveillance.''

''And tell me: Who first noticed the word 'Donahue'
burned into the front lawn? Did some clerk or tax col-
lector see it and know enough to call your office? It's
now eight o'clock. It's been light for only two hours.''

''Of course it was one of our people, but . . .''

''It doesn't sound as though they did too badly. The
KGB wouldn't have done much better. Let me see the
note.''

Gossens handed him several photographs: The top
one was of a piece of paper with a hand-printed para-
graph on it. The next three were photographs of a beer
bottle. Porterfield lifted an eyebrow and tossed them on
the desk. He read aloud.

Announcement of auction. The private papers of
the late Professor Ian Donahue will be sold to the
highest bidder on or about the first of May. Confidential bids will be accepted from qualified pur-
chasers. Your identifying number is 619352, and
your bid will be placed in the *Los Angeles Times*.

He studied the photographs of the grass, some of
them taken from the sky, some of them taken with a

special closeup lens and looking as though they must be part of a nature study.

Gossens snapped, "Well? Langley is going to want to know what the next move is."

"How far have they gotten on the lab work?"

"There aren't any fingerprints, as you might expect. Whatever footprints there might have been weren't defined enough to do anything with."

"You mean your people tromped all over the area before they'd thought about it?"

"Well—yes. But there's going to be a demonstration there in about a half hour. Something to do with nuclear disarmament, so there are going to be people all over the lawn anyway. The permit was issued two months ago. Our people barely had time to do as much as they did before—"

"What did they use on the lawn?"

"Hydrochloric acid, weak enough so that it would take a little while to burn into the lawn. It's not traceable, and it's easy enough to make, for that matter."

"And nobody saw anything?"

"No."

"Then I'd say the best thing to do is probably get in touch with Deputy Director Pines at Langley and tell him to have Management and Services start working out what our bid is going to be."

⚶ 18 ⚶

CHINESE GORDON'S BATHROBE nearly brushed the floor at Margaret's feet. It seemed to be wrapped around her twice and cinched tight in the middle, but she still looked like a small child wrapped in a blanket. He knew the next time he put it on he'd be surprised because the sleeves would be rolled up to his elbows.

"Great bathrobe, Chinese," she said, snatching up as much of the extra cloth as she could and climbing the wooden steps. "But why is everything you own brown? Aren't you bored?"

"Everything's not brown."

"Blue jeans don't count."

"Bright colors attract bees. Give me the paper."

She tossed the thick newspaper on the bed and he picked it up, wrinkling his nose. "Why's it all wet and slimy?"

"I was trying to teach the dog how to bring it in, but I don't think he understands it yet."

"Please don't say it like that. If you say 'the dog' it sounds like it's our dog. It's damned well not our dog. Immelmann adopted it, and Kepler is an accessory. It's—"

"Oh, don't be so cranky, you baby. Read the funnies." She disappeared into the bathroom and he heard the shower. Chinese Gordon turned to the classified advertising section and searched.

Business opportunity: Own a restaurant supply business. Easy, convenient terms. Worth ten million, but yours for $619,350.

He smiled as he scanned the pages.

Ultraluxurious condominiums in quiet, secure twelve-million-dollar complex, starting at $619,352.

His favorite was the display for the automobiles:

Overstocked: We've got fifteen million dollars in unsold vans! Look at this deal! A custom modified van that'll blow everything else off the road. License number 619355. The Professor's Cars. Freeway close, just blocks from ULA.

He sensed another presence in the room behind him and whirled his head to look for the dog, but it was Margaret standing over him, her hair hanging in wet strings that dripped onto his bathrobe.

"That last one is really stupid, Chinese. The others border on the suspicious, but that one is actually childish. Did Immelmann write it?"

Chinese Gordon folded the newspaper and tossed it on the floor. "I wrote it. And it's not childish, it's just blatant. You people are all so critical, so eager to deny me my simple pleasures."

Margaret wrapped the bathrobe around herself more tightly and smirked. "Oh?"

"Not those. I've got a strategy, you know. These are not subtle people we're dealing with. They're all sitting around a table in Washington or someplace right now taking themselves seriously. It's my job now to keep them off balance so they don't decide it would be an acceptable sacrifice to firebomb Los Angeles."

"Do you honestly think they'll believe those ads are offers from competitors?"

"Who cares what they think? I've got something they want. This is just a way of showing them some price tags."

"THIS is absurd." Kearns waved a hand in the direction of the newspaper but made no effort to touch it.

Goldschmidt shrugged. "Of course. But your people haven't been able to discover who placed the advertisements, have they?"

"It was done by mail—cash, three different post offices all over Los Angeles. The people at the newspaper weren't suspicious that two of the ads didn't have addresses or phone numbers. Apparently people do that all the time—just forget. So they assigned each one a box number and expected to hold any inquiries for whoever picked them up."

"What about the used-car lot?"

"They had no way of knowing it didn't exist. It could have been new. Hundreds of businesses come and go every year in a city that size, and all most of them can think of to avoid it is put an ad in the paper."

Porterfield looked around the table. It was the same group as the last time, except this time they had dispensed with the distracting presence of John Knox Morrison. He wished they could have gotten Kearns out of it too. He would add hours to this, and Alice would be waiting at home for the call from Los Angeles.

Pines, the Deputy Director, assumed his earnest expression, his brow furrowed. "As I said at the beginning of this mess, it's entirely too systematic."

Kearns snapped, "Actually, I think Goldschmidt said it, and the term wasn't 'systematic,' it was 'mannered.' "

"Did he? No matter. He was right. These people have rather carefully chosen their adversary. As strange as it seems, they've effectively launched a plausible blackmail threat to the Central Intelligence Agency. I'd say that narrows the field to one."

Goldschmidt shook his head, his eyes wide in a kind of amazement.

Pines held up his hand. "Think about it. The whole operation carried out with such discipline, such planning, but at the same time with excessive and unnecessary firepower. And now there are these ransom messages and bogus bids. As soon as I learned about it a little flag went up, and it said 'Russians.' "

"Lower the flag," said Porterfield.

"Not without some evidence. These messages are perfectly in keeping with everything in the Russian psyche —three advertisements instead of one—or none, for that matter. And the way they're phrased, the whoopee-cushion sense of humor."

"They're not Russians," said Porterfield.

"Why not?" Pines was having difficulty holding his earnest expression, which was not designed for asking questions, so he only looked as though some part of his body hurt.

Goldschmidt answered, "Because if they had the Donahue papers, they'd publish them or read them into the record in the United Nations General Assembly or hand copies of them to every ambassador in Moscow, not try to sell them back for ten or twenty million. All we have to fear from the Russians is that they'll outbid us."

"Outbid us? You're joking."

"I'm glad you feel that way," said Goldschmidt. "Now let's get to work and figure out how to handle the bidding. The main problem—"

"No, that's not the plan at all. Are you seriously suggesting that the Central Intelligence Agency pay off on a blackmail threat? A threat that the Director feels certain comes directly from the KGB?"

"So that's it," Porterfield muttered. "The little flag popped up in the Director's head, too."

Pines was in control of his expression again. "We're not here to consider capitulation. If that's the impression you gentlemen have, you're very wrong. We're here to develop an aggressive strategy that will end this problem."

Porterfield sighed, but Pines was smiling. "We'll do what we've done for the past thirty years—outmaneuver them. They have something of ours, so we will take something of theirs. The important point is that we must be precise in our response. We must retaliate at exactly the same level as the provocation so that this problem doesn't escalate. At the end of it we'll trade evenly. The Director favors the idea of hostages, perhaps three of them. There is a Soviet trade delegation at a computer show in San Francisco that begins next week. Several of the people who have been issued visas are of sufficient rank to be suitable."

The others sat silent, staring at the table. Porterfield cleared his throat. The others appeared not to notice that it sounded almost like a laugh. Pines ignored it, even when Goldschmidt cleared his throat too.

Porterfield said, "You've checked this out with the Eastern Europe desk?"

"Not yet. Of course, we will before anyone does anything. I told you, our response must be delicately tuned to be precisely appropriate to the stimulus."

⚠ 19 ⚠

THE STRONG WINDS of the morning had scoured the sky to an impossible blue and then moved on. The sunlight now beat into the bowl of Dodger Stadium, heating the seats and the concrete steps so that food and drinks spilled months ago cooked and released a perfumy essence into the air. When the third warmup pitch smacked into the catcher's mitt, a tiny cloud of dust exploded and then drifted luminous in the sunlight for a second.

Jorge Grijalvas stared about him at the stadium. He wasn't looking at any of the individual players throwing the ball back and forth. That view of things didn't interest him very much. His box had been chosen because it gave him what he called the whole view. At a glance he could see the entire infield as a unit. If he lifted his gaze he could see not people, but the crowd. He liked the crack of the bat and then the whole infield moving at once in the smooth, precise, and practiced maneuvers too quick for thought. The Dodger infield was like a special kind of machine, perhaps a trap.

Grijalvas had the same box every year. He also had a box in the Hollywood Bowl for the concert season, but

147

he always gave the tickets to friends and business acquaintances who seemed to enjoy it, or perhaps only to enjoy accepting the friendship of Jorge Grijalvas. He paid no attention to the Los Angeles Rams, because American football made no sense to him. He understood it completely, but it seemed interesting only theoretically.

Baseball was different. Here was ritual, the nobility of a single small man in a white uniform on a field of dust pitting his cunning and his reflexes against nine in a contest of concentration and will before an immense gathering of people, a colorful, variegated blur of humanity ranged from the dugout to the heavens, all breathing in unison, all gasping as he swung the blond bat.

Grijalvas smiled and pivoted his head about in satisfaction to look at his companions. He was a happy man. He was a man of substance, a *padrón*, a man who could spend the afternoon in Dodger Stadium surrounded by his friends. They were more than friends. They were *fidelios*, the faithful.

As he gazed about the stadium he could see that the food and ice-cream vendors were beginning their first sweep down the steps that separated the seating sections. Across the stadium they were stepping down the aisles at once, the aluminum cases slung on their shoulders glinting in the sunlight. He snapped a twenty-dollar bill in his fingers and held up his right arm, then glanced about for the man who would come to collect it.

He was pleased when he saw the vendor step down the aisle. It was a young woman with beautiful long brown hair that shone reddish in the sunlight, and a complexion that was white, like a ceramic figurine. She was perfect, as the day was perfect.

"Give these gentlemen whatever they wish," he said.

"I've only got hot dogs, sir." And then she smiled, and he included her in his expansive mood. She added, "Great hot dogs, though."

Grijalvas turned to his friends. "What do you think? Do we believe her?"

"How can we know?" said Juan, his face expressionless. "Is it guaranteed to be horse meat?" He winked to keep the tattoo of a tear on his cheekbone covered by his sunglasses.

She held up a tinfoil package. "This one ran third in the Belmont Stakes."

Grijalvas slapped his knee. "Give us five, and keep the change." He watched as she gave the other four hot dogs, then he said, "I want the one that won the Kentucky Derby."

"Of course. I've been saving it for you." She reached into the aluminum box and handed him one of her foil packages, then moved down the aisle. He saw her slip into the crowd and then onto the exit ramp. It must be a good day for her if she had to go back for more hot dogs already. Grijalvas looked at the infield. The first batter was striding to the plate, swinging his bat in a deliberate motion that seemed to be more mental than physical.

Grijalvas didn't like hot dogs, but he found himself fiddling with the aluminum foil. It was so much bigger and heavier than he'd expected. He opened it and peered inside. When he saw the piece of paper on top he said to Juan, "Excuse me," and walked down the steps to the men's room. Inside, he unfolded the paper and read.

"Jorge, I need a favor. The rest of this hot dog is seventy-five hundred dollars, so don't eat it. What I need is the use of your Mexican connections. . . ."

He folded the paper without reading the rest of it and put the foil package in the breast pocket of his coat. Today was not a day to think about business. Still, he was a happy man, and there was no reason not to do as this man asked if the request was reasonable. The man was a lunatic, but the world was full of lunatics, and most of them were not capable of surprising.

On the far side of the stadium, Margaret climbed the steps and sat down next to Chinese Gordon.

"How did it go?" he asked, peering through a pair of binoculars.

"He got it."

"Yeah, I saw that." He lowered the binoculars and frowned at her. "Did you save me a hot dog?"

⩔ 20 ⩔

As PORTERFIELD TOUCHED the doorknob he felt it twist in his hand, and he stood to watch the door jerk open. On the other side was a tall, alert young man in a gray suit who seemed to be decorated with bits of plastic—three laminated access badges, the plastic edge of a radio that looked like a hearing aid visible at the breast pocket, a beeper at his belt.

"Oh, God," muttered Porterfield.

"Sir?" said the young man eagerly, his left hand held to the earpiece of his radio, ready to pluck it out.

"Nothing at all." Porterfield entered the conference room and looked about him. This morning the same group had gathered, but this time they had clustered together at the far end of the long table. At the near end was another group of three men and two women who seemed to be scanning sheets of paper that were brought to them by other people Porterfield didn't know. As he watched, one of the women at the lower end of the table scribbled or marked a sheet and sent the messenger scurrying to the head of the table to Pines, who glanced at it, nodded, and returned to his conversation with those near in even lower tones.

Porterfield dodged two messengers and moved to the head of the table. The others looked up, their faces still in the expressions they'd held a moment before: Pines excited and perhaps revealing some hint of triumph at something he had just said, Goldschmidt's lined and weary face slack with something between boredom and distaste, Kearns visibly disturbed.

Porterfield said quietly, "You could fit a few more people in here if you'd have them knock out that wall."

Pines leaned back in his chair. "You can take it up with the Director."

Porterfield turned and saw the young man open the door and step aside as the Director strode into the room. Behind him came two more young men with plugs in their left ears and carrying files. The Director walked with both hands in his pockets, as though to emphasize the fact that he carried nothing, opened no doors, wrote nothing down.

"How are we doing?" he said.

"We thought we'd wait until you got here," said Pines. "The plane arrives at four-fifteen San Francisco time, which is seven-fifteen tonight."

"Plane?" said Porterfield. "This isn't that idiotic thing about the Russians, is it?"

Pines smirked, but the Director chuckled. "I don't mind a difference of opinion on strategies. Ben didn't know this plan is mine, and I give him the credit that knowing wouldn't make any difference. And I know that even if we disagree on this one, you'll all settle down and make it work."

"Of course," Pines said, staring at Porterfield. "The whole thing should be over in a few hours. The team is already in place, the arrangements are made."

"Fine," Porterfield said, pushing his chair away from the table. "Then you won't need us."

"I'm afraid we will, Ben," said the Director. "It's a good, solid move, but it's not by any means a sure thing. Every time we deal with the Russians there's a possibility of things getting out of hand—that they'll make the irrational move, the inappropriate response."

"Then I think we should take our business elsewhere," said Porterfield.

The Director's smile disappeared. "You haven't heard the plan."

Porterfield folded his arms and waited.

"It's actually very subtle. The Aeroflot airplane from Moscow arrives at four-fifteen in San Francisco. It is met by the team we had originally planned to have. The Russians have had the names and faces for months. The team leads the Russians to the VIP lounge, buys them drinks, dinner, more drinks, whatever makes them happy."

"And?"

"That's it. The Russian consulate wonders where they are, their contacts at the hotel wonder. After a few hours, Moscow begins to wonder. Nobody knows because nobody saw them arrive and nobody saw them leave. When Moscow finally comes up with Donahue's papers, the delegation is driven to their hotel and turned loose. Even they don't know they've been detained. Moscow knows, of course, but they can't make any claims because it would sound ludicrous."

"What if Moscow doesn't come up with the papers?"

"There are several contingency plans. There will be a LearJet all fueled up and ready to take them away if we need to hold them for any length of time. There will be four cars waiting if we need to split them up. Have I forgotten anything, Pines?"

"I don't believe so. We should have the papers by midnight."

"What's to stop them from using other copies?"

"That's the beauty of it. This is better than getting the papers and the men who stole them. The problem isn't the papers themselves, it's that the Russians might use them. What we're doing is letting the Russians know that they can't keep doing this kind of thing because we'll respond. They have the papers, so they know the names of a few agents, a few foreign nationals we've turned. It's too late to keep that from happening. What we're doing is showing them that we know a few agents of theirs, and maybe a few foreign nationals that they've turned. If they don't do anything, we won't do anything. After a decent interval both sides will have replaced the people who are known, and everything will be back to normal." The Director waited. "Well?"

Porterfield said, "Well—"

"No," Goldschmidt snapped. "Let me say it. The plan is stupid. Its only redeeming aspect is that it is unlikely the Russians will be able to understand the deranged message you're sending them. It's unprofessional. Who besides you was involved in this?"

Porterfield stared down the long table, watching the messengers arriving with an air of urgency, then leaving, usually with a single piece of paper that now contained a set of initials or a few words in a margin. As he watched, one of them handed a sheet to Maria Hurtado, Kearns's assistant from the Latin America desk.

Pines had handed Goldschmidt a list of names, and he was running a finger down it quickly. "Ben," he said, smiling, "you should see this." He jabbed it in front of Porterfield, who glanced down at it.

"Molnar?"

"That's the one."

"The one who was pushing the Exploding President?"

"Exploding President? What the hell are you talking about?" Pines was breathing hard through the corners of his mouth.

"It was before your time," said Goldschmidt. "Molnar was sponsoring a plan to make a dummy that looked just like the President but filled with two hundred pounds of tritonal and a layer of fléchettes."

"What the hell for?"

"To assassinate assassins. You know, at parades and ceremonies."

"But that would kill everybody around it for a hundred yards."

"Right. Well-done hamburger. If we'd gone for that one, we might have gotten the Nuclear President. I guess it's our loss. Glad to see you've found something else for Molnar to do."

The Director said quietly, "It's not fair to mark a man for life just for one bad idea. He's been very helpful on this one."

Porterfield was staring down the table at Maria Hurtado, whose face had suddenly changed. Her brows were knitted and she was frowning, but her eyes were wide with excitement as she read. Then she was standing, walking toward Kearns, her eyes still on the sheet in her hand. She reached over Kearns's right shoulder, placed the paper on the table in front of him, and waited.

The Director was saying, "We'd like to use the next few hours to develop ways of taking advantage of this situation. Actual interrogation may not be wise, but it is an option. There is a range of other options to be explored and—"

"Excuse me," said Kearns.

"One moment." The Director held his hand up majestically. "What I want is a little brainstorming. Bring in your best people. If one of you hears something that might be worth pursuing, pass it immediately to the other groups. Now, Kearns, what is it?"

"There's new information. This article appeared in the *Vox Populi* of Ixtapa, Mexico, this morning. Let me translate the important parts."

The Ministry of Education released the following figures today. There are over fifteen million students enrolled in the nation's primary and secondary schools this year. The number is the highest ever, according to Ministry sources. An especially encouraging part of the report is that while the number of students is expected to continue to grow, the number of qualified teachers has grown much faster during the past five years. There are now 619,352 full-time licensed teachers.

"How much checking has been done, Maria?" Porterfield asked.

"The *Ixtapa Vox Populi* seems to be the only paper in Mexico that carried the story. That's the biggest sign. It's a small paper with maybe thirty thousand subscribers."

"What about the report?" said Goldschmidt. "Is it real?"

"We don't know yet. The figures are reasonable at first glance. There are about fifteen million children in Mexican schools and about six hundred thousand teachers. People downstairs haven't been able to get the Ministry of Education to confirm or deny, but they're working on it."

Other messengers were arriving now, and the young man at the door was frowning as his earpiece squawked its scrambled traffic into his brain. The messengers began to form a line beside Maria Hurtado's empty chair until Kearns waved them to the head of the table.

"This one says the report definitely came from somewhere in the Ministry of Education but was released as an exclusive to the *Vox Populi*." Maria Hurtado placed it on the table and looked at the next one, then at the next. "The figure for teachers is inaccurate. The real figure is almost six hundred thirty thousand."

"Thank you, Maria," Kearns said. She returned to her seat at the foot of the table. Kearns shrugged. "It's a definite government press release, not an ad somebody bought in the paper."

"I'm not sure I'm following all of this," the Director said. "Can somebody please sort it out?"

"Sure." Porterfield studied his fingernails, then looked up. "What it means is that you'd better get somebody busy calling off the ambush at San Francisco airport."

"Right," Goldschmidt nodded. "It was a bad idea in the first place, but now we know it would just get them mad as hell for nothing. They haven't got the papers. Nobody has."

"Nobody?" said the Director.

"Not yet, anyway."

"Not yet," Porterfield agreed. "Otherwise the Mexican government wouldn't be bidding fifteen million dollars for them."

THE Director looked around himself glumly. "For this morning's session I've decided we need to develop a clearer idea of the options we have available. I've invited a few specialists to come and give us the benefit of their expertise."

Goldschmidt whispered to Porterfield, "Molnar."

"I heard that," the Director said, "as I suppose I was

meant to. The first of these people is Mr. Bob.''

"Mr. Bob?"

"Bob is his last name, and he's probably heard whatever you're thinking of saying, so forget it. He's been in on a number of ransom situations, and he's going to—"

"Does he know what's going on?"

"He's here to brief us, not the reverse."

There was a knock, and a bald man in a blue pinstripe suit entered. "Hello," the man called as he walked to the table. "My name is Mr. Bob. Are you ready for me?"

"Yes, I believe we are, Mr. Bob." The Director pronounced the name with exaggerated ease, then his brow furrowed slightly, as though he were afraid he'd said it wrong. "I'm afraid we're badly behind schedule, so I'll have to ask you to give us the basics in a few minutes."

"I can do that." He sat down beside the Director and addressed the others. "I'm here to talk money. If I go too fast, stop me. If you hear something you want more of, ask. If you want me back, call 9559. Basically, in ransom situations your best bet is the money. They won't refuse it, they won't lose it, they won't go too far from it. Always use Mr. Bob's law: 'If they've got it, you've got them.' Money talks, but only if you pay off with talking money."

Porterfield said, "What's available these days?"

"There still are only three kinds, really. There's counterfeit, marked, and treated."

"Treated?" Kearns seemed to wake up.

"Chemically treated. You can break that down in three ways, actually—there's poison, there's a biological-warfare agent, and there's a self-destruct chemical."

"You mean the money disappears?"

"Sure. It's only paper and ink. You can make it fade

with a bleach, make it go all gooey and wet with a little solvent, make it burn with a corrosive. The timing on these things is a little tricky, so you have to be careful about it, of course.''

"What do you recommend for a large transfer of funds, Mr. Bob?'' The Director hesitated. "A payoff in the neighborhood of ten million dollars? Counterfeit?''

"Well, maybe,'' said Mr. Bob. "We've got a problem with the counterfeit, though. We've got only two kinds, and what we need is three. We've got only great and awful. The awful stuff you can use only with people who haven't seen much American money. You couldn't pass it off as a supermarket coupon. The great stuff is an even bigger mistake. It's so good it takes special equipment to figure out what's wrong with it, which isn't much. No, treated money is probably the answer. We'll supply the chemicals if you'll supply the money. Chemicals are cheap.''

"You're wasting Mr. Bob's time,'' said Porterfield. "Time is money. The situation is that the money will be paid to people who are in this country and might very well take it to a bank or spend it here. They may also retain some part of what we want to ransom.''

Mr. Bob stared at the ceiling. "Let's see. No biological stuff—can't have an epidemic at home, and if it isn't a really virulent strain it doesn't always work. No poison, because you can't be sure they'd all touch it. And you say they'll keep part of the prize to protect themselves?''

"That's likely,'' said the Director.

"Then I'd say your only hope is to pay them off in one-dollar bills. It's pretty easy to spot somebody driving off in a caravan of trucks. I guess I'm not going to be of much use here.'' He stood up.

"No, wait.'' The Director held up his hand. "What

about the packaging? Can we do something with that? How about a homing signal or a radio or something?"

"Sorry," said Mr. Bob. "No extortionist in the history of the world has ever left his payoff in the container you gave him. If they've already asked for the money, they already know where they're putting it when they have it. No, this time it sounds as though the money isn't the solution to your problem." Mr. Bob nodded to them and walked out the door.

"Who's next?" said Goldschmidt to the Director. "Sharpshooters or electronic surveillance or a team of specially trained midget commandos who will be dressed as fire hydrants?"

The Director's jaw tightened and he sat quietly, as though in deep thought.

⚔ 21 ⚔

CHINESE GORDON STARED up at the luminous pearl-blue of the sky. There would be no real clouds, just a low ceiling forming in the early afternoon. He looked around him at the hundreds of small, shining cars, all waxed and rubbed to gleaming hard surfaces like colored porcelain on the green grass.

Kepler pointed to the broad white banner strung between the two trees that flanked the pasture road. "I hate that. 'Foreign Car Rallye.' You can't even say it, and if you could, you'd sound stupid. So every time you say what you can say, which is 'rally,' you feel tense about it."

"Not so loud. What do you think? Is everybody ready?"

"Sure. The bags are ready, Immelmann and Margaret are ready. And you. You know what you look like? A motorist. That coat makes you look like the kind of person who would wear that hat."

"Fine. Just be sure everybody here gets the standard issue." He moved off a few feet and turned to Kepler. "It's a pleasure to meet another motoring enthusiast such as yourself," he said, and disappeared into the crowd.

On the other side of the broad green field Immelmann carefully wiped the thin film of dust off the hubcaps of Margaret's Volkswagen. "There. It's never looked so good."

"It's a little intimidated by the Porsches and Jaguars and BMW's, I think," Margaret said.

"There are at least a hundred Volkswagens here today. Don't worry. It's not a race, it's more like a picnic. These people don't notice your ride. They just want you to notice what their ride is and be impressed. They let anything in because it keeps the crowd young."

"I suppose. I just wish it were over. This wig feels like it's squeezing my brain."

Immelmann glanced at his watch. "Soon." He unlatched the trunk and stared at the horizon, his eyes invisible behind his sunglasses. "If I can do it, I'm going to live like this."

"You're going to live in a state park?"

"This was Will Rogers's ranch. That was his house up there on the rise. He used to pasture his horses down here. You have to imagine it with all these morons and their little cars gone, and maybe a dozen horses grazing here, nothing making any noise but the birds in that grove of eucalyptus along the road."

"We'll come and see you sometimes."

"I hope you do. But you and Chinese are so much smarter than anybody else, I hope just winning this one quietly will be enough for you. I used to wonder about Chinese Gordon. Now I wonder about both of you."

"You think we're going to get caught, don't you?"

He shrugged. "We'll all know soon enough." He shielded his eyes and stared up at the sky, then turned his head slightly to listen.

• • •

IN the cabin of the Piper sat the young man who had stood guard at the door of the conference room in Langley. He wore a blue nylon jacket and baseball cap like the pilot's, but his jacket was heavy with the radio receiver that fit better into his specially cut suits. The hat was new and too small for him, so he looked like a foreigner who had never worn one before. For the first time in twenty minutes he spoke. "That doesn't sound right."

"What doesn't?" The pilot looked over at him, but he had the radio out again and he was pressing buttons on it and wincing at something coming through the earplug.

The young man bent over, peered at the map in his lap, and said, "It appears to be Will Rogers State Park. It's full of people, cars." He looked out the window at the scene far below. "There are lots of cars. Maybe a thousand, and crowds of people. It doesn't make sense, sir."

There was a long pause, then he said to the pilot, "All right. One pass over the park down there, just over the treetops, while I drop the bags. Then get up and out. They say everything is under control."

THE monotonous, distant humming of the airplane far overhead seemed to change in pitch as Immelmann watched the wings tilt for a bank. "They're coming in for it, Sunshine. The main thing is to stick with the crowd until the second when they start the climb, then run like hell. They're going to have to work at it to get out over the trees on the ridge, and that's when we have to do whatever we're going to do."

In the center of the pasture near the table where officials of the Foreign Automobile Touring Club were preparing to hand out route maps, Kepler and Chinese Gordon had finished stacking the green trash bags. Chinese Gordon heard the airplane engine begin to idle for the slow descent, then set the sign atop the first pyramid—"Free Beer"—and quickly moved away through the crowd. Damn, it was too early, they'd have to scramble. He saw Kepler setting up the second sign, "Free Soft Drinks," and heading in the opposite direction. At the pile under the trees he set up the third sign and moved up the hillside where he could see. The crowd was beginning to swirl inward already, the news beginning to ripple in all directions from the center. Seconds later, there were already competing eddies of people under the trees picking up the plastic trash bags, each containing a six-pack of cans. He could see another, smaller group near Margaret's tiny yellow car. He stared across the pasture and caught a glimpse of Kepler being buffeted aside by several people who were taking up the green trash bags and trotting off toward their cars. He had gotten only as far on his sign as "Free" before the crowd converged. When the swirl of people parted for an instant, Kepler was gone.

Chinese Gordon stood beneath the trees and watched. The momentary frenzy had begun to die down already. People were walking with the plastic bags, some loaded with six or seven that they distributed to neighboring cars.

THE sound of the airplane engine was growing louder now, and he saw some of the people near him raise curious faces to the sky. Then the airplane appeared directly above him, still gliding toward the end of the

green field marked by the white sheet with the blue
painted "X," the pilot idling his engine just high
enough to reassure himself. The plane's shadow crossed
the pasture, and four dark spots plummeted to the
ground, bounced once, and lay still. He saw Margaret
and Immelmann step to the bags as the airplane soared
over the trees on the ridge beyond the ranch house and
momentarily swept from sight. Chinese Gordon smiled
to himself as he watched them fade into the crowd.

The loudspeaker was blasting something he couldn't
understand into the hillside, which echoed it back. Then
engines started. It sounded as though all over the field
people were starting their engines. The engine noises
seemed to reverberate and merge with one another and
then grow into a loud, droning noise. Then Chinese
Gordon stopped trying to understand, because as he
watched, a second airplane swept over the field and
wheeled at the far end for another dive, its engine roar-
ing into the green basin as it searched the ground for its
prey. A few seconds later a third airplane appeared, and
then a fourth, each circling beyond the park and then
coming back in a maneuver like a strafing run. Chinese
Gordon knew he spoke aloud, but no human ear could
have heard it if he had shouted. "I knew you'd try, you
bastards." Then he stepped aside because a small blue
Fiat was already in gear and bouncing down the hillside
toward him, its driver a girl with what seemed to be a
pretty face but with eyes that didn't seem to see him.
She was staring toward the entrance to the pasture road
behind him with a demented ferocity. She missed him by
inches, then accelerated rapidly across the center of a
blanket some picnickers had laid on the ground, nar-
rowly edging out a Triumph TR6 for the privilege.
Chinese Gordon sprinted for the safety of the trees, then
hurdled a pile of fallen brush and ran through the tall

weeds that skirted the field toward the distant grove
where the van was parked.

"SOMETHING'S wrong down there," said the pilot to the
man beside him. "They're all running for their cars. We
must have stampeded them."

"Look at them," the other man shouted. "Everybody on the field is carrying a green sack." The man's
baseball cap had fallen off, and he was yelling into his
radio, "Get them. Move in. They're getting ready to
drive out." He listened for a moment, then shouted,
"All of them. Any of them."

In the second airplane the photographer held his
camera steady, his elbow propped against the door in
the stance of an expert marksman, the camera clicking
and whirring as the plane's movement brought new
targets into his sights. "What exactly is that down
there?"

His companion said, "Damned if I know. It looks
like they decided to have the Indianapolis Five Hundred
in the woods. Just be sure to get everybody carrying a
green sack."

Immelmann said to Margaret, "This doesn't feel like
a good place to be. In a minute they're going to figure
out some way of closing off the road." As he said it, the
sound of horns honking in the distance reached them.

"Into the car," said Margaret.

Immelmann sat beside her, his knees nearly to his
chest as the car began to creep across the field among
hundreds of others. An ancient Austin Healey sedan
drifted beside them in somnolent dignity, the driver
a tiny, elderly lady with blue-gray hair who held a
stemmed wineglass in her free hand.

To their right a squadron of howling Porsches knifed across the green toward the right-hand margin of the dirt road, only to find their flanking movement blocked by a narrowing at the first turn. They crouched in a frustrated line beside the main stream of traffic, sputtering and growling, the lead car rolling backward a few feet and then rocking forward again, threatening to wedge its nose between two Mercedes convertibles if so much as a yard of space should appear between them.

In the distance other cars were driving the perimeter of the broad pasture, streaming contrails of dust. "I guess we did this wrong," Immelmann said. "There just wasn't any way of knowing when they'd start up."

"Why did they?" said Margaret. "Where are they going?"

"I don't know. The way it works is that they hand out the route map when you start, and write down your starting time. At each of the checkpoints along the route they write down the time you got there. It's not a race. The idea is to be efficient, not fast. We don't have the route because we didn't register."

"Have you seen anybody get out yet?"

"Not yet. They're all just driving around or joining the traffic jam. We might be better off with the crowd. There doesn't seem to be a service road or anything."

"I'm not going out there with stolen license plates and all this money in the car. Make sure no mental defectives come up on our right." She steered the car to the right, veering over quickly while Immelmann held his arm out the window. Behind them the driver of an orange Audi hesitated and let Margaret break through the line to drive straight for the stand of tall trees along the edge of the field.

Immelmann said, "Trees ahead, Sunshine. Hard to

starboard.'' He waited a few seconds and said a little louder, ''Trees. Big ones.'' At last he said, ''What the hell are you doing?''

''The biggest trees. You said Will Rogers had horses, so that's got to be the way out.'' She drove relentlessly, the trees now looming above them like palisades.

''Horses don't live in trees,'' said Immelmann.

''No, but there have to be bridle paths, and that's where they'll be, where the trees were already big enough to have room between them, and the underbrush is stunted, and—'' The car slowed, then labored up a small slope and in among the trees. It jiggled over a line of exposed roots, then jerked up and down violently a few times as she meandered among the tree trunks. Immelmann gripped the dashboard and the door, but as they turned and bumped over a rock that was hidden by a tuft of weeds his head hammered into the roof of the car. ''Are you okay?'' she asked.

His eyes were closed. She couldn't tell if he was nodding or if his neck had gone limp. She stopped the car, and he opened his eyes and smiled.

''I said, 'Are you okay?' ''

''Better by the second. Stay here.'' He got out of the car and ran through the woods, staring at the ground. For a time she could see him running from side to side like a football player dodging invisible tacklers. Suddenly he seemed to throw himself full length on the ground as though one of them had caught him, but then she noticed the root he'd tripped on. He got up and ran again, this time out of sight beyond the trees. Overhead Margaret could hear the airplanes again, louder now that she was far from the noise of the cars in the pasture.

She wondered if she'd made a mistake. Immelmann must know more than she did about horses and riding and—if only he hadn't looked that way a moment ago, running off like a madman in the woods, with the airplanes up there, and who knew what else down here, searching. She shivered, suddenly aware of herself: Here I am. I know this woman sitting in the woods in a car, and I'm not somebody else watching her, and it's not a dream I dreamed. I am in trouble. I may very well die in a few minutes. I may die. Why does it matter so much that I'm alone in this car when it happens?

Immelmann appeared beside her, and she jumped. A wave of heat seemed to slide down her spine, but she said, "Oh."

"Follow me." He started trotting again, and she put the car in gear and drove after him. At first she felt as though it really was a dream, watching his muscular back bobbing up and down as she drove. It was as though she were floating after him among the trees. After the first few turns her body wasn't cold anymore, it was just hands and eyes gauging the space she had to weave along the meandering path, her touch on the wheel precise and accurate. Once she steered between two trees that nearly touched the fenders, but miraculously the car passed without scraping.

Finally they were through the woods, and Immelmann was standing in a clearing, waiting. She stopped the car and he got in and closed the door. "Driver, take me to the bank. Lots of room up there," he said.

Margaret's eyes followed his finger, and she drove toward the spot. It was a path, old and overgrown with weeds and grass, but now she could drive faster.

"Margaret, you're a genius," Immelmann said.

"Yes, that's true."

"Yeah, it's really a good thing," he went on, "because I've been thinking. This definitely is an old horse path. What if it leads back to the ranch house?"

"That would be annoying."

"It'd ruin my day."

KEPLER sat in the rented Chevrolet on the shoulder of the highway, three hundred yards past the park entrance. He had folded his jacket into a thick pad on the sill of the window to hold the foregrip of the rifle. There was nothing esoteric about this kind of shooting. It was all a matter of adequate preparation; keeping your pulse rate low, and making deliberate, economical movements.

The Mannlicher Model ST rifle's clip held only three of the thick, heavy cartridges, so it wasn't a question of squeezing off a few rounds to get the feel of things. He knew he wouldn't need to. All he had to do was hit something. The Winchester .458 Magnum steel-jacketed five-hundred-grain bullet would still be traveling at well over fifteen hundred feet per second when it arrived. When it got there it would still easily pierce a car door. Kepler stared into the eyepiece of the Weaver T-25 scope. The entrance to the park drive was a strange, circular scene that consisted of only about twenty feet of glittering green leaves and bristling grass, all supernaturally bright and clear because of the scope's optics, but from this distance silent, like a world seen through a closed window.

He held the crosshairs on a dandelion for a few seconds, then slowly moved down the stem and across to a rock on the drive at the entrance. He would have to use the time after the shot and before the report of the rifle reached their ears to recover from the vicious recoil, chamber the next round with the bolt, and aim again.

He rested the rifle on the windowsill and watched the

traffic on the highway. Already there were cars that must have come from the baseball fields and picnic groves on the other side of the park. When he heard the airplane engines he knew something must be wrong. There was supposed to be only one airplane, and it sounded like more. A few seconds later he saw Chinese Gordon's van pass him, going toward Sunset in the midst of a line of small foreign cars. He thought of signaling, but something else caught his eye. Already cars were streaming out of the park, much faster than he'd expected. He stared through the telescopic sight at the faces of the drivers, but their expressions didn't seem to show alarm or even worry. The third one out was laughing, and the girl next to him leaned over to kiss his cheek as he skidded around the curve. They weren't running from something, he decided. They were just idiots. Still, there should be only one airplane.

Kepler held the crosshairs on a level a few inches below the side window of the next car, and he left them there after the car whisked past. Something was wrong, and if there was a trap, this was where it would have to be. Then he saw it. A dark blue sedan pulled up beside the highway, then drifted slowly across the park entrance. Inside were four men wearing sportcoats and tinted glasses. Two got out, and one of them opened the hood of the car and stood looking down at the engine.

Almost immediately Kepler heard the faint honking of the distant cars trapped in the park. Overhead he could see four airplanes circling and swooping over the field. There were only a few choices, and none of them seemed to fit. With the elephant gun he could immobilize the car, but he couldn't move it. Something had to change, and there was only one way to do it. He emptied his lungs halfway and lined up the crosshairs on the man standing in front of the car. He wished he'd brought something smaller. There wouldn't be much left of this man's chest. He couldn't even aim low and just take a leg off, or the slug might pass through and into the engine. But when the others saw it they'd move as fast as they could, and that meant the car would be out of the way.

He grasped the stock and started to squeeze the trigger, then remembered. It would be smart to have his own engine running before he did it, even if it shook the car a little. All he had to do was hit any part of the man, and he'd be such a gruesome sight the others would drive over his body to get out of there. Kepler turned around in the seat and reached for the key, but as he did, he looked through the windshield and smiled.

Through the woods beside the road a yellow Volkswagen was bouncing along slowly, making its laborious and choppy progress over roots and stones and ruts, the weeds parting at its bumper. As it reached the highway it flashed its headlights at him and he laughed aloud. He reached over to click the safety catch on the rifle and muttered, "Gentlemen, start your engines."

CHINESE Gordon watched the line of small, bright cars rocking on the curves of Sunset Boulevard toward the canyons. He cursed himself for what he was doing. Kepler would give him another lecture on urban commando operational procedure. Nobody was supposed to change plans in the middle, no matter what happened. Now he was parked in front of the Seven-Eleven on one of the busiest corners of Los Angeles, with his motor running and his eyes on the rearview mirror.

He had to hope that at least one of the cars had gotten out. He hoped that Margaret had gotten out. It was different for Immelmann and Kepler. He knew that was a lie, too. The whole thing stank so much it didn't matter who couldn't get out of it, but the thought of Margaret in danger made him feel frantic. It wasn't his fault, he was the only one capable of firing the gun in the van. Margaret and Immelmann had to be the ones to take out the money. It wasn't his fault. Yes, it was his fault.

If only one of the cars made it out. If only Margaret made it to the highway. He watched the line of foreign cars sputtering at the traffic light. Maybe the thing to do was create a diversion. It would be easy to line up the van with the gas station across the street and make this corner look like a war zone, but not yet, not while there was still a chance they'd made it the easy way.

Finally he saw the yellow Volkswagen drive up to the intersection and swing into a right turn. Behind it was Kepler's rented car. Kepler was drumming his fingers on the steering wheel to some inaudible rhythm of the car radio. Chinese Gordon pulled the van out onto the street two cars behind him and followed.

Chinese Gordon was in a better mood now. He sang a verse of "Let My People Go" as he drove along, his eyes flickering upward to the rearview mirror every few seconds to search for the wrong kind of car with the wrong kind of passengers. He knew that in his present mood some part of him was wishing for it, so it wouldn't happen. He hoped Margaret hadn't taken too many chances to pick up the sacks they'd dropped from the airplane. As soon as he'd seen the second airplane he'd given up any thought that the sacks contained money. These people couldn't be trusted, it was as simple as that. He hoped the others wouldn't be too disappointed, but there was no getting around the fact that some things just didn't come easily. Chinese Gordon resolved to say that to them, if necessary, and any other platitudes that seemed likely to raise their spirits and ease the strains to come. As he drove the smooth, winding highway, he reflected on the enormity of human folly. He had always considered himself a reasonable man, and he'd offered these people a chance to buy him out safely for a sum that must be petty cash for them. This time he was going to demonstrate that a few of his other choices had big, sharp teeth.

⚠ 22 ⚠

THE DEPUTY DIRECTOR paced near the door of the conference room, a distant, solitary figure dwarfed by the vast maps on the walls above him.

At the end of the table Goldschmidt whispered to Porterfield, "We both said it wouldn't work. Do you think it would be more polite to be somewhere far away while they go through with it and he finds out for himself?"

Porterfield shook his head slowly and watched the Deputy Director. "We might learn something by accident if we pay attention."

"You mean from watching Generalissimo Pines pacing in his bunker?"

"Of course not. From the reports of the field people."

"Then we might as well make it interesting. I say they never show up at the drop. Is a hundred dollars okay with you?"

"My hundred says they show up at the drop and get away clean with the sacks."

"All right. What happens if Pines and the Director get lucky and pick up one or two of them?"

"Fair is fair. We give all the money to Pines."

Kearns leaned forward from across the table. "Do you mind if I get in on this?"

"Not at all," said Goldschmidt. "What's your pleasure?"

"I say the Los Angeles police arrest somebody in the field crew and Racine has to go bail for him."

"Very likely," Goldschmidt snorted. "I wish I'd taken that possibility myself. You know, of course, that if anything in this farcical operation works, Pines will win a handsome sum without betting anything?"

Porterfield yawned. "That's the best part of the game. If he doesn't get all of them and every copy of the papers, he'll lose his job—"

"Not relevant," Kearns interrupted. "He'll go back to the Mister Food Corporation and make five times as much."

Porterfield continued, "No, I don't think he'll go back there. If he loses his job, he'll also lose his bodyguards."

KEPLER popped the top of a beer can and took a gulp. "There's not a whole lot of point to doing this."

"I suppose not," Margaret said, shrugging. "I'm a little bit curious, though, aren't you? We did go to an awful lot of trouble."

"So did they, and they've been at this a lot longer than we have. It's probably four bags full of rabid weasels."

Chinese Gordon said, "We have to open them, and it has to be now. If there's a transmitter inside, we can't take the bags home."

"Agreed," said Immelmann. "Let's get to it and then out of here." He kicked one of the bags and then took a folding knife out of his pocket and began to slit the stitching on the bag's lower seam carefully, squinting to see that the blade didn't penetrate too deeply.

Kepler swallowed more beer and said, "It's a strange fact of life that there are people who look intelligent, and others who don't." He stared at the green hillside across the road.

Immelmann peered into the bag, then reached inside. "Hello. What have we here?" He handed the bag to Chinese Gordon and began to work on the second bag.

Chinese Gordon disappeared into the back of the van. When he didn't return, Margaret followed. "Well? What is it? Will it blow up?" she asked.

Chinese Gordon sat cross-legged inside, the empty bag beside him. He was frowning, but he shook his head.

"Then what is it?"

Immelmann was staring into the second bag. "There's some money. Hundred-dollar bills."

"What else?"

"Newspaper. More cut-up newspaper than we'll ever need."

WHEN Margaret awoke in the morning, Chinese Gordon was sitting in his bathrobe at the kitchen table with his hands folded. He appeared to be studying Doctor Henry Metzger, who was lying on the table beside Chinese Gordon's coffee cup. Margaret walked up behind Chinese Gordon and kissed the top of his head.

"Nice," he said. She petted Doctor Henry Metzger's head, and the cat's eyes narrowed slightly in acknowledgment. At Chinese Gordon's feet the huge dog lay on its side, the long, pink tongue draped along its jowl.

"How long have you been up?"

"Don't know. A long time."

"All three of you?"

"More or less."

"Please don't be cranky."

"We're not cranky."

Two hours later Margaret left for the market. When she returned, Chinese Gordon was in exactly the same position. The dog raised its head for a moment and stared at her, then lowered it. When Margaret crossed Chinese Gordon's field of vision, he smiled.

Margaret spent the afternoon in the bedroom. For a time she read three magazines she'd bought in the supermarket, and then she fell asleep. When consciousness returned, the first thing she saw was Chinese Gordon, still in the kitchen, staring at his cat, the weak, yellow light of the waning sun falling across the table.

Margaret got up and walked into the kitchen. She put her hands on Chinese Gordon's hunched shoulders and said, "Chinese, why are you doing this? It's okay to be disappointed, but you can't become a catatonic."

Chinese Gordon shook his head. "I'm not."

"What are you doing?"

"I'm thinking."

"What are you thinking?"

"I'll tell you when I've thought it."

"Can't I help you?"

"Sure."

Margaret sat down across the kitchen table and waited. Beneath the table the dog shifted his ponderous body and lay across her bare feet. His fur was warm, and she could feel his heart beating.

Margaret watched the electric clock on the wall behind Chinese Gordon. After ten minutes she said, "It would help if I knew what we were thinking about."

He reached across the table and held her hand. "I'm

trying to decide what to do next.''

"You could forget the whole thing. We don't really need the money. With what you got from Grijalvas we can do pretty well. We're probably lucky. We even got another ten thousand they had to wrap the newspapers in.''

"The problem is that I am not finished. I feel a strong urge to get these people for what they tried to do to us. I'm not satisfied.''

"Then you could go through with the threat. Publish the papers.''

"It doesn't feel right, somehow.''

"It does have the distinct advantage that we can do it without getting killed.''

"That's not enough. It has to feel right.''

"Then read the Donahue papers.''

"What about them?''

"Read Appendix Twenty-three.''

⚐ 23 ⚐

IT WAS A small red brick façade in the middle of a block of stores that sold antiques and gentlemen's furnishings. Its lattice windows differed from the others because the brass and wood and leather inside were partly obscured by fresh flowers. The door was a narrow maple slab with a single small window cut into it at shoulder height, and a brass plate that said, "The New Haven: Members and Their Guests."

As Porterfield opened the door and entered, the hostess looked down into the open menu she cradled in her arms as a singer holds music. Her broad, plain face seemed to contract as she looked at him, and then she opened her mouth too wide to say, "This way, please" so quietly. He followed her down a corridor paneled with dark, gleaming wood, the Oriental runner on the floor slipping slightly with each step.

The room was small and contained one round table broad enough for a dozen people, but only two straight-backed chairs, and a bottle of white wine in a silver ice bucket.

"Hello, Ben," the Director called, bobbing forward from the fireplace across the room. Porterfield counted the steps—six—and the Director took another to catch up with his outstretched hand. "Glad you were able to make it."

"Nice to see you," said Porterfield. He submitted to the handshake, the Director's left hand grasping his forearm at the same time.

"Have you been here before?"

"I don't belong."

The Director hesitated, then said, "It's about as secluded as things get unless you leave town. I get pretty bogged down in the office. I don't think I've eaten anything but commissary food in three weeks, so this is my lunch out."

"It's good of you to share it with me."

"I invited you for a chance to pick your brain in private, I'm afraid. It's time to turn to the old guard."

Porterfield nodded.

"I'll be completely open with you, Ben. I made some decisions that didn't work out. In my own defense I'll have to add that I didn't take the Donahue matter away from you and give it to someone else, I took it on myself. It seemed to me that it was too big and too crucial to delegate. There are big issues at stake here."

"What do you want me to do?"

"At the moment I want advice. You know where we stand. How do you suggest we get to safe ground?" He poured two glasses of the white wine and handed one to Porterfield.

Porterfield answered without a pause. "You have the same two problems you had a week ago—how to get rid of these people, and how to cut the Company's losses if you don't. At this stage I'd say the proportions have changed, and you ought to concentrate on cutting our losses."

"In what way, exactly?"

"First I'd get our people out of countries mentioned in the papers. I told both Deputy Directors to do it, and it doesn't seem to have made much impression. Maybe it will now. The second thing I'd do is get an appointment for a special briefing session with the President. Tell him everything so he can do something to save the friendly governments."

The Director seemed to hold a sip of wine in his mouth for a long time, as though he couldn't swallow it. At last he said, "That's a little extreme."

Porterfield shrugged. "All right."

The Director leaned forward. "Well, isn't it? I mean, think about it, Ben. This thing goes back twenty years or more, and what's involved is devastating. And then the steps we've taken to contain this thing—no, if we can't handle this ourselves, we're lost. My God, Ben, I could end up in jail."

"You asked me for my advice. That's my advice. While you're at it I'd also advise you to try again to see if you can pay these people off."

The Director smiled. "That sounds a little more hopeful. What's the strategy?"

"No strategy at all. No tricks, no traps. You give them a pile of money and hope for the best. Ten million dollars ought to be enough."

The Director's eyes seemed to water, and Porterfield watched him fluctuate between despair and anger. For the first time he appeared tired. He shook his head. "I can't do that. I can't. These people are criminals. Blackmailers."

Porterfield sipped his wine. "I hope that's all they are, because if they're not, you've already used up just about all your options."

"What you offer aren't options. They're consequences, just different kinds of defeat. What you're saying is that there's nothing I can do that will permit me to retain viable control of this adminis— agency.''

"If people in the Company start deciding that you're a disaster, you won't hear it from me. The President might ask you to sign a letter of resignation, but he won't do more than that. It might be the best way out, because if you leave even a few agents in this mess, one of them is sure to come to see you.''

"That's ridiculous. No Director has ever been placed in that position. Why you'd even suggest such a thing is beyond comprehension.''

Porterfield said, "I said it because if I were in Mexico City and knew you'd blown this, you'd already be history.''

APPENDIX XXIII: The Seismological Disaster Preparedness Task Force.

Background: During the 1960s and 1970s the government of Mexico became increasingly interested in the possibility of using modern technology and organizational methods to respond to natural disasters. After the earthquake of December 23, 1972, in Managua, Nicaragua, the Chamber of Deputies authorized the expenditure of funds for a two-year study. On August 28, 1973, a major temblor occurred in central Mexico, killing 527 and leaving two hundred thousand homeless. The confessed inability of the government to respond quickly and effectively to the problem elicited additional support within the ruling Revolutionary Institutional Party (PRI) for the idea, and the project's budget was doubled before it had begun. A geological institute was established at the University of Mexico and began collecting seismological data.

On February 4, 1976, the Guatemala earthquake killed an estimated 23,000 people and left approximately one million homeless. The proximity of this major earthquake combined with its extreme devastation prompted the introduction of several bills in the Senate and the Chamber of Deputies, all designed to contribute to the disaster-preparedness program, which was beginning to take on the character of a movement within the PRI.

On July 28, 1976, two major earthquakes destroyed the industrial city of Tangshan, China, causing an estimated eight hundred thousand deaths. Within three weeks the Mexican government transformed the former geological institute into a seismological disaster-preparedness project. As a matter of standing policy copies of these proposals were forwarded to the Central Intelligence Agency, which assigned several operatives to the project as observers and established client relationships with several others, including four geology professors, a civil defense official on temporary leave from the state of California, and an urban planning professor.

By 1977 the normal routing of projects concerning Mexico included the members of the ULTRA research team, who recognized immediately the potential value of active participation in the Mexican disaster-preparedness project. The possibility of understanding seismic disruptions well enough to predict them brought to mind the possibility of inducing them. Of more immediate concern, however, was that the Mexican government was now committed to exert its full powers to perform a realistic estimate of the nation's susceptibility to a sudden and catastrophic event. Because of its size and importance, Mexico City was to be the inevitable subject of the most intensive studies.

Chinese Gordon rested his bare feet on the big dog's warm side beneath the table and closed his eyes. "Am I supposed to read all of this?"

"Of course." Margaret was in the bedroom.

"Did you read all of it?"

"Yes."

"But I still have to?"

"Yes."

Chinese Gordon lifted Doctor Henry Metzger from the box of papers, pulled another stack out, and set the cat back down. "It's like a zoo in here."

"Then take a bath."

Chinese Gordon read on. Doctor Henry Metzger stared at him for a long time, the wide green eyes narrowing in infinitesimal gradients until at some point they closed. The dog, slumbering deeply, dreamed he lived on a great sunlit empty plain and that far in the distance his clear, sensitive eyes saw a shape he recognized as enemy. The shape was large and very dangerous, but that was part of the pleasure, and the big dog's jaws began to grind in anticipation as he dreamed that he was taking great powerful leaps toward it, building up incredible speed. As the dog dreamed, Chinese Gordon heard it first give a little growl of joy, almost like a man's laugh. Then Chinese Gordon felt the dog's paws begin to quiver as the motor neurons received the tiny false messages to run. Chinese Gordon lifted up the corner of the tablecloth and watched the great black dog, flattened on its side like a frieze of an ancient nightmare creature. The dog's thick neck muscles were clenched now, the head held forward in stiff eagerness. Chinese Gordon leaned down and whispered, "Go get it." The dog's legs began to move, his big paws churning at the invisible ground, the frantic dash bringing him closer and closer to his prey. Chinese Gordon watched the dog until the dream subsided and the dog seemed to sigh with pleasure. "Good boy," he whispered. "You got it."

Margaret stepped back from the door and waited until she heard Chinese Gordon take up the sheaf of papers again, then quietly climbed back onto the bed. She lit a cigarette and stared into the darkness. She exhaled and watched the smoke curl and fold and float upward into a shaft of light that came from the doorway. While she watched it, she smiled.

Mexico City consists of a densely populated central core surrounded by newer and less compact suburbs, to form a metropolitan area of approximately fourteen million inhabitants. The complex is precariously held together by a network of major traffic arteries, the most important being route 190, which runs southeast to Guatemala City; 85, which runs north to Laredo, Texas; 45, to El Paso, Texas; 15, which crosses the U.S. border south of Tucson; and 95, south to the coast at Acapulco. Each of these national roads passes through Mexico City and carries a portion of its daily commuter traffic. Of immediate concern to the experts of the Center for Disaster Preparedness was that any severe damage to the Distrito Federal would not only totally immobilize the capital itself but also disrupt mobile communication for the entire country. The situation is similar to that in the major metropolitan areas of the western United States such as Los Angeles, which contains the only major north-south routes as well as the western termini of the east-west routes carrying two-thirds of the interstate traffic.

Chinese Gordon picked up Doctor Henry Metzger and petted his head. Then he gave a short laugh. In the bedroom Margaret whispered to herself in the darkness, "Go get 'em."

ᐃ 24 ᐃ

PORTERFIELD PULLED THE car up to the curb in front of his house and turned off the ignition. The engine gave three violent chugs and a wheeze that sounded mortal. It had been overheating all the way home, so he'd turned the heater on. Now his suit was soaked with sweat, and his loosened tie hung limp and twisted. As he climbed out of the car the air felt cool, and the bright sunlight seemed almost gentle.

Alice came around the corner of the house with a trowel in her hand and waved it at him comically. She had her hair tied in a small bun at the back of her head, and she was wearing an immaculate pink sundress that seemed crisp and starched. She looked impossible. That had always been something that had fascinated him about Alice—she always looked so clean, like a little girl waiting to have her picture taken.

He walked up the lawn and set his briefcase on the front step. As always, it was empty, just something the president of the Seyell Foundation carried, but today it felt heavy.

"Welcome home, Ben. Lots of traffic?"

"It was what the man on the radio calls 'a tough commute.' I guess I've got to take the car in again for psychoanalysis too.''

"It did sound a little odd. Sort of growly."

Porterfield glanced at the car with disgust. It took so little to transform one from a symbol of freedom and motion into four thousand pounds of steel. As he looked, he saw the dark blue Mercedes glide to a stop behind it.

"Isn't that Jim Kearns?"

"Yes," said Porterfield. He felt a perverse annoyance that surprised him until he listened to his own thought: No. I'm home now.

Kearns got out of his car and raised his hand. "Hello, Alice, Ben. I was just passing by and saw you two standing there like an ad for a real-estate development."

"Come in out of the heat," said Alice in a tone so easy and confident that it sounded inevitable. "I was just about to make Ben a cool drink."

"Good. I'll drink his and he can go get his own."

They went inside, and Alice disappeared into the kitchen while Kearns and Porterfield sat in the living room in silence. Alice returned and said, "I'm assuming you still drink martinis, Jim. Neither of us has seen you in such a long time." Kearns looked at Porterfield.

"There are only two there, Alice," said Kearns. "Have you finally decided to cut off Ben's bad habits?"

"Far too late for that," she answered. "I'm afraid I was in the middle of repotting a plant. It's lying there looking dazed and naked right now, so I'd better finish up before I join you." They heard the back door close quietly.

"Alice is the most graceful woman I know," said Kearns, frowning at the carpet.

"She's been at this a long time. What's on your mind?"

"I'm sorry to come here like this. There was no other way. I'm one of the people who's not supposed to be seen at the Seyell Foundation. I'm afraid we've got more trouble."

"Did Pines think of another plan?"

"Not today. No. Look, you were connected to the Latin America desk for a lot of years, one way or another. We've both worked it for a lot of years. If I tell you what I know, you'll understand, and hardly anybody else would. Right now our section has about six hundred people in the field—Company people—and nobody knows how many locals and Special Operations types and stringers. In the past four days thirty-seven were supposed to check in. In the two days before that, fourteen others were due for some kind of communication."

"No word from any of them?"

"Nothing. Those fifty-one are spread from Veracruz to Buenos Aires. Some are in deep cover, running networks, but some of them are supposed to be sitting in embassies and consulates, major corporations, airlines, and so on. The only thing they have in common is that they're all family—no outsiders. Some of them have been out there for twenty years without missing a check-in."

Porterfield frowned. "Does the Director know about this?"

"I told Pines, but he said the Director didn't think it was significant. Ben, it's got to be a response to the way they blew the Donahue problem. The word got around in the only way it could have—the upper-level operational people. They're not talking to us, but they sure as hell must be talking to each other."

"Interesting," Porterfield said. "It looks like the Company's first strike. Do you suppose they want the Director's resignation, or what?"

"I wish I thought that. I really do. Everybody I know wants that, and nobody has any hope it'll happen. To tell you the truth, I'm worried. Frightened." He gulped a quarter of his drink and then stared at it as he rolled the glass between his palms. "They haven't asked for anything. Nobody has said a word. They just dropped out of sight."

"All of them? Fifty-one people?"

"So far fifty-one. After tomorrow it may be close to seventy."

"What exactly do you think they're doing?"

"These aren't a bunch of disaffected recruits just out of college. Some of these people have overthrown governments, recruited and trained armies. I'll tell you what I think. I think they've decided to establish an alibi for someone."

"If fifty or seventy or ninety people drop out of sight, any of them or all of them can go where they like."

Kearns nodded. "And even if you know it in advance, you can't tell which of them is coming, or where he's coming from."

"Of course. That has to be it. Even afterward, it would be impossible to know who burned the Director, because it could also be someone who wasn't due to check in, or someone who never checked in except with his own controller. I'd say they have nothing to worry about. In fact, the only ones who have anything to worry about are the people who might get in the way."

"You and me, for instance."

"Decent of them to give us a warning. How long will it take before a whole reporting cycle is completed and everybody who talks to Langley gets his chance to stand you up?"

"Another ten days."

"It might be a good idea to wrap up the Donahue thing before then."

⌃ 25 ⌃

"WELL? WHAT DO you think of it?" asked Chinese Gordon.

Kepler scratched his chin with his forefinger, trying not to spill the can of beer he held in his hand. "That professor didn't write this. Have you noticed?"

"Of course I noticed. The earthquake institute mapped out all the targets in Mexico City that were most important and vulnerable, and the CIA just developed the easiest ways to take them out, like a recipe. Donahue had nothing to do with it. What are you getting at?"

"This is getting a little far from the original point. A little theoretical, like the professor. I'm prepared to believe that this plan could be done in Mexico City. A hundred highly trained and experienced people go in, and each one has two backup men just as good as he is, and they can completely shut the place down in a matter of minutes. They can make everything happen that the earthquake people are afraid of."

"The report says it doesn't take a hundred guys. It says they can do the main part of it with a handful."

Immelmann said to Kepler, "You can tell that Chinese Gordon is not yet satisfied with the behavior of our public servants."

"He's disappointed."

"Miffed."

"Piqued."

"Vexed."

"Irked."

"He doesn't seem prepared to accept the limitations Fate has placed on him."

"What limitations?" asked Chinese Gordon.

"Silence, please." Kepler held up his free hand. "The village elders are considering your case." To Immelmann he said, "A tired old story of thwarted ambition."

"Complicated by extreme greed."

Doctor Henry Metzger appeared on the workbench along the far wall of the shop, stepped easily among the clutter of tools and machine parts without touching any of them, and dropped to the floor. Immelmann said, "Hey, Chinese. How does that cat get in and out of here like that? Everything is all closed up."

Chinese Gordon's jaw clenched. He said quietly, "I don't know."

"Maybe the dog has a key," said Kepler. Then he added, "This is obviously a sore subject, like being beaten up by dwarfs."

"Chinese," said Immelmann, "what you have to do is get some perspective. Considering who we were trying to blackmail, I'd say we did pretty well just to get out of it in one piece."

"You mean you're ready to give up?"

"I'm not ready to declare war, destroy a major city, or take over a country, even if the CIA provides a fool-proof recipe. I don't need the additional responsibility of owning a country at this time. Besides, I think you're not paying attention to what the report has to teach us. Not the details, but the papers as a whole.''

Kepler said, ''Just what I was trying to say before. The fact that the CIA lets the Mexican government tell it how to take over Mexico City should suggest to you that these are not people we can handle with much confidence. Not only did they behave in an ungentlemanly manner with the Mexicans, but the man who let us get these papers managed to live a whole two days afterward. Writ large across every page is: ''These Are People Around With Whom Thou Shalt Not Screw.' ''

Chinese Gordon sat motionless on the steps as Doctor Henry Metzger jumped to his lap, then climbed over his shoulder to continue up the stairs to the balcony where Margaret stood.

''I wish you'd listen to Chinese,'' she said. ''You're both being silly. We don't want to do anything as drastic as this contingency plan. We just want to remind them that we have it and understand it and that we can think of some vivid ways to reveal it.''

Immelmann said, ''When you say not drastic, what do you mean?''

''It's little enough to ask,'' she said.

''But what is it?''

''Just close down Los Angeles for a day.''

Kepler lifted his beer can and drank, then said, ''You know that if we get caught at it they'll recognize we were following their plan. It'll be the first time this year that four people hang themselves in prison on the same day.''

''We won't get caught,'' said Chinese Gordon. ''The plan is perfect.''

Margaret smiled. ''It'll make us all feel so much better.''

"IT was when I was getting those wrong numbers that time. I knew if I didn't convince myself it was the circuits, I was going to go crazy. I'd call the police and this big fat voice would come on: 'Go . . . fuck . . . yourself,' and then hang up." Immelmann shook his head and stared at the floor. "It was frightening. So I went down to Santa Monica to the big office and picked up this pamphlet and read it."

"Did you figure it out?" said Margaret, taking the pamphlet.

"No. That's the drawback. The system is so big and complicated they're the only ones who can figure it out. Just the name of it tells you that. The COSMIC Distributing Frame."

"There may be religious implications in this," said Kepler. "Most of the world's religions started within fifty miles of here."

Margaret read, " 'The COSMIC Distributing Frame at the South Grand Avenue switching station is the largest in the world, with a capacity of one million four hundred and forty thousand cable pairs and internal equipment lines.' "

"And to think they can still manage to connect Immelmann with the Holy Ghost," Kepler said.

"It sounds too big," said Chinese Gordon.

Margaret read on, " 'The miracle that makes the COSMIC frame possible is the revolutionary PACE computer-based system. With the PACE (Program for Arrangement of Cables and Equipment) only six rows of modules are necessary.' "

Chinese Gordon said, "How long is a row, and what's a module?"

"More of the universal questions that only the anointed can answer." Kepler poured a drop of beer on his own head and assumed a thoughtful expression. "No, that doesn't help."

"I'm coming to it," Margaret said. " 'No line need be more than six and a half feet long.' So it can't be very big."

"They'll have a hell of a time calling for the repairman," said Chinese Gordon. "Isn't technology wonderful?"

Kepler nodded. "Sure beats shooting a couple of thousand operators."

MARGARET'S plain charcoal gray jacket and skirt seemed to change her even more than the wig and glasses, and there was something about the way she carried the little leather case that made it look as though she might pull something out of it that would change someone's life—maybe a short list of people whose services were no longer necessary.

Chinese Gordon watched the receptionist's face as Margaret said, "Miss Briggs." The black plastic plate on the front of the desk said Carolyn Briggs, but Miss Briggs looked startled and seemed to grow pale. "Yes. May I help you?" It was so early in the morning for visitors.

Margaret's face was stony. "Kimberly Abrams, corporate headquarters, San Francisco. If a call comes in during the next few minutes, I'll be near the switching equipment. Can you point me in the right direction?"

"Certainly. Third door on your right, with the big 'No Admittance' sign." Miss Briggs had straightened in her chair.

Chinese Gordon followed Margaret down the hall,

then waited as she pounded on the door. When it opened she said, "Kimberly Abrams, corporate headquarters, San Francisco" again, and Chinese Gordon could see a young man in a short-sleeved shirt with a tie and a row of pens and pencils in the breast pocket arranged according to length. "Bill McGee," he said, and brushed an unruly tuft of hair off his forehead, not sure if he should offer to shake her hand.

She turned away from him and said to Chinese Gordon, "We'll get out of your way and let you get to work."

Chinese Gordon said, "It'll only take a minute, ma'am." He set his tool case on the floor and knelt to open it.

The young man smiled uncomfortably and asked, "Is it something I can give you a hand with?"

"Oh no," said Margaret, and for the first time her features displayed a mild amusement. "He's only changing the lock. Meanwhile, I've got to have you sign for the new key and be on my way."

She brushed past him into the room and glanced quickly about her as she rummaged inside the leather case. She had imagined it would be a wall of exposed wires and boxes that made clicking noises, but it wasn't. There were four or five computer terminals with sleek molded casings and a console along the wall. The room looked empty and surgically sterile. She wondered if Chinese Gordon would know what to do. She stared past the young man at Chinese Gordon, who was looking at the machines out of the corner of his eye as he worked. His face showed no surprise, no concern. He already had the old lock out of the door.

She handed the key to the young man and said, "Before you sign, do you understand your responsibility?"

He stared ahead with a noble, serious expression. "Yes, I do."

"Fine." She handed him a card that said only "7503, Number 4," and he selected a pen from his pocket and signed it. Margaret looked at it closely and then dropped it in her leather case. Then she pointed to the console and asked, "Is that our pride and joy?"

The young man's voice deepened with self-importance. "Part of it. The distributing frame is mostly behind those housings." He waved his whole arm to indicate a bank of plain squares that looked to her like kitchen cabinet doors. "We use the terminals to debug the programming of the switching system, but if we need to, we can access just about any base we want."

She hoped Chinese Gordon had been listening, but she couldn't be sure. He looked absorbed in what he was doing. "Very good. Now can you please point me in the direction of the Santa Monica Freeway?"

"Certainly," he said. "Just go straight up Grand past Washington and there you are."

"I'm sorry, but my sense of direction is embarrassing. Could you just point?"

"Oh, sure," he said, and pointed toward the console.

"I mean outside."

"Oh. Sorry." He blushed, then rushed forward through the doorway. Margaret followed slowly, and then he stopped himself and came back to walk beside her at a slower pace. "I'm not supposed to leave the room," he whispered. "I'm monitoring."

"You have permission this time," she whispered back, and walked still more slowly.

As soon as they turned away, Chinese Gordon backed into the room. From his tool kit he lifted a caulking gun fitted with a narrow metal nozzle that came to a point. It took both hands to lift the caulking gun to the first of the housings covering the distributing frame and insert the nozzle. It was hard for the eyes to accept that the compact cylinder was this heavy—heavier than gold and almost as heavy as lead. He pumped the trigger and moved quickly to the next housing. One after the other he pried them open a crack and slipped the nozzle in, then pumped the trigger a few times. By the third one he could tell the caulking gun was lighter, and when he had finished the console, it was empty. He closed the tool kit over the caulking gun and walked to the hallway, locking the door behind him.

Chinese Gordon had been gone no more than two minutes before Mr. McGee stepped back through the front entrance of the building. As he passed Miss Briggs his eyes didn't meet hers because he didn't want to see the disapproval he expected. He knew it wouldn't be jealousy because the woman from headquarters had been to see him, only impersonal contempt because he'd left the switching equipment. He knew that whatever it was, it would take him another week now before he'd be able to work up his confidence to ask her to go to dinner. He'd watch her and listen to the tone of her voice for at least that long before he was sure. His lowered eyes crossed her desk as he passed, and some part of his mind registered the fact that all three of the buttons on her telephone that happened to be lighted went out at the same time. When he reached the door of the switching room, he tried the knob. Then he inserted his key, and it wouldn't turn. A big drop of sweat moved down his forehead in a slow arc and splashed on the inner surface of the lens of his glasses like a tear.

On the other side of the door behind the plain spotless surface of the airtight housing that protected the first row of modules in the distributing frame, several thousand tiny random electrical catastrophes were occurring in the microcircuits. The silvery spray of mercury had landed in shivering globules on all of the main boards and caused first one short circuit, then sixty, then hundreds as each one spattered sizzling droplets of mercury in every direction, each droplet causing another short circuit. In a few moments enough of these sparks would have occurred to melt the insulation that protected the wires of the major circuits. Less than a minute later a significant portion of the mercury would reach three hundred fifty-seven degrees Centigrade, and it would begin to boil. Then the space inside the airtight housing would begin to glow with an unearthly light that oscillated from yellowish-green to blue as the thousands of exposed wires discharged electricity in infinitesimal lightning bolts through the mercury vapor.

^ 26 ^

KEPLER LIFTED THE receiver in the telephone booth and dialed the number of Mann's Chinese Theater. There was a hum and a click, and a young woman's recorded voice said, "Thank you for calling Mann's Chinese Theater. This message will be repeated in five seconds. . . ." Kepler waited, and there was another click. "Thank you for calling Mann's Chinese Theater. Our feature presentation, Woody Allen's *Bitter Herbs,* will be shown at eleven, one-twenty, three forty-five, six oh-five, eight-thirty, and ten fifty-five. No passes or discount tickets accepted for this engagement. Thank you for calling Mann's Chinese—" Kepler waited, but there was no sound except a faint, empty rustling somewhere in the wires. He hung up and put in another dime. This time there was no dial tone. He dialed the operator, but nothing happened. He put the telephone back on the receiver and glanced at the black face of his Rolex watch. It was precisely six-thirty.

Kepler walked across the street to the city maintenance yard, opened the door of the orange dump truck, and hot-wired the ignition. Trucks were so much easier than cars, with everything plain and in the open and easy to reach. He ground the gears getting it into second, but after that he got used to the stiff clutch and the sloppy transmission. The bright morning light made a glowing haze on the dusty, flecked windshield as he wound up the entrance ramp, but when he was on the Golden State Freeway he could see well enough, and soon he passed under the green sign that said "Jct Harbor Fwy South 1" and went by the Dodger Stadium sign. At that point he abruptly steered across to the left lane. Three cars shot past him on the right, and two others dropped far behind, seeming to be aware that something was wrong. He slowed down and moved onto the left shoulder and they too slipped past. In his right mirror he could see that he had a gap of at least a quarter mile before the next pack of cars reached the Dodger Stadium sign. He started the hydraulic lift of the dump truck and moved almost to the point where the two freeways separated. As soon as he saw the first pieces of gravel start to hit the pavement and bounce behind him, he swung the truck across all five lanes of the freeway, dumping the load as he went. As he drove on, he could see the gray pile of gravel stretching across the junction three feet high at the shoulders and at least six in the center lanes, like the body of a big gray fish. He lowered the bed of the truck and then he was up to speed again, heading south.

After two miles he came to the junction with Route 10, the Santa Monica-San Bernardino Freeway. At the narrowest point on the overpass he waited for an opening and then pulled the truck perpendicularly across both lanes, set the hand brake, and jumped to the ground. As an afterthought he leaned in and turned on the emergency lights. Then he reached into his boot, pulled out his pistol, shot two of the tires, and climbed down the sloping bank of ice plants to Mission Street.

At Tyler Bailey's Acres of Datsuns he was glad to see that the delivery truck was still loaded and that nobody had arrived to open the gate. He'd worried about this part of it. The Highway Department always kept two or three trucks full of gravel for the morning's work, but who could predict when Tyler Bailey decided to move his merchandise around? When Kepler had the truck started he followed Mission to Sunset and drove onto the Harbor Freeway. He was surprised to see it so empty, until he remembered that he'd already cut off the main feeder route from the north.

It was only one and a half miles to the junction of the Hollywood and Harbor freeways. He felt conspicuous driving the long rig with its load of shiny little cars, all the colors of fruit. At the place where the inbound Hollywood merged with the Harbor Freeway and swept into downtown Los Angeles, Kepler pulled over to the left shoulder again and jumped down from the cab. He climbed up on the steel track and released the chains and bars and chocks that held the little cars on the two levels. Then he got back in and waited for a break in the traffic.

When it came, he pulled forward and slammed on his air brakes so the cars rocked forward, then pushed the gas pedal to the floor. The cars started to roll off the back of the truck and skitter along the freeway, then come to rest wherever their momentum carried them. Some turned sideways, two or three he could see rolled over. One even caught fire, but he resisted the temptation to wait for the explosion. It was only two and a half miles to the Santa Monica Freeway, but another nine and a half to the place where it met the San Diego Freeway.

•   •   •

CHINESE Gordon sang a chorus of "On, Wisconsin" as he jammed the stolen school bus across the single lane that connected the San Diego Freeway with the Hollywood Freeway. As he jumped from the bus he chanted "Hold that line," but he sank into a profound silence when he reached Ventura Boulevard. It was his last stop. By now Kepler and Immelmann should nearly have finished too. In all there were seventeen spots that had to be cut off. The big problem now was the long walk home. He smiled to himself. Immelmann was going to think of that after he cut the 605, the 405, the Arcadia Freeway, and the Pomona Freeway and remembered that he was forty miles from home.

IMMELMANN gave the throttle of the Caterpillar bulldozer more gas and raised the blade a few inches to hit the signpole at its strongest point. The immense billboard tilted and gave a sickening crack, then bobbed a few times. He backed the bulldozer a few feet, then moved to the other main support. Fifty feet below on the freeway, a big tractor-trailer clattered by, with a tiny Ford drafting in its wake. Immelmann jammed the throttle and jumped from the bulldozer, then watched it rumble into the billboard.

The second pole snapped and the billboard, still vertical, moved forward into the chain link fence. The bulldozer's inexorable force uprooted six fence posts and forty feet of fencing while the billboard folded in the middle. Then the fence, the billboard, and the bulldozer, now a single tangle of metal, wood, and machinery, lost contact with the hillside and tumbled, turning once in the air to crash onto the freeway.

Immelmann shook his head. Chinese Gordon had said to use the bulldozer and to make sure they couldn't press it into service to clear the road later, but maybe he'd gone too far. It might be days before anything big enough to clear the Foothill Freeway could be moved into position, and it looked as though a whole section of the concrete had been pounded into the ground. This was unquestionably the worst one he'd done, because it also blocked the northern end of the San Gabriel Freeway where it met the Foothill. It was nearly seven o'clock already, and it would take almost to post time to walk the five miles to Santa Anita, eat breakfast, and pick the winners in the newspaper. It would be a nice day at the track, a little hot in the stands, but certainly not crowded.

MARGARET left the pile of handbills beside the gate with a brick on top of them, and the signs on the sidewalk, then posted the note: "Be Back Soon—Please Take One," and drove off. It was the last of the major Rapid Transit District bus yards, and the morning shift would arrive any minute. She had to make it onto the Pacific Coast Highway before the first of the commuters started to sense that the freeways were blocked.

As she approached the airport she could see the overpass a few blocks to her right where the San Diego Freeway crossed Century Boulevard. The freeway was packed with cars and as still as a photograph. As she drove toward Santa Monica, she wondered if she'd make it to Topanga Canyon before that route too was blocked by the overflow. It was still early enough to try, and if she couldn't swing north there, it would be better to be stranded at the beach than anywhere else. She could tell already it was going to be a hot day. It was already over eighty-five, and the sun was barely up.

She didn't have much confidence in the bus-driver

plan. The handbills said, "Emergency Strike Called at Midnight! Three Thousand to Be Laid Off. Rest to Take Pay Cut of Twenty Percent." It was hard to imagine Los Angeles bus drivers falling for that one, and they probably wouldn't. It had been designed for Central American cities, where government-owned transportation systems had gone backrupt repeatedly, missed payrolls, and tried to save themselves by hiring and laying off drivers according to no comprehensible plan. It would be easy to start a bogus strike there, but not so easy in a place like Los Angeles. It was worded that way in the Donahue papers, though, so it would help get the message through.

AT the bus yard in Long Beach three drivers were walking back and forth in front of the gate carrying signs that said "Emergency Strike." A fourth was passing out handbills to the people who came to the gate carrying lunchboxes.

A driver named Evangeline Bartlett yawned and stared at the handbill. "What is this?"

The man who had handed it to her said, "Strike. Read it."

"Who called it?"

"The union. Who else?"

"Did you vote on it?"

"I just heard about it when I got here. Ask him." He pointed to a big man with curly gray hair and a nose with small red veins visible on its fleshy surface, who was engaged in a heated discussion with two other men a few yards down the sidewalk.

Evangeline Bartlett tapped him on the shoulder. "Are you from the union?"

"No," he said. "The union steward will be back in a

little while." He said to one of the men with him, "Get this copied now or we'll run out by noon."

Bartlett turned and started to walk away, staring at the handbill, when a hand touched her arm. She looked up. It was her friend Donald.

"What's going on?"

She shrugged. "Looks like a layoff, a pay cut, and a strike." She handed him the flyer. "Enough trouble for one day."

Donald's eyes narrowed as he read the handbill. "It can't be true. It's a joke."

Evangeline's brows knitted and she walked on. "The fat man over there talked to the union steward."

"Where are you going?"

She said quietly, "It may not all be true. But it doesn't matter much which part of it is true, because it means no paycheck for at least a month. Trailways is advertising for drivers, and in about twenty-four hours you can rush down there and be three thousandth in line. Not me."

WHEN Kepler reached his car he turned on the radio and listened as he made his way along the quiet residential streets. The first station announced that "Because we've got some kind of problem with the phones here at the station," the prize for Day Seventeen of the Crazy Sound Contest would be given away on Day Eighteen: "But if you're listening out there, telephone company, send us a carrier pigeon. And make sure he brings his tools with him." Kepler held a can of beer between his legs and popped it open with his free hand. It sprayed the dashboard, but he didn't care because it didn't add much to the old spray marks. He tried another station. "It's time for Bob Byrd in his Byrdmobile to give us the bad news as he flies over the freeways. How is it out there, Bobby? A little rough this morning?''

A voice that was slightly muffled said, ''For seven o'clock in the morning it's something special, all right. At the moment I'm over the Hollywood Freeway at the Harbor and Pasadena interchange and believe me, nothing is moving. We're monitoring the CHP broadcasts, and they haven't found the problem yet. I've heard three different stories. But it's going to be a tough commute for anybody coming into the downtown slot today. I'd recommend that if you have to get there try surface streets. If you can avoid the area, do it. We've also got reports of major accidents on the inbound San Diego, Santa Ana, Foothill, and Long Beach freeways already, and the reports are coming in faster than I can write them down.''

''Sounds like you've got your work cut out for you today, Bobby.''

''No problem for the Byrdmobile, Dan. I can fly just about anywhere today and have plenty to talk about. And believe me, I'd rather be up here than down there sweating on the freeway. I'd advise everybody to leave for work as early as possible and be prepared to spend some time in the car.''

''I'd say it's time to play a real oldie, Petula Clark's 'Downtown.' ''

Kepler smiled. They wouldn't know the size of it for another half hour or so, and they probably wouldn't believe it then. The radio stations would lure as many cars as possible into the trap in that time. The disk jockey played ''On Broadway,'' then Arlo Guthrie's ''Comin' into Los Angeles.'' Kepler listened to the music, tapping his fingers on the roof of the car as he glided along tree-lined back streets. The main thing was to keep heading north and west, away from the city. If he had to backtrack even once, he knew he might be stuck all day. Already, even on these streets, the inbound lanes had begun to clog and stall, and he had to stop occasionally while a car from the other lane pulled in front of him and turned around to try another route.

It was only ten minutes before the disk jockey stopped "Summer in the City" in the middle. "We have an update on the traffic situation from Bobby Byrd up there in the Byrdmobile. Bobby?"

"Dan, the California Highway Patrol has just called Sig-Alerts in four more places. Route Five, the Golden State Freeway, is a disaster area, with four incidents. It's cut off at the Santa Monica-San Bernardino interchange, the junction with the 605, and the junction with the Hollywood south. I've just flown over those areas and I can tell you the best thing to do is stay far away from them. I've never seen anything like it. The traffic is stopped dead all over the northern half of the city, and they say there's no way CALTRANS can get emergency equipment to any of the trouble spots before at least ten o'clock. From up here the freeway system looks like one gigantic parking lot. For thousands and thousands of those cars down there I'd say there's no way to go forward, no way to go back, and no way off until the accidents are cleared. What I'd do is turn off my engine and wait."

"Not a bad idea, Bobby. Just don't try it in the old Byrdmobile. I didn't wear my hard hat today, and I don't want to feel anything heavier on my bald head today than a kiss."

"Not much chance, Danny, so you might as well put the hat back on. I'm on my way south now to check some of the other bad spots."

"We'll be checking with Bobby Byrd from time to time in case we run out of bad news. In the meantime, the CHP is advising everyone who doesn't have to drive today to please stay home."

Kepler drove on. It was becoming more difficult now. It was seven-fifteen, and the inbound lanes were stopped completely. He had to pass three blocked intersections before he found one with enough space between cars to make a left turn.

When a commercial for transmissions was over, the disk jockey said, "In case you haven't noticed it yet, today is a good day to write somebody a letter. A motorcycle policeman just drove up the sidewalk, no less, to tell us that there is a problem with the telephone equipment at the downtown switching station. So if you're waiting for a call from that special someone, don't bother, go have an affair instead. If you're beautiful, have an affair with your favorite radio personality, who signs off at ten."

Kepler could see the Ventura Freeway ahead. It was awesome. He could see thousands of cars, all twelve lanes packed with cars—even the shoulders beside the freeway were full of cars. Overhead, police helicopters hovered, the chopping drone of their engines the only sound. On the pavement of the freeway, among the shining and useless metal shapes of the cars, he could see the figures of people walking, sitting on hoods and fenders and roofs, standing in groups to talk.

As he stopped at the light beside the freeway entrance three girls walked down the entrance ramp, passing within inches of the line of cars stopped there waiting to merge with the unbroken, unmoving line of stalled vehicles.

A man in a Mercedes leaned on his horn and yelled, "Get the hell back to your car! What if it starts moving again?"

One of the girls stopped beside the man's window. Her face was calm and expressionless and sincere. "It can't, see? I have the keys."

⌃ 27 ⌃

PORTERFIELD HELD THE small slip of blue paper.
"What time did this come in?"

"The call was logged in Langley at eight forty-five, a
little over a half hour ago. Quarter to six Los Angeles
time. That's where it came from. Los Angeles." The
young man seemed pleased to be able to say something
that sounded like information. His small, glittering eyes
narrowed as he waited.

Porterfield spoke in a quiet, measured tone. "Get
copies of this to Deputy Director Pines, Mr. Kearns,
and Mr. Goldschmidt, then do what they tell you to."
The young man turned on his heel like a military orderly
and leaned forward as he took the twelve strides to the
door.

Porterfield didn't care for the young man, but he was
a necessary annoyance while the Donahue matter was
unresolved. The young man's real name was Carpenter,
but he was listed on the Seyell Foundation's payroll as
Karl Burndt, a name that didn't seem to fit and which
Porterfield needed to make an effort to remember.

Into the telephone Porterfield said, "I need a line to
the Los Angeles main office, highest priority, secure if

211

possible, but don't waste time waiting for a scrambler.
If nothing else works, I'll take a commercial line."

He glanced at his watch. It was nearly nine-thirty.
While he waited, he read the message again. "619352.
You spoiled the picnic."

CHINESE Gordon pulled his chaise longue next to
Margaret's and stepped forward to adjust the television
where it rested on the welding table. Then he moved to
the wooden stairway and accepted a can of beer from
Kepler, who was sitting on the ice chest.

Kepler scratched his stomach. "You're right, Chinese. It's ten degrees cooler in the shop than upstairs,
and that's ten degrees cooler than outside."

"It's the concrete floor," Chinese Gordon said.
"Even the animals know that." He turned to see the big
dog climbing up off the floor and settling himself on the
empty chaise longue beside Doctor Henry Metzger.

"Here it is, Chinese," Margaret called. Chinese Gordon sauntered up behind her and leaned on the cool
metal side of the van.

The television screen showed a display of cars stopped
on the freeway. The telephoto lens made them look as
though they'd been squashed together, and they shimmered in the heat waves so that in the distance the cars
seemed to be submerged in gelatin.

Printed across the picture were the words "Disaster!
The Odds Catch Up with Los Angeles." The staccato
opening of the *Noon News* theme hammered its electric
urgency like a coded message, then swelled into a deep,
sweeping flourish of importance. Then there were Gene
Turton's curly white hair and pale paraffin face. "The
biggest traffic tie-up in the history of the world, a near-

total cutoff of communication, and hundred-degree temperatures make this a special day in the Southland. More after this.'' Gene Turton was replaced by a group of young people pouring impossible quantities of soft drinks down their throats, their heads tilted toward the sun.

"I hate that Southland thing,'' said Kepler. "The Southland is way down upon the Suwannee River, not southern California. The man is an ass. If I had him here I'd—''

"Kepler!'' said Margaret.

Gene Turton was back. "This morning within a period of less than thirty minutes major accidents slashed into at least seventeen key spots on the Los Angeles freeway system and put a stranglehold on traffic, marooning millions of commuters and choking the life out of the city.''

"Calm down, Gene,'' said Chinese Gordon.

"At the same time, what appears to be a freak accident at the South Grand Avenue switching station knocked out the telephones of some ten million homes and businesses in Los Angeles County, leaving the Southland deaf and dumb. A *Noon News* minicam team cornered the mayor in his office only an hour ago, and he had this to say.'' Gene stared at something off-camera for several seconds, and then the mayor appeared in a glare of lights that threw black shadows behind him on the wall and made his eyes shine like those of an animal caught in a car's headlights.

"I'm asking the governor for emergency assistance, in the hope that he will ask the President to declare the county a disaster area. This will make possible the use of the National Guard to help get us out of this mess, and might also make the business community eligible for economic assistance if they suffer significant damage from this day's events. It's only eleven, and we've got a long day ahead of us.''

A reporter's arm appeared and a microphone was thrust under the mayor's chin. ''Have you communicated with the governor yet?''

The mayor scowled. ''No, I haven't. The telephones don't work. Remember?''

Gene Turton's face appeared again. ''For the first time ever, all flights are being diverted from Los Angeles International Airport because of what's happening here on the ground. *Noon News* has learned that, because of the monumental traffic problems, nobody has been able to get in or out of LAX for several hours. The terminals are already full of stranded passengers, and the airlines are now afraid that if they do land they'll have to take off empty.'' Gene Turton's eyebrow lifted slightly as he stared into the camera. ''No one could be reached to tell us how passengers were to be transported from the Ontario, Burbank, and Orange County airports, or how the airlines expected people booked on outgoing flights to get there.''

Chinese Gordon patted the dog's head. ''Can I sit down, boy?'' The dog stared at him but didn't move.

Gene Turton continued. He was gazing earnestly into the camera, which zoomed so close that his face nearly filled the screen. ''There are unsubstantiated reports of a bus drivers' strike, and other major stories that broke this morning. Throughout the day we'll have camera teams in helicopters on the spot wherever news is happening, but it may take days to sort out everything that's happened. We do know a few things that we can pass on. One is, don't try to drive anywhere unless it's a genuine emergency. By 'emergency' I mean that someone's life is in danger. There are over four million automobiles stuck out there now. Don't let yours be one of them. In the meantime, be patient and keep your sense of humor. In a day or two we'll laugh at this the way people in New York laugh at the 1965 blackout, and people in Buffalo laugh at the blizzard of '77. Let's show the world that Los Angeles is a place where people help each other, hmm?''

^ 28 ^

PORTERFIELD LISTENED TO the Director's voice, holding the telephone an inch from his ear. With the other hand he poured himself a half glass of Scotch and put the bottle back in the desk drawer. His eyes were on the television set built into the bookcase.

"I asked the man to play it down, and he wouldn't do it. You've got to remember I didn't tell him to kill it, I asked him not to make a big deal out of it on national news, as a favor to—"

Porterfield interrupted. "That wasn't a very good idea."

"What are you talking about? It was the man's duty as president of the network. Schenley is supposed to be a responsible man. For God's sake, I've let him into Langley for briefings."

"That wasn't a good idea either. He'd castrate himself on camera if a sponsor would pay for it."

There was a pause, then the Director said, "Well, it's coming on. I'll talk to you later."

The print on the television screen said "Special Report." The face was Gilford Bennett's. Porterfield sipped his drink. It would have to be Bennett, the network's veteran commentator, who had stayed on the radio after the others had pulled the plugs and gone home because he hadn't believed that Dewey had defeated Truman. He was retired now, but he appeared a few times a year to interview heads of state or narrate special reports about the space program. His familiar old face with the scholarly, serious eyes and the thin, pinched nose like a pigeon's bill held the usual sardonic expression as once again he returned to view with lofty amazement one of the difficulties mankind had failed to solve for itself since he'd ceased to take a personal interest.

"This hastily prepared special report is about a disaster—a disaster of massive proportions that hit the second largest city in America today. It was real enough to cause economic, political, and social consequences that will be felt for some time to come. But it was different from other disasters, because thus far there have been no casualties. There has been very little physical damage, and nearly all of that was to property owned by public entities and giant corporations that can take their losses without blinking an eye. The disaster? Why, the disaster is that nothing happened."

Porterfield stared at the screen. A camera in a helicopter showed a stretch of several miles of freeway with cars parked on it, and people sitting on them and waving.

Gilford Bennett said, "This is the Santa Monica Freeway in Los Angeles, California, at two o'clock today. It was blocked by several major accidents at about six-thirty this morning, and nothing on it has moved since then. Traffic jams are nothing new for Los Angeles, the city that invented freeways, but this jam is different. What you're seeing is not a special sight today, because at this time every major freeway in Los Angeles County,

a metropolis approaching eleven million people, looks
just like this. Most of these people have been with their
cars on the freeway since around seven this morning.
People who left for work later than that aren't down
there because there wasn't room for them on the freeway. Instead they took surface streets, and this was the
result.''

The scene changed to a residential street lined with
tall palm trees. The street was crammed with parked
automobiles. People walked among them, talking.
Others sat in their cars, staring glumly forward through
the windshields. ''This is Riverside Drive, a few blocks
from the network's studios in Burbank. Our producers
didn't exactly pick it, they just didn't have the use of
enough helicopters to get a camera crew any farther
away than walking distance.'' At that moment a dark
green Jaguar sedan abruptly pulled out of line, bounced
over the right curb, and drove over front lawns and
across driveways and through hedges. A battered Ford
station wagon followed it, and then other cars tried,
until something too far up the street for the camera to
catch blocked them. A Volkswagen Rabbit, the last car
to leave the street, sat absurdly in the middle of a bed of
bright purple flowers.

''If you didn't see any reason to join your friends and
neighbors in the biggest traffic jam since Hannibal
brought the elephants over the Alps, you could have
called up your boss and told him you weren't coming to
work, right? Wrong, because in Los Angeles today a
freak accident has also closed down the telephone
system. Public transportation? Los Angeles has never
had a very good system to begin with, and it consists entirely of buses that don't do as well in the traffic as these
automobiles. But even so, today happened to be the day
Los Angeles bus drivers went on strike. The reason? We

don't know, because none of the union leaders could be called on the telephone, and none could be located physically. Chances are, they're out there somewhere, caught in the traffic with everyone else."

Gilford Bennett's face reappeared, and his expression was the one he used while interviewing engineers about NASA hardware. "We have Mayor Quentin Sample of Los Angeles in the studio of our Los Angeles affiliate right now, waiting to speak with us. Mr. Mayor, what can you tell us about the worst day in your city's history?"

"Well, Gil, we have teams of inspectors and assessors all over the county right now trying to tally up the damage. We don't have anything like a real estimate, just examples. So far nobody seems to have been killed, but it's a hundred and three degrees out there, and we've had reports of police in helicopters evacuating a number of people to hospitals with heat exhaustion, and at least one possible heart attack. Other than that the only real damage is economic, thank God."

"You mentioned examples. Can you give us a few?"

"Every industry in Los Angeles has lost a day of business. On an annualized basis that's a half percent of the year's output for the entire region. But that would be an optimistic way of putting it. I'll give you a few examples. Tied up on the freeways would be approximately ten to twenty thousand trucks carrying perishable food, which will be garbage by the time they can move again. At this time studios have filed permits for twenty-three major motion pictures in production this week. Some of them have shooting budgets in excess of a million dollars a day. The costs don't stop if they don't shoot. Los Angeles is the center of the record industry, the aerospace industry, the television industry, and has a huge proportion of the nation's insurance and banking business. I could go on for hours, but you get the idea. The economic losses will be incalculable.''

"I may as well put the questions to you that you'll be hearing from now on. What caused it, and what are you going to do about it?''

"What caused it seems to me the frightening part. It was just chance—the odds. Every day of the week some freeway in the area is jammed by breakdowns, or something. Today seventeen major accidents occurred all at once just before the busiest time of the day, and at the same time an equipment failure cut off telephone service. We've had every one of these problems before, but not all at once.''

"But I'd been told you were asking the governor to apply for federal aid on the grounds that Los Angeles had been hit by a natural disaster.''

"What has hit Los Angeles is a force of nature that is exactly the same as a flood or a fire or an earthquake. It's the natural law of probability. Given four to five million vehicles traveling on those freeways each day, a certain number of accidents will happen. It was mathematically unlikely that one would happen at each of seventeen major interchanges simultaneously on any given day, but the odds caught up with us. Mathematics is a force of nature too.''

"An interesting idea, but it certainly contradicts some of the tenets of insurance law.''

"All right. I don't care if the President or anybody else agrees with me philosophically. We've got a disaster, and it doesn't matter what caused it. If this same disaster had been caused in some other way, the federal government would help with the cleanup, emergency loans, and so on. What if it had been something else? A minor earthquake would have about the same results. If this had happened in San Salvador or Mexico City the check would already be in the mail."

The telephone was already ringing. Porterfield picked up the receiver. "Yes, I heard it. No, it's only a coincidence. Don't worry. There are only a certain number of municipal disasters he would think of. It was just a matter of time—you know, the odds."

⚤ 29 ⚤

PERSONALS

619352. No need for more dramatics. I've read the book. Talk to me, and maybe we can start over.

"Is that supposed to mean something to me?" Jorge Grijalvas opened his fingers and let the page of newspaper float to the desk.

"It means quite a bit, actually. You wanted to ride that silver saddle in the Pasadena parade. Now you'll be able to afford to buy a horse to put under it. That'll make you look a lot taller."

Grijalvas drummed his fingers on the desk. "Mr. Gordon, this is the third time you've come to me. In the first instance you graciously allowed me to buy back my own merchandise, recovering some of my losses. The second time I was able to make a telephone call for seventy-five hundred dollars. I've enjoyed these transactions, I'll have to admit, but I'm a busy man. What is it, exactly?"

Chinese Gordon said, "I've been having a hard time

222

selling something. My customer agrees to the price, but when the time comes he just doesn't seem to be able to part with the money.''

"What you're selling is drugs. Why didn't you come to me?''

"It's not drugs.''

"What, then? If it's worth anything, I'll buy it.''

"It's not transferable. I've got some evidence about somebody who can't bear to see it in print and has lots of money. I offered him a perfectly good chance to buy it back, but he set up a trap.''

Grijalvas covered his eyes with his hands and chuckled. Chinese Gordon could see a gold pinky ring with a ruby the size of a pea. "Blackmail. I'm afraid you've learned the first lesson, Mr. Gordon. People who have lots of money are seldom the best targets for extortion. They have little to fear from the police, and if necessary lots of money buys lots of professional assistance. It's a fool's game.''

Chinese Gordon nodded his head. "That's about the size of it, Jorge. My customer has so much professional help I don't know where he gets it all. Sometimes I'm afraid he'll spend so much just to make his payroll that there won't be enough left for fools like me.''

"Take my advice and get out of that business. You'll never see any money, and the richer your target is, the more likely he is to have connections who would be happy to hunt you down and kill you just to do him a favor.''

"I guess you'd know, wouldn't you?''

"I would know.''

Chinese Gordon stood up and shrugged. "Well, I'll think about your advice, Jorge. God, I hate to give up on this one, though. I've gone to so much trouble already, and all that's left is taking the money. That's the hard part, and that's why I wanted to cut you in for it—you know, lots of money buys lots of professional assistance.''

Grijalvas stared at the newspaper again. "How much professional assistance did you want?"

"Hell, you'd have been able to ride the winner of the Preakness in your parade and have yourself declared Rose Queen besides. The price for handling the payoff is a half million dollars.''

Grijalvas studied Chinese Gordon. This was not a man whose first offer would be more than 10 percent. Who had secrets worth five million? Grijalvas succeeded in keeping the tension out of his voice. "Just who is this person?"

"Well, actually it's several people, but I've decided that the one I want to deal with is this one, because he's the only one I have a picture of." Chinese Gordon handed him a black-and-white photograph of a man with graying hair, shaking hands with another man. The photograph had been clipped from a magazine.

"Where did this come from?"

"I cut it out of a kind of newsletter in the library. He works for the National Research Foundation, handing out money to colleges and things."

Grijalvas smiled. "That sounds like good practice for what you want him to do. What's his name?"

"John Knox Morrison."

Grijalvas shook his head. "I'm very sorry, Mr. Gordon. I can't get involved in this kind of thing. There's too much risk. A man like that might have called the FBI already, and there are not a few private corporations he could hire that specialize in handling embarrassing situations for wealthy families. But good luck to you."

"Jorge, I think you're making a hell of a mistake."

"I've made a safe, prosperous life out of just such mistakes. But if you succeed and find yourself with a large amount of marked money to trade, I'll be happy to help you out for very advantageous rates."

When Chinese Gordon climbed into Kepler's car he was humming "La Cucaracha."

"Well," asked Margaret, "will he do it?"

"Of course he'll do it." Chinese Gordon peered into the cooler in the back seat and examined Kepler's supply of beer. "He can't get to ride Seabiscuit to the moon on the Fourth of July if he doesn't use some ingenuity."

"What?"

"He'll do it."

THE Director stepped into the conference room, smiling. Pines followed, closing the door behind him, but not before Porterfield saw the two large men taking their posts outside in the hallway. He whispered to Goldschmidt, "Are those two yours?"

Goldschmidt shook his head. "I've never seen them before. He doesn't want professionals. He thinks those football players will do him some good."

The Director tossed a file on the table, but it landed harder than he'd intended, giving an audible slap and letting a single sheet skitter out and float to the floor. He bent over and picked it up, and when his face reappeared over the edge of the table, the smile was still there. "This will be quick, and you can all go on with your business. Ben, you were right."

"About?"

"The people who have the Donahue papers are still willing to talk. We've still got a chance to salvage this situation. We heard a response to our advertisement last night."

"Good. How much do we have to give them?"

"They want five million dollars."

"I'm disappointed in them. They could have gotten twice that. But I'm glad you decided to get it over with."

Pines nodded. "It won't be long now."

The Director said, "Of course, there will be some mopping up to do, and undoubtedly we'll have to meet again when we've received the results of whatever interrogations occur."

"Interrogations?" said Kearns. "What interrogations?"

Pines snapped, "Well, after all, we do hope to be able to take at least one or two of them alive. We ought to have the expertise to do that much."

Porterfield closed his eyes and sighed. Goldschmidt said quietly, "You're going to try to trap them again."

The Director extended his hands in front of him as though he were holding up an invisible object for inspection. "Not *try*, my friends. This time we've got them. Last night they placed a telephone call to Morrison and set up the payoff."

Porterfield opened his eyes. "To Morrison."

"Yes. John Knox Morrison. His name was in the papers, so they must have thought he was important. They called him at home, and of course the call was recorded. This time we know where and when in advance, and we're going to take this thing seriously."

Kearns was tapping the table with a pencil but didn't seem to be aware of it. "Has the voice been analyzed?"

"Yes," said the Director. "That's going to be your favorite part of it, Jim. It's not a voiceprint we've ever seen before. But there was the tiniest trace of an accent, and the analysis people say it's definitely a Spanish accent, and definitely Latin American. So that puts this group squarely in your bailiwick. This operation may very well solve some problems for your section."

"I'd like to recommend that you reconsider," said Porterfield. "In spite of the accent, these people might be domestic. We have to remember that the other thing they stole from that building was cocaine. If they're domestic, then paying them off won't have any consequence that we need to worry about. It may even induce them to stop taking risks and retire."

Pines smirked. "And what if they're a Latin American terrorist group? We've already given them lessons on taking over a major city. We give them five million dollars to help overthrow some friendly government? Brilliant."

"I second Ben's motion," said Goldschmidt.

"Me too," said Kearns.

Pines shouted, "I'd like to remind you people that this isn't some damned men's club. Nobody's voting on anything here."

The Director held up his invisible object again, but this time it seemed to have grown. "I'm afraid that I really do have to take this decision on myself. I can't see myself as the first Director to yield to the temptation to take the easy solution and pay to keep someone quiet about the Company's secrets."

"Not by a long shot," said Goldschmidt. "They've all done it. Half the world's diplomatic corps has been on the payroll for twenty years, and the KGB pays the rest."

"That's hardly comparable to paying five million dollars to a gang of criminals, foreign or domestic. Besides the possible consequences, it's just not cost effective. Five million dollars is a lot of money."

Porterfield cleared his throat. "Have you ordered an accounting on this operation yet? I don't mean what it's cost Los Angeles or what it might cost the Company if the Donahue papers come out. I just wondered what we've spent so far."

The Director contemplated his imaginary object again. "Oh, I suppose we could—"

Pines interrupted, his head shaking with what could have been rage, but seemed to be somehow debilitating, like a palsy. "No. No audit has been done, and nothing of the kind has been considered. This isn't some project we're working on. This is war. Five million or ten million or ten billion don't mean a thing."

"They do if you lose," said Kearns.

Porterfield was watching the Director. His arms were still held before him, but his hands had gone limp, as though he had dropped the object he'd been holding. He seemed to be contemplating Pines.

⩓ 30 ⩓

JORGE GRIJALVAS SAT in the back seat of the Lincoln Continental, watching the last of the great patches of green irrigated land sweep past the window and disappear. It was all desert now, the earth a dusty brown with slabs and outcroppings of gray rock visible in places where it broke through the thin, powdery covering of soil. The sky behind his head was a glowing pink already, but the high rocks ahead were still in the strong, direct rays of the late-afternoon sun.

He turned to Juan and started to explain again. He spoke patiently and precisely so that the others, who were older, could listen without appearing to. "This man is rich, so there's no question he'll bring a number of armed men with him. Just to carry so much money he'd need help."

"I understand," said Juan. He adjusted his dark glasses again, a gesture that had already become unconscious. He had been proud of the tear tattooed on his cheekbone until Mr. Grijalvas had taught him that it was a mistake, the mark of a loser. There was no honor in the mere fact of having been in prison.

Grijalvas said, "This man will be a coward. He's

229

ready to pay the money because he's afraid not to. He's also afraid to pay it, and if he sees a chance to avoid it, he won't have any pity. The men he's hired will be the ones to watch. They'll be feeling foolish because they didn't kill him and take the money themselves. The only way they can give themselves ease now will be to try to kill us. If he shows the slightest sign of wavering, they'll try it."

Juan said, "And what if he doesn't give them the chance, and we get the money?"

"Then there will be a number of men walking away from this who are accustomed to being paid for carrying guns and who know that we have five million in cash."

"I understand."

The car crossed a bridge over a dry streambed that was choked with rocks and small, spiky plants. In a half hour they would cross another, and then the patches of green would begin again. This time they wouldn't be irrigated fields of alfalfa and hay, but the first of the carefully tended golf courses of Palm Springs. Grijalvas looked out the window. From the quiet, air-conditioned interior of the car it all looked still and inviting, like a painting. The bright sunlight made the jagged rocks stand out in relief, throwing long, dark shadows on the empty flats. Outside the car the air was beginning to lose some of its ferocious dry heat. By the time they reached the first of the stoplights on Palm Canyon Boulevard it would be down to a hundred degrees. By the time John Knox Morrison ventured out of his refrigerated hotel room it would be in the seventies, a calm, clear, pleasant night.

CHINESE Gordon said, "Well, Palm Springs it is. That's the last turnoff."

Margaret sighed. "Do you have any idea how hot it is? Why in the world would people come all the way out here when they could climb into an oven just as well at home?"

"We know why old Jorge is here. It's not a bad choice, either, considering what he knows. It wouldn't be hard for him to outnumber the police."

"And you still expect to be able to take the money away from him afterward?"

Chinese Gordon shrugged. "No matter how many people he has there, he has to split them up when he leaves. If he gets the money and we see a chance, we may do it tonight. If not, tomorrow is another day, and it's always a long, lonely drive to Los Angeles."

Chinese Gordon let the big Continental drift off into the distance, dropping the van back to the speed limit. It was several minutes before Margaret realized that what he was humming was "Tenting Tonight."

JUAN sat erect and proud, as the companion of a powerful man should. He tried not to look directly at Mr. Grijalvas but to keep his eyes forward, staring at the hundred feet of rock and gravel in front of the car's headlights. Beside the road a gnarled joshua tree appeared, like something crouching to gather energy to stretch itself, then floated back into the darkness. The headlights caught a patch of yuccas clustered in the rocks ahead, and he could see a haze of dust drift across them. A few seconds ahead another car must have passed by here, disturbing the still night air. He could see Mr. Grijalvas's silhouette in the periphery of his vision, and he unconsciously shifted his posture to imitate it.

Mr. Grijalvas said, "It is now exactly twelve-fifteen."

Juan knew what that meant. Morrison and his men would already be at the valley station of the aerial tramway. In a moment they would leave their car and climb into the gondola, then ride it up the long cable to the mountain station at the top. It was easy to see why Mr. Grijalvas was who he was. Morrison's ride to the top would take fifteen minutes. His ride back would take another fifteen minutes. During that time he couldn't change his mind or come back or do anything but dangle a thousand feet above the desert floor in the little glass box. In that half hour Mr. Grijalvas could take the money from Morrison's car and disappear. That, at least, would be what Morrison thought, but that was only part of it. Juan thought about the new car he was going to buy. After that, there would be other things, but they would occur to him while he was driving the new car.

JOHN Knox Morrison stood in the parking lot and stared at the little blue-and-yellow corrugated steel building on its concrete platform. It looked tiny and insubstantial at the foot of the mountain. The small pool of yellowish light from the flood lamps made the garish building and the pitiful red flowers look unreal. Around the globes of the streetlights in the parking lot huge moths and bugs fluttered and buzzed, their bodies making tapping sounds as they battered against the hot glass. He waited while his companion, Morton, joined him. He glanced back once at the car to see that Morton had left the newspaper on the hood, then walked toward the little metal building.

At the stairway he could see the end of the tramway cable. He sighted along the thin wire, following its sagging length to where it turned up again and became in-

visible against the dark mountainside. Far above him at
the top of the mountain he could see another little pool
of bilious yellow light. From here the dim incandescence
brought back some long-forgotten memory of a carni-
val, with the smell of stale popcorn and cotton candy
and crowds and the strong sweat that came with the fear
of falling from some whirling metal machine that jerked
the body upward and pressed it against worn metal
safety bars with the centrifugal force of its demonic
spinning. He wished he felt more comfortable and could
say something to Morton, but Morton was as alien to
him as this place. Morton had the calm, efficient, un-
imaginative look that some of the operational people
had, not feeling anything, not really seeing anything.
There was also the nagging suspicion that somehow
Morton had been chosen by some awful mechanical system in Langley that was based on the similarity of their
names.

He followed Morton to the ticket booth and then to
the wooden deck, where they waited while one of the
tiny lights moved down the mountain toward them, then
grew into a set of lighted windows, then resolved itself
into a little rectangular box floating down the cable.
Morrison listened to the heavy machines behind the wall
of the building, a cyclical sound like wheels turning and
an armature thumping. He listened for a flaw, an un-
even sound that he could invest with his uneasiness, but
it only sounded heavy and powerful. Then he remembered that in a few minutes this place would be dangerous, and this machinery was going to take him up and
out of it. He felt a terrible eagerness as he rushed into
the tram gondola. As it jerked forward and swept away
from the deck, it swung gently on the cable. He clung to
the hand grip in front of his seat and stared down at the
little blue-and-yellow building. It was beginning to look

small already. As he watched he saw the tiny headlights of a car come up the road and enter the parking lot. He resisted an urge to drop to the floor of the gondola and kneel out of sight.

A recorded voice came over a speaker in the ceiling. "Welcome to the Palm Springs Aerial Tramway. We'll be going from the Valley Station, elevation 2,643 feet, to the Mountain Station, elevation 8,516 feet, a trip approximately two and a half miles long and over a mile straight up. The car is suspended on a cable about three inches thick and is driven by the turning of a large wheel . . ."

THE Continental coasted into the parking lot and moved up the line of cars near the little tram station and stopped behind a tan Chevrolet with a rental agency sticker on the bumper and a newspaper on the hood.

"All right," said Grijalvas. "Very quickly now."

Juan walked to the Chevrolet and looked into the back seat, then opened the door and pulled out two suitcases. He walked purposefully up the steps to the tram station, onto the wooden deck, and into the waiting gondola.

"Fine," Grijalvas said, and Miguel drove the car to the edge of the lot near the entrance to the road.

ON the hillside above the parking lot an agent spoke softly into his radio. "There's something wrong. One of them took the suitcases into the tram station, and the others didn't leave."

A bored voice answered, "Then wait. We've got the road blocked, so they can't go anywhere. He's probably going to count it or something."

"But there's nothing to count."

"You don't say. Won't he be surprised. Look, we have to wait until Morton has Morrison safely into the chalet up on top before we do anything. Nothing changes that."

JUAN stepped off the gondola and walked along the sidewalk outside the restaurant, where Morales and Figueroa were waiting to take the suitcases. He watched while they carried them a few yards down the hillside, then reappeared in the light.

The three walked beyond the glass doors to the foyer of the chalet, but as they did, Las Crusas was already on his way out of the gift shop and moving toward the telephone booth. The four men converged on the spot. Juan could see Morrison and another man standing outside the booth waiting for an elderly woman with bluish-white hair who was on the telephone.

The four men pulled out their pistols when they were within ten feet of Morrison, and fired. Morrison jerked backward against the wall, his body jumping as the bullets tore into him. Morton crouched and reached inside his coat, but the first shots punched his head back, and he toppled against the telephone booth and sprawled on the floor.

As Juan and his three companions ran toward the door, the old lady said into the telephone, "If you didn't hear that, it was everything going wrong. They're both dead."

The four men burst through the doorway and scrambled down the hillside toward the suitcases. Morales and Figueroa snatched them up and ran as Juan turned to see if anyone was watching from the windows. It was done—no head was visible. Making it at night on the trail down the side of the mountain would be difficult, but the four-wheel-drive truck was waiting for them on the flats. They'd drive along Andreas Canyon to Indian Road, then eastward toward Indio.

Juan ran and caught up with the others, who were trotting now. In the darkness he could hear the rhythmic sound of their deep breathing as they moved down the trail in single file. The trail wound around a large slab of rock, and Juan wondered when they would slow down. In this darkness, after a few twists and turns they were already invisible. The sounds they made seemed loud, but there was no ear that could hear them.

Juan heard a sharp metallic click in front of him that must have been one of the suitcases hitting something, but it sounded like the pump slide on a shotgun. Then there was a clatter of metal sounds that seemed to come from beside the trail and behind him at once. Suddenly glaring lights went on and he saw Figueroa caught in the center of a glowing circle. Figueroa froze, his hands before him as though he were riding a bicycle. Then there were bright flashes of fire that seemed to come from everywhere at once, and Juan saw Figueroa's body swatted away into the darkness as though a wind had carried him. He didn't see anything else happen. He felt a terrible, wrenching pain and he was on the ground and his breath was gone, but when he tried to gasp for another it didn't come.

ᐯ 31 ᐯ

CHINESE GORDON WATCHED the black Cadillac make the left turn into the road that led to the aerial tramway. He said to Margaret, "How many is that?"

"Four, if you count the one that came in right after Grijalvas."

"I'm counting it. There were five men in it, mean, ugly men."

"You couldn't tell if they were mean and ugly."

"No, but they were right on time, and what are five men in suits doing driving to the aerial tramway together at midnight? A basketball team on a wholesome junket?"

"How about a law firm?"

"I'd say they're blocking off the road behind old Jorge. I guess that's that. Another trap." He turned the key and started the van.

"At least we had a good dinner."

"Sure. Jorge has—had, I mean—good taste in restaurants. I loved it."

"I was watching you, and you didn't put a pound of pepper on everything the way you usually do."

Chinese Gordon smiled. "Yeah. I hate all that pepper."

Margaret stared at him as he put the van in gear and pulled out onto the highway. He drove toward Palm Springs, humming the drinking song from *The Student Prince*.

"Chinese?"

"Hmm?"

"Look, I don't think this is any of my business, but I love you very much, and someday I hope to marry you if I ever can find one shred of evidence that you're not criminally insane. Then this would be my business, because I'd like to cook for you."

"Feel free to plumb the depths."

"Well, I thought the reason you used all that pepper was that you'd gotten used to it somewhere you'd been where the food was awful—like Viet Nam or Thailand or maybe Africa. I never said anything about it because I thought it might make you sad or even mad."

"Hell, no. The food in some of those places is terrific. The secret history of the world is that the French concentrated on placing chefs in all of the major cities, and the British concentrated on taking over those places so they could get something decent to eat. If you spend time in England you begin to wonder if all animals are made up entirely of innards."

"Don't change the subject. Why do you use all that pepper?"

Chinese Gordon pulled the van into the parking lot of the Palm Canyon Motel. "This place look good to you?"

"Fine. Why the pepper?"

"I'm not in a good mood. I just lost a chance at several million dollars."

"Me too. Why the pepper?"

"If you must know, and apparently you must, I put the pepper on because of Doctor Henry Metzger."

"He likes pepper?"

"He hates it. If I don't put pepper on things, then as soon as I turn my back, he eats whatever is on my plate."

"What about the dog?"

"He doesn't even wait until I turn my back."

GRIJALVAS glanced at the face of his watch, the numbers glowing green in the darkness. "By now Morrison is dead and the others are on their way down the far side of the mountain. It's time to deal with the ambush he will have set up down here."

Grijalvas and his two men spent a few seconds wiping the smooth surfaces inside the car with handkerchiefs. Joachim left the motor running and the headlights on. The bulb had been removed from the dome light in the ceiling, so when they opened the doors beside the edge of the parking lot they were still in near darkness.

The agent on the hillside whispered into his radio again. "They're out of the car now. It looks like they're walking into the bushes, but the car's still running and the lights are on."

The voice from the radio said, "Don't do anything. Our highly skilled team of medical analysts agree that they're taking a piss. They think they're about to start a long drive." Then there was the sound of laughter in the background.

"But one of them's carrying a briefcase or something—"

"Wait a minute. They're calling from the top." There

was a pause while the agent strained his eyes looking through his infrared night binoculars to see the men who had left the car.

The voice came back over the radio, much louder. "Move in. Take them now. Do you hear me?"

The agent turned to give the signal, but the voice on the radio continued, "All units, move in now." He looked down at the Continental. Six cars were converging on it from different parts of the parking lot. On the sloping hillsides surrounding the area bright spotlights switched on and shot long beams across the basin, some sweeping slowly along the thick brush near the car, others jumping spasmodically to the road and then to the bare hills, then to the parking lot. The agent said, "We'll have them in a minute. What's up?"

"The car's a decoy. The trace on it brought back confirmation that it's stolen. They've probably got another one parked someplace."

"Did you get Morrison and Morton off the top?"

"No. Four guys who looked like Mexicans walked in and killed them before the evacuation team could move in. We haven't figured out why yet. We thought they'd wait for Morrison to come down the tramway."

"Maybe they looked in the suitcases."

"Not a chance. They were still carrying them down the mountain when they bumped into the evacuation team."

"So at least that much came off. Thank God for dumb luck."

"What luck? There are only two trails down, and we had people on both of them."

The agent heard the roar of an automatic weapon below him, and he jumped up to see one of his men standing beside the Continental, spraying the bushes with an Uzi submachine gun, a bright tongue of orange flame and sparks sputtering from the muzzle. He shouted into the radio, "Somebody tell that shithead down there to stop firing, if you can hear me. He's going to blow all our heads off."

A man got out of a nearby car and ran up to the man with the Uzi, who had paused to insert a fresh magazine. They walked back to the car together.

The agent said into the radio, "Oh, no, cowboy. Don't get too comfortable in that car. It's time for a sweep. Everybody hear that? I want five cars, bright headlights, at intervals of five hundred feet. The rest of you on foot. Keep to the high ground, and don't let them get out of this valley. Now get going."

Along the ridges on both sides of the road he could see spotlights moving now, methodically sweeping from side to side, crossing one another, but always inching up the road away from the aerial tramway station toward the main highway. The first of the cars moved up the road slowly, with men in the back seat aiming spotlights out both side windows.

Moments later the second car moved off, its headlights falling just short of the first car's taillights. It would be impossible for anything larger than a gila monster to escape, the agent thought.

GRIJALVAS and his two companions scrambled through the bushes above the aerial tramway station. They would stay on the rocky ridges all the way up the road until they managed to find the car that was waiting for them, and then come in on both sides of it. The ambushers would never expect to be attacked. They'd be waiting for the Lincoln Continental to appear on the road with the money in it. But the Continental had been abandoned, and the money was on its way down a

mountain trail miles from here. It would be safely in the
back of the pickup truck in another half hour, guarded
by some of Grijalvas's best men. Morrison was dead,
and in a few minutes the ambushers would be dead. Grijalvas had no doubt there would be ambushers. He had
chosen this place because it invited Morrison to arrange
a trap. It was the best way to ensure that Morrison
would bring the money; Morrison wouldn't want to
take the chance that the blackmailers would sense the
trap and escape to reveal whatever it was they knew
about him.

Grijalvas led his companions up the hillside a few
yards and studied the shapes of the dark ridges to see
which would make the best trail. There was no reason to
make this an evening of bruised shins and twisted
ankles.

Suddenly the narrow valley was bathed in light.
Floodlights blinked on and long cones of blinding
brightness pierced the air, moving about erratically. The
nearest was no more than a hundred feet from where
Grijalvas stood. He tapped Joachim's arm and scrambled over the ridge to the slope beyond. The three
moved quickly, putting as much distance between them
and the road as they could. After they had gone a half
mile, Grijalvas heard the rattle of an automatic weapon
in the distance.

He said, "It's all wrong. There are too many of them.
They're too organized."

His companions said nothing, only followed him over
the broken ground, Joachim carrying the briefcase containing the three Ingraham automatic rifles, and Jesus
carrying the extra ammunition clips.

A few hundred yards farther and Grijalvas swung to
the left in a path parallel to the road. There could be no
question of attacking the men waiting to block the

road—there could be twenty of them, all heavily armed. It was all wrong. Even a man like Morrison couldn't arrange this. He must have called the FBI. There was an army around that tram station. Grijalvas broke into a run, and the two men followed. They seemed to have no trouble staying within a pace of him even with the heavy metal they carried. Grijalvas's lungs ached after three hundred yards and his breath came in gasps, but Joachim and Jesus seemed to run easily and tirelessly. Finally Grijalvas tripped on a jagged rock and fell to his knees. The two ran on for twenty feet, then stopped to wait while he staggered to catch up.

They walked in silence for a time, then Grijalvas managed a trot. After five minutes Grijalvas's wind gave out again and they walked until they came to a low rise and could see the cars passing on the highway into Palm Springs. Far to the left Grijalvas could see the yellow glow of the sodium lamps at the aerial tramway station and the brighter white beams that swept the land around it.

It was important not to let himself get too confident now that they were out of the immediate vicinity of Morrison's trap. In a short time they would begin searching the highway in cars, and that would bring other problems. He was glad he'd heard the firing of automatic weapons near the station. The police wouldn't fire aimlessly into the underbrush because three men who might not even be armed had gone into it. They'd shout something through a bullhorn and then fire, so it wasn't the police. He hoped they had some way of learning that Morrison was dead and the money was gone. If they weren't police they would have no reason to keep searching this area. Instead they'd make a futile attempt to catch up with Juan and the others, because they had the money.

He walked toward Palm Springs, keeping as far from the highway as possible without losing his bearings. Joachim and Jesus followed without speaking. It took an hour before they crossed the first road on the edge of the town. From here on it would be difficult. There would be lights now and soon sidewalks, and buildings that would block their movement but wouldn't give them a place to hide.

He stopped on the shoulder of the road beside a high chain link fence. "Let me think about this for a second."

Joachim said, "We could steal a car."

"Maybe," Grijalvas agreed, "but by the time we get far enough into town to find one that's parked, we'd be risking a lot for nothing. The car Figueroa left for us is what we need." He stared at the fence. "This looks like a golf course." He shielded his eyes from the glare of the streetlamp and peered through the fence into the darkness. He could see a thick stand of trees and a gentle rise in the ground beyond that looked as though it couldn't be natural. He set the toe of his shoe in the fence and lifted himself up. From there he could see that the top of the mound was flat. "It is a golf course. Come on."

Joachim pulled himself up and stared at the mound. "Are you sure? I don't see a flag."

"Maybe they take them in at night."

They climbed the fence, the two younger men pushing Grijalvas over with difficulty. At the top he caught the tail of his coat and managed to disentangle it only by tearing the bottom seam. When they were on the ground beyond, they walked among the trees and skirted the open fairway. The quiet of the night air was broken only by the distant swish of cars passing on the main highway. Sometimes they could see the headlights, tiny and dim at first, then growing brighter as the car approached, then gone again, leaving only the red tail-lights diminishing in the darkness.

They went through another stand of trees and then past sand traps and across a wooden bridge over a narrow pond of still, greasy water. Finally they stood on a green, and at the end of the long, straight fairway they could see the lights of the clubhouse. Grijalvas said, "I guess we'd better get the guns out now. That's where the gate will be, and it looks as though they must have a restaurant or something open. Keep the guns under your coats and let me talk if anybody stops us."

Joachim opened the case and handed two of the short, heavy weapons to the others. He wiped off the case with his handkerchief and ran with it back to the pond. When he returned, the three walked up the edge of the fairway toward the building. As they approached they could see people through the large, lighted windows, sitting at tables. As Grijalvas watched, a man at one of the tables stood up, holding a stemmed glass high, and spoke for a few seconds, then sat down again. To my friend Mr. Gordon, Grijalvas thought. The man to whom I owe my five million dollars.

They turned left at the tee below the clubhouse and walked up the path to the parking lot. A young man in a tight red jacket rushed up and said, "Can I bring your car up for you, sir?"

"No, thank you," said Grijalvas. "It's parked down the road." As he walked on he surveyed the parking lot. All of these cars—fifty or more—would have their keys in the ignition or under the sun visor on the driver's side. It was something to keep in mind, but his own car wasn't far off now, and it wouldn't be a good idea to let his tired feet make the decision for him. They moved down the driveway to the street.

There was a sidewalk now, and after five minutes they passed another pedestrian, an elderly man in a tight red jogging suit who was walking a small, fluffy white dog that stopped to sniff each tree, each fence post, then scurried on to the next with nervous excitement. When they overtook him the dog yapped twice and the man jerked the leash, turning the little dog around to face him. "Cut it out, Nancy."

Grijalvas could see the place where the car was parked. He could recognize it because there was a dessert shop called Mamie's across the street that was always full and always seemed to have a line of people waiting outside the door. He could see the queue stretching down the steps and nearly to the door of the jewelry store in the other half of the building. There must have been ten people waiting to get in. There was very little to do in Palm Springs at night, he thought.

As they approached the restaurant, Joachim saw the car first. He quickened the pace, but Grijalvas didn't stop him. It was late and they'd walked a long distance and with all the people waiting to eat pies and cakes at Mamie's they wouldn't attract attention.

When Grijalvas reached the car Joachim had the doors open and was starting the engine. As Grijalvas slipped into the back seat he glanced across the street again at Mamie's. At that moment the man at the head of the line stepped aside to speak to another man, and Grijalvas saw the sign in the window: "Closed."

"Get going fast," he shouted.

Joachim pulled the car away from the curb just as a bullet punched through the rear window and whined out the open side window behind Grijalvas's head. There were more shots, but Grijalvas was lying on the back seat as Joachim accelerated down the empty city street. Grijalvas lifted his head cautiously to peer through the spidery cracks in the rear window, and he could see a line of six or seven men strung out across the street, firing at the speeding car. Twice he heard bullets thump into the trunk, but the car squealed along a curve in the road and then he couldn't see the men.

He said, "As fast as you can, Joachim. They don't seem to want to give up." He watched the speedometer over Joachim's shoulder as the needle reached the one-hundred mark, then devoted his attention to checking the load of the Ingraham he held on his lap. Out the rear window there was only darkness now. The car seemed to sway with each touch on the steering wheel and to swoop down the gentle inclines. The broken white lines on the road had merged into a single smear.

Minutes passed, and still there was no sign of another set of headlights. They had moved into the desert now, and when they roared onto Route 10, Joachim swung into the westbound lane without slowing. When they shot past the sign for Banning, Grijalvas could hardly read it. He said, "Slow down now. There might be police from here on."

After they'd passed Banning, Grijalvas began to feel more comfortable. It wouldn't be long before they came to Redlands, where he knew a man who could hide the car and give him another. From there East Los Angeles was only about an hour away.

All three noticed the lights at once. There was a red and yellow flashing, and rose-colored flares were burning on the road. As they drew near they could see that the lights were at the entrance to the Dinosaur Memorial. The burning flares lit the gigantic scaly torso of the life-sized tyrannosaur and made his glass eyes glitter with red. There were two white tow trucks, one parked beside the belly of the brontosaur, and the other blocking the right lane of the road. The flashing lights made the cluster of dinosaur effigies look as though they were moving.

Jesus said, "It looks weird. Way out here in the middle of nowhere."

Joachim said, "The only thing that's weird is you. It's for kids. There must be an accident."

As they watched, the second tow truck pulled out and blocked the left lane, and a man with a flashlight ran in front of them and started waving it.

Grijalvas said, "Can you get around them?"

"No. There's a steep drop off the shoulder on both sides. The tow trucks are probably here to pull somebody else out."

The man with the flashlight waved them into the entrance of the Dinosaur Memorial. They drove into the parking lot and saw that there were two other cars ahead of them, moving slowly toward the exit that led back to the highway. "Just a little detour," said Joachim.

When the first car reached the exit gate it stopped. The second car pulled up behind Joachim and stopped. Joachim honked his horn. The first car's lights went out. He leaned on the horn. Suddenly the doors of the front car opened and men started to jump out of it. Joachim saw the first one out kneel and level a pistol in his direction. The car behind Joachim moved up and pushed Joachim's into the car ahead and held it there, its motor whining and the tires spinning.

Grijalvas reacted instantly. He swung the Ingraham to the rear window and fired it, blowing out the remaining glass and demolishing the windshield of the car behind. He could see the two men in the car; their bodies were covered with blood and tiny nuggets of shattered glass. He yelled, "Put it in reverse," but he turned to see that Joachim had opened his door and was struggling to get out of the car. Joachim sprang out away from the car and took two steps, firing a burst toward the front car. Grijalvas saw the kneeling man kicked backward, and Joachim pivoted to return. He dived toward the open door, but a bullet seemed to turn his head in the air, and his body crashed against the side of the car, making it rock. Jesus fired wildly from the window at the car in front.

"Take the wheel," Grijalvas shouted, but Jesus seemed not to hear. Grijalvas climbed through the gaping space where the rear window had been and rolled off the trunk to the ground. He looked around him and could see the two pickup trucks blocking the road behind, and the car blocking the exit. Above loomed the bulbous bellies of the gigantic dinosaur statues.

As he looked, a burst of fire caught Jesus from somewhere on the other side of the car. His dead hand hung out the window above Grijalvas's head.

Grijalvas took a deep breath, then blew it out of his lungs. He crawled quickly toward the front car. When he reached the trunk of the car he stood up and fired a burst into the interior. Suddenly he realized there was no one inside. He opened the door and climbed in, sliding toward the driver's seat. He had his hand on the key when the man crouching in front of the car stood up. For an instant Grijalvas thought he might somehow be able to start the car and run over the man in time, but the man was already taking aim while he was thinking, and then he knew it was too late. He started to raise his hands, but the gun flashed. He carried with him into the darkness the sight of the man, and far over his head, the long neck of the brontosaur moving outward into the clear sky, and the tiny head with its little mouth gaping in surprise.

⚊ 32 ⚊

IT WAS THREE-THIRTY on Monday morning when Porterfield first noticed the car. He heard the idling engine at the end of the street as he was sitting alone in the darkened living room. He pushed the curtain aside and looked out to see the car move down the street as slowly as a man's walk and then stop, its headlights out. After a few seconds a man emerged wearing a dark sweat shirt and a knitted watch cap that was pulled down to his eyebrows. After he was out he bent over and picked up something from the back seat, then walked up the sidewalk with it. As he passed under the streetlamp, Porterfield released the curtain and made his way to the bedroom. The man had been carrying a thick stack of newspapers.

On Tuesday afternoon Porterfield left the Seyell Foundation office an hour early. That was the second time he noticed the car. When he turned the corner onto the street, the car was stopped in the same place. As he approached, the driver started the dusty brown Ford Galaxie and moved slowly down to the next corner and turned out of sight. There was no question in his mind that it was the same car. The ticking sound of the un-

250

balanced fan when the engine idled was the sound he'd heard the night before.

Porterfield said to Alice, "Do you know if our paper-boy—I guess I should say paperman—lives around here?"

"I see him quite often, but I've never spoken to him," said Alice. "Isn't that terrible? He's such a sweet-looking little boy, but there's something about seeing someone at five o'clock every morning in your bathrobe. The only way you can tolerate it is to avoid conversation."

Porterfield nodded. He was thinking about hunting turkeys. An old farmer had once told him the way he hunted wild turkeys was to take a walk in early summer to a clearing in the forest carrying a broom handle painted dark gray. He'd prop the broom handle on a fallen log or in the low branches of a bush and leave it there. The turkeys would get used to seeing it so that soon they'd strut within a few yards of it. By fall it would be so familiar to them that they didn't seem to see it anymore. On the first day of the turkey season the farmer would sit in the clearing. He swore the turkeys never noticed that the broom handle had been replaced by the barrel of a shotgun.

On Wednesday at three-thirty in the morning Porter-field heard the car's ticking fan as it turned the corner onto the street. It was easier to hear on Wednesday because Porterfield was sitting in the lawn chair on his neighbor's patio, and the redwood fence did nothing to muffle the sound in the still night air.

Porterfield stood up and looked between two boards of the fence. As usual, the man got out of his car and then reached back in for his stack of newspapers. This time when the man passed under the streetlamp Porter-field squinted to see his face. The watch cap was pulled down low over his brows, but Porterfield could see the small, dark eyes and the wide mouth under the bristling blond moustache.

The man walked up the sidewalk of Porterfield's house, then walked around to the window beside the driveway. Next he moved across the front lawn to a clump of bushes at the corner of the neighboring house. Porterfield watched him walk from house to house, examining shrubbery, standing under windows, and sighting angles and distances.

When the man turned and walked up the driveway toward Porterfield's garage, Porterfield slipped through the gate of the redwood fence and along his neighbor's hedge to the street.

It was nearly ten minutes before the man returned to his car. He opened the door and placed his stack of newspapers on the front seat, then slid into the seat beside them. He started the car and let it drift quietly down the street to the corner before he turned on his headlights.

Porterfield said, "Make much extra money peddling papers, Lester?"

The man jerked in his seat and half turned to gape over his shoulder. "Porterfield." After a second he seemed to collect himself. He steered around the corner and accelerated. "Not much money in papers these days, Ben."

"You're supposed to be in Guatemala, Viglione."

Viglione turned his head to the side and said, "No, you're wrong. Special assignment, temporary duty."

Porterfield chuckled. "Lester, when I heard we might be having this kind of trouble, I thought about who might show up, but I didn't think it would be you. I guess I should have. It's your specialty. But I didn't think anybody would take the chance of letting you in on it. You came to see me. Is someone at the Director's house?''

"What are you talking about? I'm just here for a conversation."

Porterfield sighed. "Lester, what is all this stuff back here?" Porterfield picked up a short, heavy hardwood stick connected by a few links of chain to a second stick. *"Nunchaku."* He opened a paper sack and poured several star-shaped plates of steel onto the back seat, so Viglione could hear the clinking. *"Shuriken.* What else? Piano wire, push knives. What is it with you, Lester? Don't they sell nine-millimeter ammo anymore, or are you just getting overconfident?''

"I'm not here for that."

"If it had been anything else they'd never have picked you."

"We worked together in the old days."

"I guess I remember you better than you remember me. Pull over up ahead and let me off, or I'll be half the night getting home to bed."

Viglione slowed the car and coasted to the curb. Porterfield swung his legs out on the left side and said, "I found the picture."

Viglione's right hand moved toward the pile of newspapers. Porterfield could see the gleam of the black metal finish of the pistol as the fingers fumbled for the handle, but Porterfield's right arm was already in motion. The *nunchaku* hissed in the air and the chain swung the club into the back of Viglione's head, making a hollow thud. Viglione's head kicked forward, but his hand came up with the pistol in it. Porterfield crooked his arm around Viglione's neck and pushed off on the door frame with both feet, twisting his body at the same time. Viglione's neck snapped with a sickening crack, and Porterfield released his hold. He knew Viglione was already dead.

Porterfield muttered to himself, "You'd have a hard time killing an old lady with those things." Then he spent a few moments wiping the handles of the *nunchaku* and collecting the papers from the back seat: the notations Viglione had made of the times Porterfield left home in the morning and returned at night, the crudely sketched map of the house and grounds, and the photograph of Alice.

⚼ 33 ⚼

PORTERFIELD WALKED DOWN the empty hallway, past closed doors with numbers above them but no signs. At five-thirty in the morning there were few people in this wing. Porterfield had made too many of these early morning trips to Langley in the past two weeks. The president of the Seyell Foundation had no business in the complex at Langley, and each time the car came for him Porterfield knew there was a chance he'd be spotted. Half the governments of the world might have people watching the roads in this area to see who came and went.

"Porterfield." The voice was quiet and familiar. He turned and waited while the tall black man came abreast of him, and they walked on together.

"You keep turning up pretty far from Miami, J.K."

"It's hot there right now."

"It's always hot there."

"So I always get out when I can. I have to go back tonight, but I wanted to see you first. I've got something to show you."

Porterfield stopped. "You wanted me?"

J.K. nodded. "This is probably the safest place." He opened the thick file folder he was carrying and pulled out two eight-by-ten-inch black-and-white photographs.

Porterfield studied the pictures. They were both photographs of crowds of people in airline terminals. In the first one a group of passengers was moving along a corridor toward the camera, carrying small bags and briefcases. In the foreground was a middle-aged man with a high forehead and broad cheekbones and wearing a dark suit. "Who's this?"

"He works at the Czechoslovakian embassy in Bogotà. He's here legally and everything, but we've been taking lots of pictures of those flights lately. In the other picture the mark is the stewardess. She seems to be a courier for somebody, but at the moment we're just watching. Forget those two. Take a close look at the other people, the ones in the background."

Porterfield held the photographs at arm's length and lifted them close to the light in the ceiling. "Damned eyes aren't as sharp as they used to be." He squinted at the faces. "Okay, I see him. It's Albert what's-his-name."

"Cotton. The flight list says he's somebody else, but they seem to have made a mistake."

"Did he follow this guy from Panama City?"

"That's the mistake. According to the Latin America desk, Cotton is still in Panama City. This was a flight from Toronto."

Porterfield studied the second photograph. "I'm getting good at this, now that I know the game. How many monkeys do you see in this picture? Oh, yes. There he is. The one with the moustache is Lester Viglione. I worked with him once, years ago."

"He's on a Special Ops detail attached to the

Guatemala secret police, the ones that were supposedly disbanded. Now they only work nights."

Porterfield shrugged. "It leaves him the daytime for travel."

"He hasn't been in this country for over ten years."

"Who told you all that?"

"I have lots of friends, because I do lots of favors." He put the photographs back in the folder and said, "Both of those were people who got wind of your little problem, asked permission to come home, and were refused."

Porterfield said, "Thanks, J.K. I'll take care of it. Keep it to yourself."

"Take care of it? You know what I think they're doing? I think they're coming to see the Director. And if I just happened to notice these two in a couple of pictures, how many others are there? They'll have to stand in line to get a shot at him."

"Thanks, J.K. I'll take care of it. I owe you another favor." Porterfield turned the corner and left J.K. standing alone in the empty corridor. Porterfield made another turn and stopped at a plain door marked only with the number 412, and knocked.

Goldschmidt's voice shouted, "Come in," and Porterfield opened the door. "Hello, Ben. Did you come all the way out here again for this fiasco voluntarily, or did that fool order you to come?"

"The Director wanted us all there." He glanced at his watch. "We've got a couple of minutes. You can make a call for me."

"Sure. What is it?"

"Arrange to have some medical people standing by for an in-house autopsy, probably within twenty-four hours. The papers can say suicide or something."

"But they only do that when an agent is killed."

"I know. Better make sure there's room for two."

WHEN Porterfield reached the conference room, Kearns was sitting alone, staring at an oversized brown square on the table.

"What's that?"

"It's a menu. Under it there's an order sheet that says 'Director's Breakfast.' Apparently we are here for the Director's breakfast. Is that a good sign or a bad sign?"

Goldschmidt entered and nodded at Porterfield, then said to Kearns, "Bad. It means we'll be here for four or five hours."

"But did the Palm Springs thing work?"

Porterfield shrugged. "Order champagne and see if anybody crosses it out."

The door swung open and Pines held it while the Director passed him, not slowing his quick, jerky strides until he reached the head of the table. He sat down and Pines handed him a file folder, which he flipped open and studied in silence.

The others waited. Pines walked around the table and picked up the menu and handed it to Porterfield. "Just write in your orders and they'll be here to pick it up in a minute."

"I'd like to know whether I'm going to feel like eating," said Goldschmidt.

Porterfield handed the menu back to Pines. "Just coffee for me. I should be back in Washington before there are too many people on the street."

The Director looked up from his file and began talking as though he'd heard nothing. "It's now two-thirty in the morning in California." He paused. "The first phase of this ended about a half hour ago." He held his arms out and grasped the round, imaginary object between his hands, then stared through it at the opposite wall of the room. "The initial reports give us some cause for hopefulness and some cause for—for disappointment."

"Who got killed?" asked Goldschmidt.

The Director seemed to lift his invisible globe out of the way as he stared down at the file again. "We seem to have lost four men. John Knox Morrison and Kevin Morton were shot down in some kind of chalet at the top of a mountain near Palm Springs. The other two seem to have been hit within the last hour at . . . it says here 'the Dinosaur Memorial.' Is that possible?"

Pines said, "Yes, sir. It's a tourist attraction on the main highway between Palm Springs and Los Angeles. Big statues of dinosaurs in the desert."

The Director looked at him. "How odd. At any rate, we don't have their names yet. They were apparently part of the team that was supposed to block the escape of the terrorists. I haven't been informed yet about the details."

Goldschmidt said, "A dinosaur stampede?"

Porterfield leaned forward. "You said something about hope. You mean the papers have actually been recovered?"

"Not yet, but the report we received indicates that there were seven terrorists involved, and the operational group allowed none to escape. At this moment our people will be using every means to discover their identities. Raids will be conducted before morning."

Goldschmidt shook his head. "Eleven people killed in public places—four of ours, seven of theirs, and nothing to show for it. And these raids you're talking about, no doubt the people left to guard the papers will throw down their arms and come quietly."

"This is the easy part," Pines said. "We're certain that this is a small, tightly knit terrorist cadre from somewhere in Latin America. They may not come quietly, but believe me, they'll come. We have nearly two hundred operational men out there already, and there will be more before the first raid."

Porterfield glanced at Kearns, who was staring absently at the menu, his mouth hanging open. "And how many people involved in the support and communication?"

Pines said proudly, "Over a thousand. As the Director told you two days ago, this time we took the threat seriously."

Kearns winced. "But that means over twelve hundred people know what's happened?"

"What do you mean?" asked the Director. "Of course these are handpicked people."

"There is no such thing as twelve hundred handpicked people," Kearns said. "You don't even know the names of all the ones killed. That means the people with them didn't know their real names either."

"If there's someone you're worried about—"

"You!" said Kearns. "Before this happened there were people whose lives were in jeopardy all over Latin America, and who knew it, and knew you were doing nothing to protect them. Now you've got twelve hundred—"

Pines interrupted. "If you're going to bring all that up again, we might as well just give up."

Porterfield said quietly, "You could do what we've been asking you to all along, pull the people home who have a reason to be afraid. It may be too late to negotiate with the ones who have the papers, since you've betrayed them twice."

The Director smiled. "But we've got them, blasted

them off the face of the earth. We're going to go through with the mopping up.''

Porterfield's eyes suddenly seemed to lose their luster. The lids half-covered them, and he stared at the Director with a look that might have been boredom. He seemed to be old and tired. "Is that your final word?"

"Of course."

Goldschmidt slowly stood up, pressing his palms against the table to support himself. His face was pale and he was sweating. "Excuse me, please. I just remembered I got a number wrong on an important telephone call I made a few minutes ago." He walked to the door and stopped. "For the record, I'd like to say I agree with Ben." He opened the door, then said, "But I forget—that's ridiculous, isn't it? There is no record." He left, closing the door behind him.

Pines said to the Director, "I wonder if we shouldn't all take Mr. Goldschmidt's lead. Mr. Porterfield and Mr. Kearns have given their opinions. They didn't wait for the reports from California, but I don't think that would change anything. Would it, Mr. Kearns?"

Kearns shook his head and stood up. "I don't think so." His voice changed, and he seemed to be pleading. "Don't you see? We don't have to worry about one little gang of terrorists. We've got the makings of a revolt inside the Company. Seventy-eight people so far, and any one of them knows more than Donahue did. Any one of them can do more than these terrorists have done. Any one of them—"

"Thank you," said the Director and stood up. Kearns took one long look at Porterfield, then turned and walked out of the room.

Pines walked to the Director's seat and picked up the file from the table. Porterfield remained seated, leaning down to lift his briefcase slowly to his lap. His face had not changed. He looked at the two through half-lidded eyes.

The Director smiled compassionately at Porterfield. "Ben, I admire your guts. I always have. You're an old pro who's spent a lot of time in the field and is used to doing things on your own and relying on your own wits to stay alive. But I can't have you doing this to me. You see what the problem is?"

Porterfield was silent for a moment. The hand in his briefcase stopped moving. "Yes. I do." The Director and Pines looked at each other. Porterfield said, "You are both people who aren't up to what you're doing."

The Director flipped his hand at Pines, urging him to leave. Pines turned on his heel and took a step, but there was a sharp, spitting sound and his head jerked and he walked into the wall. He took another step and collapsed. The Director looked down at Pines. The side of his head was already oozing blood. It ran down his temple to his neck and then to the floor to form a pool that grew as he watched.

The Director froze, as though he couldn't step across the body. Then he bent over and looked at it closely. He pointed at the floor. "I suppose that mess is his brain. I see the bullet hole, and that's what came with it, isn't it?" He turned to face Porterfield, standing straight. "You've done it now. I'm sure you know. There are people waiting for us outside the door."

Porterfield stood up. "Yes." He aimed carefully with both hands, and the gun spat again. The Director's head slammed against the wall, and his body fell forward to the floor.

Goldschmidt opened the door and slipped into the room. "The meeting's over?"

Porterfield walked to the Director's body and nudged

it with his toe. "Did you take care of the arrangements?"

Goldschmidt shook his head. "I didn't have to. Yesterday afternoon Pines ordered the autopsy team to report this morning." Goldschmidt stopped and studied Porterfield. "They were expecting to lose agents on this."

Porterfield picked up his briefcase and moved toward the door. "Can you take care of the cleanup?"

Goldschmidt sat on the table and stared down at the bodies on the floor. "I've already talked to the people at the gate. You didn't come here this morning."

"What about Kearns?"

"He was the one who told the Director's bodyguards to take a break."

⚞ 34 ⚟

Washington—(UPI)—In a press conference at
noon today the White House announced the deaths
of William Blount, Director of the Central Intelligence Agency, and Deputy Director Arthur Pines,
reputed to be Blount's most trusted assistant. The
two officials were victims of an automobile accident which occurred while they were beginning a
surprise inspection of several outlying installations
in the vicinity of the CIA headquarters at Langley,
Virginia, shortly before dawn. Within seconds of
the accident an escort vehicle reached the scene and
rushed the victims to the nearest medical facility, a
CIA emergency station near Langley. Both were
declared dead on arrival. Autopsies have been conducted by the agency. As yet there has been no indication of foul play, but a White House spokesman
said that the President has ordered the agency to
conduct a thorough investigation, saying that in the
deaths of two key members of the intelligence community the possibility can never be ruled out.

Chinese Gordon tossed the newspaper on the floor.

As Kepler reached for it, the huge dog lunged past him, pushing his arm aside, and scooped up the newspaper in its jaws, then bounded for the open door of the garage.

"What the hell was that?" said Kepler.

Outside they heard Margaret's voice. "Oh, sweetie, what a wonderful big boy you are. Thank you," she sang.

"She's trying to teach him to bring the paper in," Chinese Gordon muttered. "He doesn't get the idea yet. He keeps grabbing it and running out the door. That's the third time today."

Kepler popped the top of a beer can and stared at Chinese Gordon. "You really ought to break him of that."

Chinese Gordon's jaw tightened, the muscles on the side of his face working convulsively. He said quietly, "I'd like to do that. I'd like to. What do you think of the car accident?"

Kepler sipped his beer. "You train the cat too?" Chinese Gordon looked up to see Doctor Henry Metzger walking backward, laboriously dragging a large turkey leg through the kitchen doorway onto the balcony.

"Margaret probably gave him a treat," he lied. He remembered leaving it out on the counter when he was making room for Kepler's beer in the refrigerator. "He likes turkey."

"He must."

"What about the car accident?"

"It would be hard to know what really happened to them, but I agree with the President. Foul play can never be ruled out—or something like that. That good big sweetie out there nearly tore my arm off fetching the paper out into the alley, so I don't remember the exact words. I suppose they might have gone along to watch their agents spring the trap on the late lamented Jorge Grijalvas and gotten taken out.''

"Doesn't sound likely, does it? I mean, those two weren't career spooks, they were appointed. They were both fat-assed businessmen a year ago.''

Margaret walked in the door wearing large saucer-shaped sunglasses and a bathing suit. The dog followed her, with the newspaper still clenched in its jaws, leaping with pleasure and uttering muffled grunts. "Here's the paper,'' she said. The dog rushed up and dropped the newspaper on the floor. It was wet and had been chewed through in the middle.

Kepler looked down at it. "Smart as a whip, and a mouth like velvet. If we could get him to fetch those Donahue papers, our problems would be over.''

Margaret passed on up the stairs. At the top she called, "Chinese, you can't give Doctor Henry Metzger a whole turkey leg. He'll choke on the bones." Then she said more quietly, "Come on, Doctor Henry, let me cut that up for you.''

Kepler sipped his beer and studied Chinese Gordon. "That's curious," Kepler said. Then his eyes seemed to brighten. "No, I guess you're right. Those two were too important and therefore worthless for a night operation in the great outdoors. Let me look at the newschow and see how much of it I can read." He gingerly peeled off part of the front page and examined the article. After a few moments he said, "In-house doctors, in-house autopsy, only CIA people on the scene. If they weren't at Jorge's final fiesta I'd say they were burned by their own band of merry men.''

Chinese Gordon nodded. "Okay, if that's true, what does it mean?''

"A man whose animals outsmart him should not pretend he's Socrates. Stop asking me questions you think you know the answers to.''

Margaret leaned over the balcony and said to Chinese Gordon, ''Immelmann's on his way, and I told him to bring a fresh newspaper.''

Kepler said, ''Good, you can show him your dog's reverse fetch.''

Chinese Gordon shrugged. ''I don't know why I waste my time talking to you. Margaret, tell him your theory.''

''What I think is that these two did not die in a car accident. They didn't die at Palm Springs either. Therefore they were killed. The CIA is hiding the way it really happened, so they must have killed them. It doesn't matter why they did it, what matters is that there are new people making the decisions now who know that the Director was killed.''

''So?''

''So even if it had nothing to do with the Donahue papers, they'll be much more interested in keeping them a secret, because they have a whole new reason to worry about setting off an investigation.''

''I suppose so.''

''You suppose so?'' said Immelmann from the doorway. The dog rushed to Kepler, snapped up the soggy newspaper again, and ran with it to Immelmann. ''No thanks, old fella. I brought my own. Hey, Margaret, you're doing great with him.''

''Yeah,'' said Kepler. ''She's teaching him to take out the garbage.''

Immelmann said, ''Well, what did you decide? Are we going to take them up on it?''

''Up on what?'' said Chinese Gordon.

''I thought that was why you wanted me to bring my

newspaper. Didn't you read it? They made us another offer.''

Washington—(AP)—Benjamin Porterfield, who recently left the Mr. Food Corporation to become president of the prestigious Washington-based Seyell Foundation, announced to the Foundation's trustees today the results of the independent audit he ordered upon assuming the post. The audit, conducted by the Maryland firm of Crabtree and Bacon, revealed that the Seyell Foundation has approximately five million dollars less than had been reported in last year's audit. Mr. David Welby of Crabtree and Bacon said that it is customary for audits to be conducted whenever there is a change of power in a foundation of this kind, and that there is no implication of dishonesty on the part of previous officers of the trust.

"Actually," said Welby, "it's a series of bookkeeping errors made ten to twenty years ago and perpetuated. Tax-exempt organizations are regularly audited, but mainly to see whether someone is doing something he shouldn't. Nobody, including the government, is interested when a foundation reports its assets too high." When asked for examples, he mentioned that there was an entry in the list of assets of $619,352 for a house owned by Theophilus Seyell. Welby became curious because the location of the house in New York would indicate a higher value, and later learned that the house had been given to the city in 1954, and the cash value included in the foundation's report as a cash asset. "It's sort of pitiful," said Welby. "The money was counted twice but never existed."

•   •   •

PORTERFIELD sat behind the gigantic desk in the Seyell Foundation office and stared across the room at the wall where the portrait of Theophilus "Just Plain Ted" Seyell hung above the door. He had already decided it had to go. In the days when Just Plain Ted had occupied this office, before it had been dismantled and transported to Washington, that space had been taken up for thirty years by a portrait of Seyell's father, painted from Seyell's description by a young artist of limited talent. Seyell's father had been long dead by the time Just Plain Ted had become rich enough to require an ancestor. He'd reacted to the need with his usual common sense by hiring the artist who would work cheapest, a man who made his living dashing off caricatures at Coney Island for a quarter each on Sunday afternoons. It was the first time the man had been able to afford to work with oils on canvas, and the result was something like a police reconstruction of an old man wanted for long-forgotten crimes involving piracy on the high seas and the deflowering of virgins. When Just Plain Ted had seen it, the story went, he'd pronounced it satisfactory and paid the artist the thirteen dollars he'd agreed to. Then he'd said to one of his vice-presidents, "Hang the old son of a bitch up there where I can gloat at him now and then."

During the inventory of the Foundation's records the old painting had been found behind a filing cabinet in the basement, and Porterfield had decided that the time had come to hang it again.

Kearns walked into the room and sat down in the armchair in front of the desk.

Porterfield raised his hand. "Thanks for coming.

And tell Goldschmidt I saw the articles in the paper. They should be fine.''

Kearns nodded. "The transfers are going pretty well. If we can assume that the people who dropped out of sight have the sense to take care of themselves until this thing is cleared up, we'll be able to protect just about everybody."

"I don't suppose anything turned up since I talked to you?"

Kearns stared at the pattern on the carpet. "You knew it wouldn't. These people all worked for Jorge Grijalvas. Nothing about him seems to have any political implications. He was just an old-time gangster. He did pretty well in the Los Angeles drug trade and had a lot of very nasty people on his payroll, but there's no way we can hunt down all of his connections. Every piece of paper he and his friends owned has been examined, and none of it is worth anything. We did get a hell of a haul in weapons and cash, and quite an assortment of drugs, of course."

"Just what we need."

"There's no sign of the papers, no sign that he ever had a van rigged with a twenty-millimeter automatic cannon. We thought that somewhere he might have some ammunition for it, a few spare parts, something."

Porterfield sighed. "I keep wondering about all this. Grijalvas doesn't fit."

"Maybe someone he met in the drug trade, somebody big enough to think there was a point to this, just hired him to handle the dirty part of it. He must have had some pretty serious international transactions."

"All along they wanted money instead of political concessions but were willing to let a man like that get his hands on the cash."

"If they were big enough to hire him, they'd be big

enough to make sure he didn't rob them. They're capable of shutting down the city of Los Angeles when they feel like making a point.''

"And yet they needed to send him to Palm Springs, and without the papers to trade, not so much as a photocopy. If they had any notion there was a possibility we'd pay off, wouldn't they have given him that much? It might have helped him and would actually strengthen their bargaining position.''

"With us, not with him.''

"Exactly.''

"He was just a sucker?''

Porterfield leaned back in Theophilus Seyell's chair and gazed at the vaulted ceiling. "He's dead, isn't he?''

The telephone on the desk buzzed and Porterfield leaned forward to pick up the receiver. "Yes?''

Mrs. Goode's voice said, "I think it's the call you were waiting for. When I asked who it was, he said, 'Captain Greed. Put Porterfield on.' ''

"Thanks, I'll take it.'' Porterfield pushed the button on his telephone and said, "Hello, Captain. This is Ben Porterfield.''

The voice sounded young, the accent flat, maybe Californian and maybe Midwestern but definitely American. "No time for amenities. Do you really have five million dollars in cash?''

"Yes.''

"Bring it with you to Washington National. I'll expect you within a half hour, alone.''

"See you then,'' said Porterfield, and hung up the telephone.

"Who was that?'' said Kearns.

"Nothing very important, I suppose, but I've got to keep seeing these damned professors or people are going to wonder if the Seyell Foundation is what it appears to be. I've got to meet one of them at the airport in a half hour."

"He calls himself Captain?" said Kearns as he stood up.

Porterfield chuckled. "If that were the worst thing about him he'd be practically normal. I'll talk to you in a day or two."

As soon as Kearns disappeared, Porterfield buzzed Mrs. Goode. "Please get me a taxi. And don't tell anyone about that telephone call for twenty-four hours. If I haven't gotten in touch by then, tell Goldschmidt. Meanwhile, tell Alice I had to go to London and I'll call her." He put on his suitcoat and straightened his tie, then went to Theophilus Seyell's closet and pulled out the two large suitcases. They were heavy, but with the small casters on the bottoms he could wheel them most of the way, he thought. It would have been easier if he could have afforded some help, but he'd have to manage. He couldn't take the chance that someone in the Company would change his mind without warning and see a chance for another trap. This time it had to be ended. Goldschmidt and Kearns, at least, were old guard. He'd sometimes trusted his life to their decisions. But they'd both been in Langley too long. There was no way to tell how they would react when it actually came down to experiencing the feeling of losing.

⩓ 35 ⩓

PORTERFIELD STOOD ASIDE and let the cabdriver haul the heavy suitcases out of the trunk but waved the waiting Skycap away from them. He wheeled the two suitcases along the walk, bending slightly at the knees to reach the handles while the porter leaned on his two-wheel dolly, shaking his head in disdain.

The pneumatic doors hissed and admitted Porterfield to the lobby. He made his way to a row of plastic seats along the window and sat down, his knees pressed against the two suitcases. He was sweating from the exertion, and his wristwatch had worked its way around to the inside of his wrist. As he adjusted the watch he confirmed that time was still with him. He had two minutes to spare, enough time to reach a telephone and call Langley. Porterfield let the thought exist for a moment, then dismissed it. Nothing had changed except that his fifty-nine-year-old body was preparing to remind him that it wasn't in its prime. The quick reactions, the flexibility and force were gone, and now the way to stay alive was to think farther ahead.

The air was filled with the constant murmur of voices and the hum of conveyor belts and the rumble of bag-

gage carts, but when the public-address system was
activated there was an immediate change, a low hiss
that seemed to muffle the random sounds and swallow
them up. "Mr. Porterfield," said the calm, unchang-
ing female voice, "please pick up a white courtesy
phone. Mr. Porterfield, please pick up a white courtesy
phone."

He stood up and looked around him. There was a
white telephone a few yards away on a counter that
jutted from the wall. He considered pushing the suitcases over to it but decided not to. They were so big that
he'd attract attention pushing them around the lobby,
and if they announced his name enough times someone
who knew him might hear it. He rushed to the telephone
and turned to face his suitcases as he said, "This is
Mr. Porterfield."

The telephone sounded dead. A second later there
was a ringing. He waited, and it rang three times before
there was a click. There was faint music and a recorded
male voice said, "Please stand by."

Porterfield watched as a young blond woman and
three small children walked up and sat down behind the
suitcases. He found himself humming along with the
recorded music. The male voice came on again. "Please
stand by."

The middle child, a fat little boy wearing a T-shirt
that said "Redskins," straddled one of Porterfield's
suitcases as though he were riding a horse, jumping up
and down and slapping the side with his hand. Porterfield winced. "Please stand by." The mother looked on
with bovine serenity as the little boy discovered that the
suitcase had wheels under it. He leaned forward like a
jockey and pushed off the floor with his feet, coasting a
yard into the middle of a passing family of Japanese
tourists, who eyed him with benevolent amusement. The

smallest child, a little girl in a bright red dress that had a bow in the back, tried to climb onto the second suitcase.

"Please stand by." Porterfield's jaw tightened. The little girl's legs weren't long enough to mount the suitcase. She struggled to get on, beginning to whine. The oldest child, a boy about ten who had reached the age where his body was thinner and longer than his little brother's, lifted his little sister and set her on the suitcase, then began to push the suitcase along the row of seats, barely missing the feet of an elderly man who was studying his ticket with a fretful look on his face.

"Please stand—" There was another click, and the female voice said, "May I help you?"

"I'm Mr. Porterfield."

"Please hold on." The three children were now riding the suitcases back and forth over the floor, their mother laughing and clapping her hands. Porterfield felt his collar beginning to tighten. The telephone clicked again. "Mr. Porterfield?"

He tried to sound calm. "Yes?"

"Your ticket is waiting for you at the American Airlines counter. Please don't wait in line, go directly to the check-in area. You only have a few minutes."

He hung up the phone and walked toward his suitcases. As he approached the nearest one, the oldest boy pushed the suitcase too hard. His little sister glided along for a few feet, then the case turned abruptly and toppled over. The little girl's eyes widened as she fell off, and Porterfield saw her knee hit the floor. She lay there for a count of five as she gathered her breath for the scream.

Porterfield arrived in time to bend over her and say, "You're okay, honey. Let's get you up." He lifted her to her feet, and she stared at him with a look of indecision.

The mother made her way slowly to the little girl, saying, "See? See what happens?"

Porterfield righted his suitcase and stepped toward the other as the little boy scooted away from him. Porterfield said, "Sorry, partner. Got to catch a plane."

The little boy shouted, "No! I'm not through."

Porterfield turned to the mother for help, but she had picked up the little girl and was glowering at Porterfield with some irrational sense of injury. "Come on, now. I'm in a hurry," he said and lifted the little boy to the floor. The little boy struggled and let out a yell of frustration, then ran to his mother.

Porterfield sighed and wheeled the suitcase beside the other one, then pushed the two toward the American Airlines counter. Behind him he could hear that the two younger children had agreed on a decision and were now screaming in concert, competing for their mother's attention.

Suddenly Porterfield heard footsteps behind him, then something jabbed his shoulder. He turned to see a man in his thirties, tall and thin, with his hair in a windblown fluffy halo around his head, and wearing tinted glasses.

"What did you do to my kids?"

"Not a thing. They were playing and one of them fell." Porterfield turned and started to push his suitcases forward.

The man grabbed his arm. "Oh no you don't."

Porterfield stood straight, then slowly turned to face the man. The man looked surprised when he saw Porterfield turn, as though he had somehow misjudged and was beginning to sense his mistake. Porterfield's eyes narrowed and his mouth assumed a look that could have been a smile. He said quietly, "I am about to miss a flight, and it's very important that I make it. Ask your wife what happened.''

The man hesitated, then raised his voice. "You can't treat my kids that way.''

Porterfield's hand moved so quickly that only the most curious observer could have noticed. It was at his side, and then it was on the man's shoulder. It appeared to be a friendly gesture, the collar of the man's shirt hiding the fact that Porterfield's right thumb was slowly crushing the man's trachea. Porterfield's smile broadened and he leaned close to him, whispering conspiratorially, "I'm really in a hurry and I don't want to be bothered. Go back to your cow of a wife and the three little pigs and tell them you scared the hell out of me.'' Porterfield let up on his grip, and the man's mouth hung open. He gasped for air, his hands going to his neck.

Porterfield gave him a final pat on the shoulder and whispered, "Go on." The man staggered back a step, then seemed to regain his composure. By the time he reached his disgruntled family his weak-kneed walk had acquired what could have been a swagger.

At the desk Porterfield said, "You have a ticket in the name Porterfield?''

"Yes, sir,'' said a young man in a blue blazer and handed him an envelope.

Porterfield glanced inside. San Diego via Los Angeles. It was going to be a long night, he thought.

"Check your bags, sir.'' It wasn't a question.

"Fine,'' said Porterfield, and accepted the two baggage stubs.

"Gate 78,'' said the man. "You'd better hurry.''

Porterfield walked quickly across the lobby toward the bank of escalators that led to the metal-detectors and then beyond to the airplanes, not looking back.

• • •

PORTERFIELD spent the time on the airplane reading magazines. There seemed to be nothing on this flight except the journals for money fanciers—magazines that contained excruciatingly detailed accounts of the economic exploits of men who were photographed with their coats off but their shirts unwrinkled and their ties clasped beneath stiff, immaculate collars. These men were all referred to as "CEOs" who had moved from one company to another because of their love of a challenge. There were other magazines that seemed to be all advertisements for objects that cost thousands of dollars and were handmade by European craftsmen. They were all special, some in limited edition, some numbered and signed, some just called rare. There were also beautiful advertisements for hotels in cities where he'd spent time—most of them tropical cities on the ocean, where large, futuristic buildings along the beach were crowded from behind by filthy shacks made of sheet metal and discarded plywood anchored in the rain-soaked mud. He slept for the last hour of the flight and awoke feeling calm and rested. As the airplane descended, he gazed out the window at the array of lights in the Los Angeles basin, fluttering and blinking in the distance. He reached into his pocket and glanced at his ticket again. He'd have only a few minutes to catch the airplane to San Diego. He would have liked to telephone Alice, but this was their home ground and they'd be watching him for that. Besides, Mrs. Goode would have reached Alice hours ago.

The crowd of people leaned and wobbled and bumped each other as they made their way down the aisle toward the door. Porterfield waited for an opening and joined them. He knew Los Angeles International

Airport, and his baggage was checked through to San
Diego, so he felt calm and resigned. The flight to San
Diego was only forty-five minutes, and then this would
be over. They'd have some way of throwing off any trap
he might have set for them, but the exact nature of it
didn't pique his curiosity. He only hoped it didn't de-
mand that they kill him.

He yawned as he stepped across the threshold into the
carpeted corridor and walked toward the terminal. He
walked to the television screen mounted on the pillar in
the center of the room and looked for his flight, then
went to Gate 19, picked a bench away from the crowds,
and sat down. It would only be a few minutes.

He heard the voice on the public-address system, and
it sounded exactly like the one he'd heard in Washington. "Mr. Porterfield, please pick up a white courtesy
phone. Mr. Porterfield."

Porterfield walked down the hall and picked up the
telephone. To his surprise, there was a voice on the
other end. "Mr. Porterfield?"

"Yes."

"Please come to the American Airlines desk at Gate
72."

Porterfield said, "I'll be right there." He smiled. It
was simple enough. There would be another ticket
waiting for him, and another flight to another city. It
was the trick, the way they'd planned to break up the
trap. It wasn't bad. They'd have redirected his baggage
with the change in reservations. They were watching
him now, he was sure. There was no way he could let
anyone know where he was going.

At the end of the corridor he entered another large
waiting area, the mirror image of the one he'd passed
through moments ago. As he made his way toward the
desk at Gate 72 something seemed to be wrong. There

was no young man in a blue blazer to meet him, only
another passenger waiting there. He noticed that the
passenger was a girl with long brown hair and a rather
good figure, then she turned toward him and he noticed
that she had large, clear green eyes. He moved up beside
her to wait for the attendant to return.

Suddenly the girl turned and threw her arms around
him, smiling. "Daddy!"

PORTERFIELD stood still while the young woman embraced him hard, her hands moving to his back. He
said, "You don't really have to frisk me. You saw me
get off an airplane."

"That's true, but you probably have a little card on
you that says you can even shoot people on airplanes
when you're in the mood, and electronic underpants
that jam the metal detectors."

"Interesting idea," he said, returning the woman's
embrace so she could finish her search.

She reached into his breast pocket and extracted the
envelope with his ticket in it, then appeared to study it.
"Okay, time to move on." She walked across the lobby
and Porterfield followed. They walked to the line of
people waiting to board the flight to San Diego.

As they waited in the line, Porterfield said, "We seem
to have made the flight. Are you going with me?"

She stared at him. "I'll be with you. Other people
too."

As they neared the portal at the narrow corridor
leading to the airplane, people huddled closer, and
Porterfield felt himself bumped twice. He decided not
to speak. She didn't seem to care if he asked questions,
but in the press of the crowd he knew she wouldn't
answer. As they reached the doorway she grasped Por-

terfield's hand and pulled him to the side.

"Something wrong?" he asked.

"No problem. Come on." Then he noticed that she no longer held his ticket. She must have handed it off to someone in the crowd, he thought, but he resisted the temptation to look down the corridor to see which one it might be. He followed her across the lobby again, and they sat down together.

She lit a cigarette and said, "I noticed you're not wearing a bulletproof vest."

"Should I be?" He smiled. His sportcoat had panels of Dupont Kevlar sewn into it, so it would stop any bullet smaller than a .45 caliber.

The young woman shrugged. 'It's your wardrobe, but I would have thought something like that would be required if you want to dress for success in your line of work."

"Or yours."

"I'm flat enough as it is. But the point is this. You're not some kind of kamikaze, are you? Eager to die for the cause?"

"I'd prefer not to. What's the cause?"

"We thought you might be a little cranky about what's happened."

"If the money is all you want, I don't think we have much to worry about. I didn't set any traps. I didn't know I was going on a flight. If I had, I wouldn't have known where. Most people would have assumed it would be any place but Los Angeles."

The young woman looked away from him through the large plate-glass windows. The airplane was slowly moving toward the runway. She blew smoke in the air, then pushed her cigarette into the ashtray. "I hope you're telling the truth, but we'll know in a minute when we try to get out of here."

They stood up and walked to the escalator, then rode it down to the ground floor and stepped onto the moving walkway. In front a family wearing Hawaiian shirts blocked them from passing, but the young woman didn't seem to care. They stood on the long conveyor and drifted sedately toward the main foyer. In a moment, Porterfield knew, they'd be past the bank of metal detectors. From here on there would be danger. Armed men could reach this part of the airport from the parking lots without even passing security guards. He said quietly, "Did you have the courtesy to make a return reservation for me?"

She said, "Here. You might as well have this." She reached into her purse and produced another airline ticket.

Porterfield accepted the ticket and studied it, then said, "This plane leaves in forty-five minutes. Am I going to make it?"

"As your travel agent, I sincerely hope so. You will unless you managed to get word of your itinerary to someone."

"How could I do that?"

"The airplane has a radio, and I'm sure you also have a little card that says you can use everybody's radio."

"No, my electronic underpants cause static."

The couple in front of them wearing Hawaiian shirts whispered together. The husband shook his head, but the wife said loudly, "He said 'electronic underpants.' I heard him."

When they reached the end of the conveyor the young woman walked across the main foyer and through the exit to the sidewalk. Hundreds of people were moving into and out of the airline terminal, taxis stopped and started, pudgy little buses deposited streams of passengers. Porterfield said, "What now? We drive to a desert shack and hold me hostage for another''—he glanced at his watch—''thirty-eight minutes?''

"Some other time. Our desert shack is being re-modeled, so the paint's still tacky in the guest room. You'll have to drop in and see us later. We're expecting to be able to entertain more lavishly soon."

"Thank you. I'd enjoy that. What do we do while we're waiting?" He stepped back to allow a cabdriver to swing a suitcase onto the curb.

"Nothing," she said, and put her arm in Porter-field's, walking him to the bench beside the wall. "Sit here, relax. Some nice men in cars out there in the darkness have rifles trained on you right now. Some others are in the airport waiting for you to make a move, so you won't be lonely. Right now I have to leave you, but I'll be back." She turned and walked down the sidewalk and into the terminal again.

Porterfield looked out at the thousands of cars in the lot, then scanned the five-story parking ramp across the drive. He could see nothing for certain—there were silhouettes of heads in many of the cars, and people stood on some of the tiers of the parking ramps, some fumbling with baggage, others just loitering, apparently without another way to pass the time before they ex-pected an airplane to arrive or leave. Probably she hadn't lied, and at least one of them was there to blow his head off if something went wrong. There was no reason to doubt it, and he knew he wouldn't do any-thing different if there were no one watching.

The plan wasn't bad, he thought. Even if he'd man-aged to shake the woman and get to a telephone, there was no way he could have done anything. He could tell the San Diego field office that a person arriving on the seven-thirty flight would pick up two brown suitcases that he had baggage claims to match. It would have taken longer than the three-quarter-hour flight even to organize a team, and then they'd see fifty or sixty people arrive and pick up two brown suitcases each. They had no way to arrest anyone or even examine the suitcases. Meanwhile, Porterfield would be here with guns trained on him. It wasn't bad. He smiled as he glanced at his watch again. It was after seven-thirty already, and the baggage would now be rolling down the ramp in the San Diego airport. He waited.

The young woman appeared again far down the sidewalk. He watched as she walked toward him. She had one hand in her purse, fumbling around for something. His jaw tightened, then the hand emerged and it held a cigarette and a lighter. He leaned back on the bench and sighed.

She stopped in front of the bench and lit the cigarette. "Stretch your legs, Daddy. You've got a long flight ahead of you."

"That's a relief." Porterfield stood up. "My wife will be pleased. I left word I might be gone for a couple of days."

"You people have wives?" She seemed startled.

"Sure. Wives, kids. Of course, my kids are grown up and married. We even had a dog, but he died a few years ago."

They walked on in silence between the metal detectors, along the moving walkway, and up the escalator to the boarding area. Finally she stopped him. "Wait. Here's the locker key. Inside the locker is the original set of papers. You've got a minute or two. Don't bother to be careful about the briefcase or the papers. There aren't any fingerprints on anything."

He stared at her. "That's not necessary. We have copies."

"But we wanted you to know, and we thought that if you had them back—"

"Know what?"

"That it's over. As of this minute, we're out of this business. There's no reason now to hunt for us."

Porterfield handed the key back to her. "Do me a favor. Just take it with you and burn it. Burn the other copies you have. Forget you ever saw it." He turned and walked to the boarding gate.

∧ 36 ∧

GOLDSCHMIDT SAT IN the massive leather armchair in front of Porterfield's desk. Far behind him on the wall above the door the portrait of Theophilus Seyell's father stared into the room like a malevolent voyeur at a window. Goldschmidt said, "If we devote sufficient time and energy to it, the problem can be settled."

Porterfield leaned back and studied Theophilus Seyell's father. It was an impossible face, the features a child's imagination would create to complete the specter that seemed to materialize at night among the clothes in his darkened closet. "There isn't any problem unless we invent one. Everyone who might have been vulnerable has been rotated. Most of the people responsible for the papers are dead."

"But there are still interests that need to be insured."

Porterfield nodded. "Of course."

"I'll start organizing a field team as quietly as possible. My own people may be the only ones I can afford to use right now, but—"

"Don't bother."

"Given the time and the resources, anyone can be hunted down. And these people have too much money to remain invisible for long."

"No. I'll handle it."

"Ben, be reasonable. The first time we heard of these people it was because they attacked a college campus with an automatic cannon. For all we know they're brigade strength and spending the five million on military weapons."

Porterfield shifted his gaze from the portrait to Goldschmidt. His tired eyes narrowed. "For all you know they're from another galaxy and live on whipped cream." He looked back at the portrait. "We can't open this thing up again on a grand scale or the word will go out to the operational people. The rest of this is going to take me about a week. After that there won't be any terrorists and the papers will never see the light."

"Is that all you're going to tell me?"

"You don't need the extra headache."

"Then I'll talk to you in a week." Goldschmidt stood up and walked across the broad Oriental carpet to the door. He stopped and pointed up at the portrait. "Fascinating, really, isn't it? That a man with Seyell's money and power would choose to have a thing like that on his wall?" Without waiting for an answer, he went out and closed the door.

Porterfield took a scrap of paper and wrote on it, "Enjoyed the pictures you showed me the other day. I'd appreciate it if you could order me a set from last Thursday in Los Angeles. I'd especially like shots of my daughter and me. I'd do it myself, but once you get on the mailing list you never get off."

He sealed the paper in an envelope and dialed the intercom. He said, "Karl, I'm afraid I have to send you on an errand in Miami today. Come on in and I'll explain it."

•   •   •

IN the garden of the Biltmore Hotel the only sound came from the rhythmic advance of the tide over the sand of Butterfly Beach. The sun had stopped at the horizon line and seemed to have flattened on the glassy surface of the ocean like the yolk of an egg, and now the purple blossoms of the jacaranda trees glowed whitish in the sky.

"This is it," whispered Chinese Gordon. "Zero minus sixty seconds and counting. We can still call Mission Control if you don't want to marry an inert and unpromising object like me."

Margaret held up her bouquet of ranunculus and poppies like a microphone and intoned into it, "This is Houston. We have ignition. I repeat, we have ignition."

Margaret's father, a tall man with wavy gray hair at his temples and a bald pate that caught the weak glow of the sun, walked up to them, lifting his feet three inches off the ground at each step in unconscious guilt at crushing the soft carpet of grass. "It's just about time for me to do my only official act in this. I hope I give her away without making any mistakes. She's the only daughter I've got, so I'd better not make a mess of it."

"Daddy, you're walking like a chicken. How much champagne did you have?"

"Mr. Kepler and Mr. Immelmann have made sure we were supplied. Liberally. Magnificently."

Chinese Gordon said, "I'll be good to her, Doctor Crisp."

"Don't call me that. I've been a proctologist for over thirty years now, and every time somebody calls me Doctor I think the worst is yet to come. Call me Baird."

"Baird. Stop that," said Mrs. Crisp as she came around the corner of the bungalow with Immelmann. Behind them the judge, a short, fat man, was putting on his black robe. Kepler straightened the judge's collar and patted him heavily on the back. "There you go, sport. Want me to dust off home plate for you?"

The judge beamed. "I think I'll manage. I've done over two thousand weddings, you know—career total."

"Ever figure your won-lost record?"

The judge stepped onto the grass, smiling and holding his arms out in their flowing sleeves to herd everyone into position. High in a eucalyptus across the lawn with scarlet bougainvillea vines woven into its dark green leaves an invisible bird began to sing.

"How beautiful this is," Mrs. Crisp said to her husband. "And look, far out there on the ocean. The lights on that ship are gorgeous, red and green and blue. It looks like a sailing ship. Magical."

Kepler said to Immelmann, "She's got a great eye. Never seen an oil rig before."

Immelmann glared at him and said to Mrs. Crisp, "You're right. We're very lucky. Must be anchored out there waiting for the right wind to take it out to sea— maybe to Hawaii or even Tahiti."

Kepler whispered, "Anchored nine miles out with fifteen hundred feet of pipe. The good ship *Standard Oil*."

"Dearly beloved," the judge's melodious voice rolled in the still air of the evening, "we are gathered here this evening to witness the joining together in matrimony of Margaret Anne Crisp and Leroy Charles Gordon. It is a solemn occasion and yet a happy one. . . ."

Mrs. Crisp whispered to no one in particular, "I've never seen a civil ceremony before. He's very good."

The judge, with faintly antiquated diction, ceremoniously repeated to the small group of smiling people the traditional wisdom concerning love and the founding of families and the sharing of responsibility. Mrs. Crisp looked with wide, soft eyes over his head at the eucalyptus tree, nodding slightly to herself.

He asked Leroy Charles Gordon if he took this woman to love, honor, and cherish as long as they both should live, and Leroy Charles Gordon said he did. Then he asked Margaret Anne Crisp if she took this man, and she said she did.

As the judge raised his voice to pronounce them man and wife, Dr. Crisp turned his face away from the couple to catch his wife's eye and noticed that it was Kepler, the one who looked like a professional boxer, who had tears in his eyes. Dr. Crisp wasn't surprised. It was always the tough ones who fainted at the sight of a needle or a sigmoidoscope. He turned back toward his daughter. At that moment she seemed the most beautiful creature he'd ever seen—her mother's large, soft eyes and tiny waist. She seemed impossibly delicate in that little blue dress. Then he looked off toward the sea, his own eyes beginning to cloud over.

It was then that he saw the other couple standing apart under the broad, umbrella-shaped magnolia tree. The man seemed to be about his own age. Could it be that Leroy's parents had been able to make it here to Santa Barbara after all? Suddenly everyone moved at once. People were shaking his hand, and Margaret gave him a bone-crushing hug. There was laughter, and the judge floated among them in his dark robe, obscuring one person, then another in the dusk. He lost sight of the two people under the magnolia tree for a moment as Immelmann forced a glass of champagne into his hand.

As Doctor Crisp lifted his champagne glass he saw that Margaret had noticed the two newcomers too. She seemed to drift toward them into the deeper darkness under the magnolia tree. She must have recognized them, he thought, so in a moment there would be introductions. The only thing he could do that might be any use was to hunt for Immelmann or Kepler. Each of them seemed to have his own red-coated barman with a tray of champagne glasses following him around the lawn like a caddie on a golf course. Whoever these people were, they'd apparently come some distance to see his daughter married, and they were going to be made welcome. He scanned the shapes in the dusk and recognized Immelmann's girlfriend, the one he called Sunshine. She'd help him get things organized. She seemed to be a sweet girl, although she was a little too shy for conversation. She had a striking appearance, almost like one of the blond starlets of the fifties, and she stood out in the dim light well enough to help him get people together. What kind of parents would name a girl Sunshine?

MARGARET passed into the shadow of the magnolia tree. She said quietly, "Mr. Porterfield."

Porterfield moved toward her, and she winced, but he was saying, "This is my wife, Alice." Margaret felt her hands beginning to tremble but she didn't have time to pay attention to it, because the woman seemed to materialize when Porterfield named her, as though she were part of a dream.

The woman stepped into the light, and Margaret could see she made no sense either. She seemed to be the kind of middle-aged lady who must spend her time running charities and going to concerts. Her graying hair was still lustrous, worn tied up behind, showing her tiny emerald earrings. The woman embraced Margaret and said, "Your wedding is just lovely, dear. I'm so glad we got to see it."

Margaret heard voices murmuring behind her, and she grasped the chance. She turned her head to see Kepler talking to a waiter. "Kepler, there's someone I want you to see."

Kepler sidled up to them. When he was about eight

feet away he said quietly, "You."

Margaret said, "This is Alice Porterfield. Can you introduce her to everyone?"

Kepler hesitated for a moment, then said, "Sure. Of course. I'd be delighted." He took Alice Porterfield's arm and they moved off onto the lawn.

She heard Porterfield chuckle in the darkness. "That was very good."

"He wouldn't hesitate to kill her, you know. I don't know if she's really your wife, but you can't want that."

"She's really my wife. About thirty years, and I love her very much."

"What a cold-blooded bastard you are to bring her here."

She could see Porterfield shake his head, but his face was obscured. He said, "She's safer here than she'd be at our hotel. We both enjoyed your wedding."

"How did you know who we are?"

"Now and then some people I know take pictures in airports. It's usually international flights, but not always, so I thought I'd ask. There were three very good pictures of you and me. I have other friends who can call up the records of the Department of Motor Vehicles, including pictures on licenses, and others who can lift a fingerprint from a used airline ticket. It's a long story."

"You must be exhausted. What are you going to do now?"

"Drink champagne, meet your parents, maybe dance a little if Alice is willing to put up with me."

"You said to burn the papers, but we didn't. We still have them."

Porterfield touched her arm. "Of course you do. Hang onto them. Your job is to protect them for us. Stay healthy, live a long life. Have lots of kids so there will always be somebody around to take care of those papers. As long as there is, we're not going to worry, because you're never going to reveal them.''

''Because you know who we are.''

Porterfield let the implications settle into Margaret's consciousness, then said, ''Now let me join Alice and celebrate your wedding. I doubt that there's anybody here who more sincerely wishes you a long and happy life.''

''Thanks,'' said a male voice behind him.

Porterfield didn't move his head. ''Is that you, Chinese? After all I've read about you in the past few days I'm glad to finally meet you.''

''Thick file?''

Porterfield shrugged. ''You and your friends have done a lot of soldiering in a lot of places. American ex-sergeants who turn up as majors and colonels in Africa or Asia make the people at the regional desks curious. But you're too rich now for anything but early retirement.'' He shook Chinese Gordon's hand. ''Congratulations. She's a beautiful girl.''

⚤ 37 ⚤

IT WAS FOUR o'clock in the morning when Chinese Gordon climbed out of bed in the bungalow in the garden of the Biltmore Hotel. Margaret stirred in her sleep and then tugged the extra covers up over her bare shoulder. Chinese Gordon studied her as he pulled on his pants. The sight of her made his breath catch in his throat. She seemed so tiny and vulnerable, and yet there was something about the way her lips turned up slightly at the corners in a serene smile that made him want to touch her.

He had to go out now, though, before the hotel gardeners arrived, or it would be too late. He tiptoed to the door and pulled the key quietly from the lock. He opened the door and held it until the dog passed out into the garden.

Chinese Gordon and the huge black dog walked across the wet grass in the darkness, then down the stone steps to the cool, damp sand. Every few seconds there was a crash of surf and then a hissing as the wave subsided, boiling and bubbling, back into the ocean. Then there was a long lull, and he could hear the loud, excited panting of the great black dog beside him as they walked down the beach.

Chinese Gordon said, "You can run now, boy."

The dog stood still, and he could feel its eyes looking up at him in the moonlight.

Chinese Gordon knelt on the sand beside the looming shape of the dog. "You're not locked in a hotel anymore, you big vicious bastard. Enjoy yourself." Chinese Gordon patted the dog's back and stood up. He began to trot, and the dog trotted with him. They loped down onto the smooth, hard sand at the edge of the surf. Sometimes the water would wash up to Chinese Gordon's ankles, and he would splash through it. It seemed to excite the dog, and he would run out into the surf and run back, circling Chinese Gordon easily. When they passed the first jutting point they were out of sight of the hotel. Before them a mile of empty beach stretched into the darkness. Chinese Gordon's heart was pounding in his chest. He shouted to the dog, "Now run. Go get 'em."

The great black dog galloped ahead of him down the beach, his long legs taking leaping strides, his paws kicking up little sprays of sand behind him. Chinese Gordon sat down and watched. In the moonlight he could see the dog diminish in the distance, a small black shape on the white sand streaking off in a meandering pattern as though he were trying to cover the whole beach, step on every spot.

Chinese Gordon lay on his back and looked up at the stars, letting his wind come back to him. In another hour the sun would come up. He rested, feeling his breathing deepen and the pulse in his temples slow. At last, above the sound of the ocean, he heard the thumping of the dog's paws and the huffing of his breath as he approached.

Chinese Gordon sat up and looked into the dog's broad face. "I guess it's time we started back." He raised himself to his feet and began to jog back up the beach. The dog seemed to hesitate until he called, "Come on, boy. Come on, Porterfield," and then he heard the sound of the big animal's heavy paws as it moved up beside him in the darkness.

About the Author

THOMAS PERRY studied English at Cornell and has a Ph.D. in English from the University of Rochester. He and his wife live in southern California, where he is assistant coordinator of the General Education program at USC. His first novel, *The Butcher's Boy*, won both the 1982 Edgar Allan Poe Award, given by the Mystery Writers of America for the best first novel, and the Commonwealth Club of California silver medal for literature. *Metzger's Dog* is his second book.